SHADOW LOVER

Lori Handeland

Bestselling Author Of *Second Chance*

"A powerhouse of a story full of deep human emotions, betrayals, and revenge....This is one you don't want to miss!"

—Rendezvous

STRANGERS IN THE NIGHT

Rachel stepped into the storm, oblivious to the downpour soaking her to the skin. Drawn toward the shadowy figure sitting alone in the middle of the overgrown garden, she made her way over the wet ground. Just as she reached him the storm came upon them in earnest, thrusting Sedona into complete darkness.

"Michael?" she whispered and felt rather than saw him tense.

She went to him then and laid her hands on his bare shoulders. Her first contact with his flesh sent shivers through her that put the electrical storm above them to shame. She could feel the powerful muscles tighten and relax as she ran her hands down his arms. Leaning forward, she put her cheek against his wet hair; her breasts flattened against his back.

Michael's body went still at her touch, and Rachel was afraid he meant to bolt again. She circled her arms around his neck, holding him to her. At that moment lightning blazed, thunder crashed and the lights in the house behind them went out, painting the very air around them black.

Suddenly, he turned and jerked her toward him to plunder her lips ruthlessly with his own.

Other *Love Spell* Books by Lori Handeland:
SECOND CHANCE

LOVE SPELL NEW YORK CITY

For my husband: the most wonderful man in the world. Love at first sight is true.

LOVE SPELL®

March 1995

Published by

Dorchester Publishing Co., Inc.
276 Fifth Avenue
New York, NY 10001

Printed in the United States of America.

Grateful acknowledgment to the following:
Dr. Joan Z. Handeland of the Beaumont Clinic, Green Bay, for sharing her medical expertise
and
Sgt. Cyndi Thaldorf of the Oshkosh Police Department for sharing her knowledge of law enforcement.

Any mistakes are, as usual, mine.

SHADOW LOVER

Prologue

"I want you dead."

The words, spoken in a calm, conversational tone, sent an icy trickle of dread down Michael Gabriel's spine. Slowly he turned away from the rim of the precipice and the three-thousand-foot drop to the Colorado River. He met the heated gaze of Robert Matthews. The man Michael had believed was his friend stood close—too close—behind him.

The first blow glanced off Michael's chin. He staggered sideways, careful, despite the ringing in his ears, to stay away from the deadly edge.

"What the hell?" he muttered, then ducked to avoid another well-aimed punch.

Michael deflected the next blow with his forearm. The impact resounded throughout his body, and he staggered backward, moving a few inches closer to the edge he strove so desperately to avoid. Now he knew why Robert had insisted that they view the river from such a dangerous and isolated position.

"What's the matter with you?" he shouted.

"Nothing that killing you won't fix. You betrayed me, Gabriel, and I'll never forget it."

Robert backed away for a moment, and Michael watched him closely for any hint of another attack. He'd known a confrontation was coming; that was why he'd agreed to come on this camping trip to the north rim of the Grand Canyon. In the desolate area few tourists braved so late in October, they could resolve any lingering anger in private.

When Robert suggested they go on the trip, Michael had hoped his friend finally had understood the ways of their world. Success was everything, regardless of the cost. Michael might not like those rules, but he had learned to live by them.

"Calm down and listen to me," Michael said, then glanced over his shoulder to gauge the distance between himself and the edge. His heart rate accelerated; he turned back toward Robert and took a step forward.

"I—ah—"

His next words were cut off when Robert charged forward, hitting Michael in the chest with his shoulder in a running body slam. Michael fell backward, his hands grabbing reflexively for a hold on something—anything. He found Robert's shoulders and clung.

Together, the two men tumbled over the edge and fell into the nothingness beyond.

Chapter One

"Bobby!" Rachel cried. "Where are you?"

"I'm here, little sister. I'll never leave you."

"That's what you said when you left for New York. But you never came back."

"I wanted to. But it was him. He betrayed me. He killed me." The voice—deep, resonant, well-loved—took on a pleading note it never possessed in life. "You have to do something, Rachel. If you don't, I'll never rest easy. An eye for an eye. A death for a death. I want vengeance."

Vengeance, vengeance, vengeance . . .

Rachel Taylor awoke with a cry on her lips, the final words from her dream still echoing in her ears and filling her soul. For a moment, still half lost in the hazy world of sleep, she sensed Bobby near. She reached out to touch him, to hold on to him so she would never lose him again. As always, her eyes stung with tears at the realization that her adored brother was indeed gone forever.

Forcing back the wave of emotion, Rachel glanced around the empty room. She blinked in confusion until she recognized the studio. She had fallen asleep while rehearsing. The tension from her first big career break combined with nervousness over her secret plans had exhausted her beyond endurance.

She sighed and prepared to get back to work. Then a sound so faint as to be eerie invaded her consciousness. Rachel cocked her head, straining her ears to ascertain the direction and cause of the noise.

Music. Instruments. A voice. Someone must be using another studio for practice. But who?

Her brow furrowed with curiosity. All the weeks she'd been working on this project, staying late every night in her effort to perform above and beyond what she'd ever done before, she had never seen or heard another soul in the building. As far as she knew, she was the only person using the recording studios after hours.

Tantalized by the music, she stood and moved from the room and into the hall. The sound was louder there. The singer must be using one of the practice rooms, not one of the soundproof recording studios as she was. Rachel edged toward the back of the building, drawn forward by the exquisite notes as though she had no will of her own.

Broken only by shadows from security lights and the music drifting on the silence, the darkness pressed in on her. She continued to move toward the music, allowing the incomparable voice to wash over her. Pausing for a moment, she closed her eyes and experienced the pain, the joy, the love portrayed in the lyrics. The voice sent shivers up her arms and across her scalp. She opened her eyes and continued on. As she got closer to the source, the myriad tones solidified into a now familiar melody—the song she had practiced earlier that evening. But the pitch was definitely male, hauntingly familiar and the most beautiful sound she had ever heard.

Rachel's heart thumped with recognition and she stopped. She had studied that voice very well over the past few years. She knew its every nuance. She wanted nothing more than to meet the owner of that voice face-to-face. Yet now that the time had come to confront Michael Gabriel and put her plan into motion, she froze on the very threshold of the half-open door.

While revenge and ambition warred within her, Rachel continued to hesitate. She knew very well that if she went ahead with what was in her heart, she could destroy any chance for the successful career she'd always wanted.

A face flashed before her eyes, now lost to

her forever. Rachel's shoulders snapped back as her chin came up, and she knocked on the door in front of her. It was slightly ajar and creaked open another inch at her touch. The singing stopped immediately, and a second later the recorded music snapped off.

Just as Rachel reached for the doorknob, taking a deep, calming breath in preparation to meet her nemesis, the door slammed closed in her face. The audible click of the lock resounded in the now silent hallway.

Rachel stared at the smooth metal panel in front of her, blinking with surprise. Then she frowned. He wouldn't escape from her so easily.

She clenched her fist and pounded on the door, allowing her irritation to lend force to her blows. There was no response.

"Hey, I know you're in there," she shouted. "I heard you singing." She paused and listened.

Nothing.

Rachel swallowed and attempted a calmer tone. "You sing beautifully, by the way."

Her straining ears picked up a slight scraping sound, as though a chair had been pushed across the floor when someone stood abruptly.

"I'm Rachel Taylor. I think we're playing the lovers in this film. Could I come in? I've been anxious to meet you."

When silence continued to meet her repeated requests Rachel raised her fist again and slammed it once against the door.

"All right. If you want to play the crazy artist, that's fine with me. I thought if we sang that song together it would do a lot for the movie. But never mind."

She waited, her heart beating loudly in her ears as impatience warred with nervous anticipation. What would she do if he continued to ignore her? Several moments later a deep voice answered from behind the locked door.

"What you want is impossible."

Rachel sighed with relief. At least he was talking to her. "Nothing's impossible."

"Our singing together is."

The voice was as beautiful speaking as it was singing, so much more so in person than on the recordings she had listened to avidly. She had a sudden mental image of Gregory Peck in *To Kill a Mockingbird;* this man's voice had that same languid, mellow tone that made her toes tingle with the awareness of something wonderful. Rachel bit her lip, irritated with her weakness for beauty. She had no room for that now.

"Why can't we sing together?" she asked, though she knew perfectly well. If she wanted to gain his trust she couldn't let on how much she knew about him.

"I don't allow people to see me."

Rachel was silent for a moment. "What's that supposed to mean? You're an actor. People look at you all the time. It's part of the business."

"Not my business." He laughed shortly,

though the sound held no humor. "Not anymore."

Rachel leaned closer to the door, straining to hear through the barrier.

"Aren't you the male lead in this movie?" she asked.

"Yes. But no one will see me in an animated feature. My voice is all that's needed. I demanded and received complete anonymity when I signed on for this movie. I've found my voice is worth the price of any eccentricity on my part."

The absence of sight enhanced her perception of tone, and Rachel recognized the sadness tinging his voice. The same tone had shadowed her own voice for the past three years.

But something was wrong here. She hadn't expected him to be sad. In her perception of him he played his problems to the hilt, preying on the sympathy of the public to enhance his mysterious, romantic image. She doubted the facial scars she'd read about even existed. Or, if they did, how bad were they, really? A sudden urge to learn the truth consumed her.

"Let me in," she urged softly.

Silence met her words, and she had the distinct impression that he no longer stood beyond the locked door. She remembered the back entrance to her own practice room and swore softly. He had slipped away from her.

Clenching her hands in frustration, Rachel fought to stay calm so she could think. She had come too far to allow her plans to be ruined now. Desperation won out and propelled her through the hallway toward the back exit. She would confront him on his way out of the building and somehow find a way to gain his trust.

A shadowy form moved up ahead, and she squinted against the dimness of the darkened building. Someone was there, perhaps a hundred feet in front of her. She knew exactly who that someone was, and she increased her pace accordingly.

He certainly was big. Though he was dressed in black, she could still make out his immense height and broad build. Long, ebony hair brushed against an equally dark shirt as he ran.

He was aware of her pursuit, but never once did he glance back. Despite Rachel's all-out pursuit, he was fast; he burst through the heavy fire door yards ahead of her. Black met black as he leapt into the night. The door slammed shut with a deafening roar seconds before she reached it.

She threw her shoulder against the portal, groaning with the weight as it inched outward with agonizing slowness. Michael Gabriel must be very strong to fling open something so heavy with apparent ease. Rachel fell through the gap into the fresh, dark air.

The parking lot was empty.

Her breath coming in short, harsh gasps, she

searched the night. The red sheen of taillights in retreat were all that met her anxious gaze.

Michael Gabriel leaned his head against the car seat and exhaled slowly, willing his pounding heart to calm down.

That had been close. Too close.

He felt like a fool, running from her like that. But what other choice did he have when she chased him? From now on he would bring Roger inside while he worked, rather than having him remain with the car. Since Roger was paid well to do anything Michael asked without question, there wouldn't be any argument from the bodyguard about the change. Michael had learned in the past three years that money, or the promise of money to be made, could buy many things, especially loyalty. And Roger was nothing if not loyal to the core.

But Michael worked best when alone, and the presence of anyone, even Roger, would probably hinder him. He would never have come tonight if he'd thought someone besides himself haunted Danfield Studios. He'd have to speak with the producer tomorrow and clear up this misunderstanding. If Harold P. Stanhope wanted to use Michael Gabriel's voice, he would have to ensure that there were no more disturbances.

"What was that all about?" Roger turned his head slightly to catch Michael's gaze in the rearview mirror.

"Nothing," Michael mumbled, looking away.

"Then why did you come out of the door like that? No, wait—I'd rather know who the brunette babe was coming right behind you."

Michael's head snapped up at the question. "You saw her?"

"Sure, I watched in the mirror. Couldn't really make out her face, but she had a nice body. My type, I'd say. Can you introduce me?" Roger's lips curved into his idea of a smile.

"Hardly. You know I don't see anyone but you. She heard me singing and came pounding on the door. She's the female lead in this picture."

"Interesting." Roger watched him closely in the mirror. "What did you say she wanted?"

"I didn't," Michael said shortly. But when Roger continued to glance at him suspiciously, he let out an irritated sigh. Roger was like a kid with one last piece of candy—he never gave up when he really wanted something. "She thought we should do the title song as a duet," Michael said. "I told her that was impossible."

"Well, since she chased you down, I don't think she believed you."

Michael grunted and Roger, familiar with his moods, subsided into silence.

Michael put his palm against his chest. Why hadn't his heart slowed down? The running certainly wouldn't make him this breathless; not when he ran several miles a day on his indoor track. He breathed deeply, in through the nose, out through the mouth, as he'd been taught to do in therapy. Slowly his heart rate returned to normal, and the pounding in his head ceased.

He had spent the three years since his accident building a wall around himself, impenetrable to everyone but Roger. The physical pain had faded, but the scars remained, not just on his face but within his soul, as well. Michael knew he used his ruined visage as an excuse to remain in seclusion. He didn't deserve to enjoy a real life after what he had done. Every day and every night, questions hounded him. But the answers to those questions were as impossible to secure as Michael's lost dreams.

He made a good living doing projects that required only his voice: cartoons, commercials, books on tape, and now an animated feature. He had been hesitant to take on a job of such magnitude, but when he read the script he knew he had to accept. The story of two lovers, one from the future, one from the past, traveling across time to be together in the present, had touched him so deeply, he found it hard to say no. The movie had the potential to be a blockbuster, and he'd allowed his buried ambition to resurface long enough to consider the part.

The black Lincoln Continental slid through the security gate at the front of his house. Seconds later, Michael left the car and, ignoring

Roger's concerned glance, went directly to his rooms upstairs.

Sitting at his desk, he pulled from the top drawer a photo given to him by the studio and placed it in front of him. Rachel Taylor was no beauty. But she made up for that fact with the liveliness shining in her turquoise eyes and an endearing, heartfelt smile. From the first Michael had been drawn to the love of life he recognized in her face, a love he had shared until three years before. And her voice—God, that voice made him want to lose himself in her forever.

With a curse, Michael threw the picture back into the drawer and slammed it shut. Why on earth had he contracted for this movie? He had all he could do to live up to the demands required of him for the film, and now this woman wanted him to work with her face-to-face. He could see that what she said was true: If they sang together, the finished product would be far and away better than anything they could accomplish separately. But stepping back into the world he craved, if only for the good of the movie, was something he could never do. He had his reasons for remaining in the darkness—damn good reasons—and he wasn't about to give in to the siren call of life at this late date.

Michael stripped off the dark clothes he favored and stepped into the shower. As the hot, pounding water beat on his upturned face, he groaned and remembered.

Awakening in the hospital after the accident, he was unaware of the extent of his injuries. At first he was too drugged to fathom what had happened, and when he was finally well enough to understand he railed at a fate that had left him disfigured but alive.

The morning after he first awoke to undrugged consciousness the plastic surgeon had entered his room.

"Mr. Gabriel, your parents asked me to consult on this case. I'm sure your doctor has told you that your other injuries, the broken leg and arm, will heal normally given time. But the abrasions on your face are another matter."

Michael held his breath. The surgeon's expression as he perused Michael's chart did not inspire confidence.

"Are you aware that you have the type of skin that forms keloids?"

Michael nodded and reached up to touch the sterile gauze still protecting the deep scrapes across the left side of his face. Dread filled him and he knew, even before the doctor spoke, what his prognosis would be.

"Nothing can be done, Michael. I'm sorry," the surgeon said, and Michael could see that the man was truly sorry. But sorry wouldn't return Michael's face to normal, and time, in this case, would not heal all wounds.

The surgeon continued to speak, and Michael listened with only half an ear to the diagnosis he knew by heart. "Your skin forms heavy ridges of scar tissue at the slightest abrasion. Any type of surgery will only worsen the scars. Modern medicine cannot fix everything, and keloids are one of those things."

Michael nodded, remembering another doctor telling his mother the same thing when he was six years old. She had rushed Michael to the doctor's office when his knee had formed ridged tissue after he fell off his bike and scraped himself. The condition that had been a minor annoyance in childhood had suddenly become the scourge of his adulthood.

The police arrived on the heels of the surgeon. Michael, still reeling with the knowledge that a career for which he'd spent a lifetime preparing was in tatters, had not known what to say to their pointed questions.

When he learned he was being investigated for murder he had lost his temper and shouted until hospital security removed the police from his room. But they had returned with their questions and accusations, making the hell of Michael's life an inferno of self-doubt and self-loathing.

Michael shook his head sharply to clear away the memories of that other time and twisted off the water with a flick of his wrists. He didn't want to think about the investigation, or Robert, right now.

Michael stepped from the shower and quickly toweled himself dry. Usually he was exhilarated after an evening of rehearsal or recording;

tonight he felt drained of all energy. Climbing into bed naked, he closed his eyes and sought oblivion in vain. Sleep would not come.

Instead, images of Rachel floated through his mind. Her voice—talking, cajoling, singing—her face, her body.

Damn.

He sat up in bed, reaching toward the night table and flicking on the light with a short, angry movement. He would have to do something to banish these dream visions from his brain. Shoving his legs into a pair of well-worn sweatpants, he left his room, bare of chest and foot.

Traveling through his darkened house as he'd done many sleepless nights before, Michael easily reached his living room. Moonlight poured through the many skylights, shining on the grand piano in the center of the polished wood floor. Seating himself on the bench, Michael began to play. Soon his voice rose in company to the music.

Several hours later he gazed up at the stars visible through the glass above. Despite all his efforts to forget, he could still hear her voice, see her young, hopeful face. Michael Gabriel lay his head on the keys of ebony and ivory and, as the harsh chord his movement had wrought faded into the night stillness, he wondered where his sudden fascination with her would end.

* * *

After watching the car disappear into the night Rachel turned and allowed the fire door to slam shut behind her. The heavy thud echoed her mood.

She grimaced and kicked the door in childish retaliation. Though she had been thwarted in her physical pursuit, she was far from vanquished. In the morning she would find a way to meet with Michael Gabriel. Convincing him to sing with her was the perfect way to get close to him, and from there it would be a short road to the destruction she anticipated. Maybe, if she went about things right, they could finish the movie first, and then she could have success and revenge in one perfect package.

After gathering her purse from the abandoned studio and quickly leaving the building, she settled into the red Mustang convertible that had once been Bobby's pride. Between the manufactured coolness of the air-conditioned studio and the bone-dry, hundred-degree-plus temperatures of a summer in Phoenix, she looked forward to the fresh air on her face. The engine roared to life, and she sped along the deserted road, her shoulder-length hair whipping in the wind.

Home waited only a short ride away. Rachel enjoyed the quaintness of the small Spanish-style house, which she had bought for its proximity to Danfield Studios. Ever the innovator, Danfield had built its new studio in the desert just outside Phoenix in an effort to escape the hype of Hollywood, as well as the astronomical price of land and escalating taxes of California. But Phoenix did not boast an abundance of freeways, like most other large cities. As a result, getting from one side of town to the other took a ridiculous amount of time, and a long drive home late at night was out of the question when she was worn out from work. Purchasing a house five minutes from Danfield Studios solved the problem. She told herself a steadily increasing bank account made the house an investment. But, in reality, she had fallen in love at first sight with the view of the desert from her kitchen window and had decided to make Phoenix her place of residence from that moment on.

Rachel unlocked her front door and stepped inside, immediately kicking off her shoes and tossing her purse and the mail onto a nearby table. A black kitten appeared as if from nowhere and pounced on her foot. She had bought the kitten soon after the house, unable to bear coming home to the empty rooms. Bending down, Rachel lifted the ball of fluff until it was even with her face.

"Did you miss me, Minnie?" she crooned, laughing when the small animal began to purr, all the while swiping at Rachel's nose with sheathed claws. "All right." She plopped the kitten down on the floor. "Time for dinner."

The kitten followed her into the kitchen,

losing interest in nourishment when she spotted a dangling thread on the tablecloth. Rachel filled a bowl with kitten food and placed it on the floor before retreating to her bedroom.

The events of the evening had exhausted her. Usually she was unable to sleep after an evening of rehearsing. But tonight she didn't think sleep would elude her for very long.

Rachel eased the straps of her sky blue cotton sundress from her shoulders. The material slid down her body and pooled in a heap around her ankles. She stepped out of the dress, vowing to pick it up the next morning when she found the ambition.

Falling on the bed wearing nothing but her briefs, she tugged the covers to her chin and wiggled her toes with pleasure. Sleeping was one of her favorite pastimes. She didn't have to be at the studio until ten tomorrow, and she planned to take advantage of the late call.

After twenty minutes of tossing and turning she sat up with a groan. No matter how hard she tried to empty her mind, his voice called to her each time she drifted from wakefulness. She saw his tall, muscular body outlined in the doorway, his black hair swaying as he moved with dancerlike grace. But the only face she could conjure to pair with those images was one from a newspaper photograph she had come across several years earlier. In that picture Michael was in the midst of his first great career success—young, confident, energetic. His skin carried the bronzed tone that hinted at an Italian ancestor hanging on a lower branch of his family tree. The high sculpted cheekbones, strong nose, and dark eyes increased that possibility. He was classically handsome, and Rachel could see why he had been cast so often during his early career in the role of a brooding, dangerous hero. She could also understand why his career crashed when reports of his disfigurement reached the press.

Rachel sighed and ran a hand through her tangled hair. Why couldn't she sleep? She had gone over her plan countless times. Just because she had come so close to the object of her desires was no reason to panic. She had to be as cold and calculating as Michael Gabriel himself if she wanted to accomplish what she had set out to do.

Shrugging on an emerald silk robe that reached to mid-thigh, she padded with easy familiarity through the darkened house until she reached the small piano she had bought the week before. Soon music broke the stillness, and shortly after her voice joined the serenade.

Several hours later Rachel walked to the window and stared up at the moon. His voice continued to haunt her.

"Tomorrow," she whispered as she gazed at the stars. Tomorrow she would meet him face-to-face, and then her fascination with him would end.

Chapter Two

Rachel awoke the next day feeling as though she hadn't slept a minute. She'd gone to bed in the early hours of the morning, and what sleep she'd managed to catch had been disturbed by dreams of memories, shadows, and ambitions.

When she'd left her home in Kansas at the age of eighteen Rachel had been intent on becoming an actress and following in her older brother Bobby's footsteps. Though he had made his way in the Big Apple, her dreams led her to sunny California. She had the naive belief that her incredible voice would be her ticket to stardom, despite her somewhat ordinary looks.

Life hit her in the face after only a week in L.A. She saw enough beautiful faces with the talent to match to sink the *Titanic* all over again. Her small-town innocence made her an easy target for those who had been in the business long enough to become hardened. She lost a lot of parts to so-called "friends" who undercut her with directors behind her back. Her trust destroyed, she learned quickly to keep to herself, with her mind firmly fixed on her goals. She was determined not to return home to a lifetime of "I told you so's." Gritting her teeth and tightening her belt, she found a roommate and begged a job.

The first four years were tough, but she persevered, exchanging letters and phone calls with Bobby in New York, thriving on his encouragement. Despite the seven-year difference in their ages, Rachel and her brother had always been close. She missed him terribly and was thrilled when he told her he planned to visit her in L.A. after taking a camping trip with a friend to the Grand Canyon.

She waited for him at her apartment the day he was supposed to arrive. Even when the hours passed and he didn't come she never feared for him. Bobby had always been a free spirit, believing clocks and schedules weren't meant for the artistic. He would arrive when he arrived.

Then the phone rang. She jumped up, certain it was Bobby, calling to say he was in town. With a smile she picked up the receiver—and her world shattered around her.

Then her goals changed; she still wanted to

be a star, as much for her own sake as for Bobby's, but she took on another goal as well—to get revenge against the man who had ended her brother's life.

Rachel pushed aside the depressing thoughts and went to the bathroom for a drink of water to unstick her tongue from the roof of her mouth. The sight of her reflection in the mirror, complete with dark circles and pale complexion, made her groan.

"I guess I should be thankful I don't have to go on camera like this," she mumbled to the apparition who faced her.

After a steaming shower, several cups of coffee, and extensive use of a cover-up stick, she looked presentable, though she felt no better physically. Promising herself she would go to bed early that night, Rachel hurried from her house.

A short time later she drove through the gates of Danfield Studios, waving to the guard on duty. Parking in her assigned space, Rachel took a moment to be grateful for the wide-branched tree shading her car. Though it was only ten in the morning, the summer air sizzled with the promise of the coming heat wave.

She spent the rest of the morning recording the title song for the movie. Patiently she waited, knowing her producer, Harry, would arrive in the early afternoon to hear what had been done. She would corner him then and try to bring him around to her way of thinking in regard to Michael Gabriel. If she could get Harry to go to bat for her, it would be a whole lot easier than trying to convince Michael on her own.

But her preoccupation with her co-star influenced her performance, and when Harold P. Stanhope entered the studio the director was still unhappy with the song.

"Shouldn't this be done by now?" Harry's voice, as always, echoed in the small confines of the recording studio. "I came here expressly to hear the title song. What's the problem?"

Shooting her a this-is-all-your-fault look, the director attempted to explain. Rachel didn't wait to be cast in the role of the incompetent artist but quickly walked up to Harry and touched his arm.

"Harry." She smiled warmly at the older man. "I can explain, if you'd join me in the hall for a moment."

"Of course, dear."

His smile was warm and welcoming, as Rachel had known it would be. For some reason she had gained Harry's regard. He admired her voice and talent, but she also had the feeling he saw her as the granddaughter he'd always wanted but never had. Rachel knew Harold P. Stanhope was a tremendous force in the entertainment industry, and that lesser beings cowered beneath his superior power, but he had been nothing but open and kind to her, and she was at ease with him. If she had an occasional twinge over what she planned to do to his male star, she stifled it with the knowledge that blood was thicker than ambition, at least for her.

Rachel preceded Harry into the cool, silent hallway, then turned abruptly.

"This isn't going to work, Harry."

He blinked, obviously confused by her statement, though his smile remained fixed in place. "What isn't?"

"I can't sing these songs or speak the dialogue in a vacuum. I need to work with the other actor."

Harry's friendly smile suddenly faded, and his face became closed and cold. She could understand why others became fawning idiots at the first sight of his displeasure. "Impossible, Rachel. We've discussed this before, and you agreed to the terms."

"That was before I knew how difficult it would be to sing and speak like a woman in love when I have nothing to sing and speak to but a wall."

"You're an actress. Act."

Rachel made an impatient sound, then took a deep, calming breath. "You're not being fair."

"I'm sorry. The contracts have been signed, and his is very explicit."

Rachel was silent for a moment as her mind searched desperately for some way to elicit Harry's support.

"We were both here last night," she said softly.

Harry's gaze searched hers, obviously trying to see if she spoke the truth. He sighed in resignation. "You saw him?"

"In a manner of speaking."

"What the hell does that mean?" Harry said, frowning darkly. "Out with it, girl. It's always been your straightforwardness I admire. Let's have some of it now."

Rachel fought not to flinch at Harry's assessment of her character. She had been anything but straightforward with him regarding Michael. But she couldn't give up now, not when she sensed a break in the producer's defense of Gabriel's working requirements.

"I heard him singing and spoke with him through the door of his studio. Then he ran away." Harry started to speak, but Rachel pressed on, her words tumbling out fast and furious, her face reflecting the earnestness of her plea. "Harry, he and I should be singing that song together. If I could sing with him, I know the recording would be wonderful. Putting our two versions together later in the studio just won't cut it. Can't you see that?"

Harry stared at her for a long moment, and hope fluttered to life within her. Then he shook his head, straightened, and turned away. The tiny bit of hope sputtered and died. "You might be right, but he'll never agree. As I told you before, I signed a contract that states his requirements to the last detail. I can't afford to break my word."

Without another word, her producer returned to the studio, leaving Rachel alone. She stared after him for a moment, then straightened with undiminished determination. "You may have signed a contract with him, but I didn't. If I have to sit in this studio for a week, I *will* meet with Michael Gabriel."

Michael awoke refreshed in the early afternoon following several hours of sleep—an unusual occurrence for a man who rarely slept an hour at a stretch and, as a result, was always tired. For once his dreams had been peaceful, restful, filled with visions of light and music. He couldn't remember the last time he'd dreamed of anything but the accident and the pain and guilt that had followed.

But he did have a little matter to discuss with Harry. Since he had specifically outlined rehearsal and recording times in his contract and had stated that during those times he required the studio completely to himself, he wanted to know what Rachel Taylor had been doing in the building last night. When he was done with Harry, Michael was sure Rachel would never bother him again.

A heavy weight of sadness descended upon him at that thought. But he shoved it back inside where the rest of his emotions dwelled.

Then he forced himself, as he had to do on many mornings, to get out of bed and dress.

As he stared into the mirror and shaved the heavy dark stubble from his chin, Michael wondered at the continuing weight of despair plaguing him. What was wrong with him this morning? He'd gotten past the point of feeling sorry for himself long ago. He only wanted one thing, didn't he? Now and forever, to be left alone with his guilt and his secrets?

A tap on the door preceded Roger's entrance by a fraction of a second, and thoughts of Rachel fled to the back of Michael's mind.

"Are you up yet?"

"I thought I was awake." Michael tilted his head and wrinkled his brow in feigned confusion. "Don't tell me; this is all a dream and I'm sleepwalking, right?"

Roger looked at him strangely. "Funny guy this morning. I take it you're in a better mood than usual."

"What makes you think that?"

"Well, most days I have to pull you out of bed and listen to your growling until I drive you to the studio. Then I'm treated to a few hours of peace and quiet."

"Well, that's going to end."

"Why?"

"You'll have to come inside with me from now on. I want to make sure the studio is empty before you leave. I don't need a repeat performance of last night."

Roger shrugged. "You're the boss. But I've seen guys a lot worse off than you in prison, Mike. I think you're nuts to keep yourself locked away all the time.

Michael ignored Roger's words as he had on the countless occasions his friend had voiced the same opinion. Roger was only aware of the public story regarding Michael's accident and the police investigation that had followed. He didn't know what really had happened that day when Michael lived and another man died. No one did. No one but Michael—and the dead man.

Michael knew better than to hope for anything more in his life than he already had. If the truth be told, he was grateful he could continue working in the business he loved, even if he was no longer fit for a career in front of the cameras.

He had his mother to thank for the little bit of his career he had salvaged. A few months after his accident, when his depression was at its deepest, she had sent him a video of *Jungle Book,* his favorite movie as a child, along with a scathing letter that said he should "get his 'act' together." Mom had always been able to get to the heart of the matter.

He had resisted temptation for another month and then come to the conclusion he had to have a way to support himself. Since he was trained for nothing but a career in the performing arts or waiting tables, Michael succumbed to the inevitable. After making a few calls he recorded some demo tapes, and within a few days had work lined up for several months. He had been singing and speaking behind the scenes ever since.

It didn't take Michael long to realize he needed someone to help him if he wanted to remain out of the spotlight. He found Roger through a work release program for rehabilitated drug dealers. Roger had been through too much in his life to be put off by Michael's scarred face or surly manner, and the job Michael offered paid too well to refuse for any reason. They had been together for two years, and the relationship worked for both men.

Michael shook off his memories and glanced at Roger, who waited patiently. The bodyguard was used to Michael's habit of sliding into the past with his memories for moments at a time. Roger had gotten so accustomed to it, in fact, that he rarely commented on the lapses anymore.

Michael picked up their thread of conversation where they had left off moments before. "You should know by now that I'm not going to change my mind about the way I live my life. Let's drop it." He walked to his desk and sat down, pulling some papers from a drawer. "Get Harry on the phone for me, would you?"

Roger hesitated, as though he wanted to argue further.

"Today, Rog." Michael continued to peruse the papers without looking up.

Roger left the room without further comment, and a short while later the intercom on the desk buzzed.

Michael pushed the button. "What line?"

"He won't be in all day, Mike."

"His secretary doesn't know where he is?"

"She said he was unreachable."

"Right. He's avoiding someone, probably me." Michael scowled. "Okay, thanks."

He returned to his paperwork, but his mind wouldn't remain on the task at hand. If Harry was avoiding him, then he knew why Michael was calling. And the producer obviously didn't plan to do anything about the situation, at least not right away. *Which means Rachel will be dogging my every move at the studio from this point on.*

Michael shoved back his chair and stood, striding to the window and pushing back the dark curtain. Blinding Arizona sunlight made him wince.

He could stay away from the studio until Harry solved the problem. After all, his contract was quite specific on this matter. But he hated to hold up production and get the reputation of a troublemaker. He was already pushing his luck with his eccentric work requirements. He'd just have to follow his original plan and bring Roger with him to work. If anyone was capable of turning away a determined woman, Roger was that man. The bodyguard had made a science of discouraging even the most resolute reporter over the past two years; an actress with a mission would be a hoot. Then the only problem left to deal with would be Michael's own overwhelming urge to see her.

Rachel's day had not gone well. The director, disgusted with her lack of enthusiasm for the song, had put off the session until the following week. She had shrugged philosophically, irritating the man beyond measure. But she knew something he did not: By next week she planned to be singing a duet.

Instead of going home for a few hours as she usually did, Rachel remained at the studio. If he came again tonight, she would be ready. After her conversation with Harry she half expected one of the guards to throw her out. When no one knocked on the studio door she wondered if the producer had looked the other way and given her the chance she desperately wanted. As the silence increased around her, she continued to go over her lines. Sometime after dark the pressing stillness signaled her that she was alone.

A short time later male voices sounded nearby. Rachel, who had been listening for just such a sign, jumped up from her chair and headed out of the room. She hurried down the hall toward the source of the noise.

Again the building was dimly lit, and Rachel's isolation loomed as an almost tangible force. Unease flooded through her, and she hesitated. What did she know about this man really? Except that he was a murderer. And she was alone with him in a deserted building. But what choice did she have? She needed to talk to Michael Gabriel. He was here. Right now. Rachel began to walk again, determination in her stride. She would accomplish what she had set out to do. She wouldn't let fear get in the way.

As she neared Michael's studio, a dark, hulking shape detached itself from the doorway and materialized in front of her. The fear returned full force. With a gasp, Rachel backed away several paces.

The shape followed, stepping into a shaft of dim light and taking on the form of a man—or, rather, a mountain. He was close to seven feet tall and must have weighed three hundred pounds. Long, iron-gray hair swung in a ponytail down his broad back. Large biceps pushed at the sleeves of a black Harley-Davidson T-shirt, and faded jeans strained their seams around his heavily muscled thighs. The black-and-red snake tattoo on his forearm shimmered and slithered in the shifting light.

This must be Michael's bodyguard, Roger. She'd read about him in some magazine or newspaper article she'd ferreted out while researching Michael's life. She knew from her study that Roger was an ex-con who had served time in prison for drug dealing. Rachel opened her mouth to greet him and then hesitated. She had never spoken with anyone who had been in prison before. What did you say to a Hell's Angel, anyway?

"Aah, h-hello," she stuttered.

Brilliant, Rachel, and oh, so impressive, too, a little voice mocked.

She took a deep breath and continued more steadily. "I was hoping to speak with Michael."

The mountain stared at her unnervingly. What was going on behind those black, all-seeing eyes?

After what seemed like hours he cracked his knuckles, the sound echoing loudly in the dark corridor. His gaze never wavered from her face as he answered her in a low, scratchy voice. "Can't help you."

"I know he's here." Rachel nodded toward the practice room.

The man smiled and revealed a mouthful of bright white teeth. Then he emitted a deep, rumbling sound that held a hint of menace.

Rachel started. Was he laughing? The sound made her feel anything but amused.

"He might be here, and he might not be. But the reason I'm here is to keep you out, so I'm afraid you've wasted your time, babe."

Rachel flinched at the word *babe,* delivered with a twist of sarcasm, but decided she didn't have the nerve to object to the term. She resisted the urge to turn tail and run. "Can't I just talk to him for a minute? I won't be long."

Roger shook his head slowly. His ponytail twitched—right, left, right, left. "He sees no one, and I'm paid a ridiculous amount of money to make sure things stay that way." He spread his huge hands wide and shrugged.

Rachel remained silent, her mind working quickly for another way to accomplish her goal. She was so close. Last night she had sensed a wary interest in Michael's voice when she'd spoken of the great things they could accomplish together. Rachel understood the draw of ambition very well. That emotion had been the guiding light of her life—until three years ago. Then revenge—equally powerful, she'd learned—had taken its place. Remembering that power, she wondered if she might be able to awaken Michael's buried ambition and use it to further her own ends. If she could convince him that working with her would improve their performance, she might get close enough to him to accomplish her true goal. She just needed to talk to him one more time. She could make him see the light if she only had another chance.

Rachel smiled and drew a small white card from her pocket. She held it out to Roger between two fingers. For some reason, the thought of his touch made her extremely nervous.

"This is my phone number. Could you at least ask him to call me so I can try to persuade him?" She smiled harder, her face aching from the effort. She could tell Roger wasn't fooled, but she kept the smile plastered on her lips anyway. "It won't kill him to talk to me over the phone. Tell him if he calls and still wants to say no, I won't bother him again."

"I'll tell him, babe. But don't wait too long for an answer."

Roger reached for the card, purposefully brushing her fingers with his own as he gazed mockingly into her eyes. Then he tucked the card into the back pocket of his jeans and folded his arms across his chest before leaning back against the door. Rachel felt him watching her all the way down the long, dark corridor as she returned to her studio.

Michael listened to the rise and fall of Rachel's voice as she spoke with Roger. The sound tickled along his spine, arousing him as nothing else had for three years. What was wrong with him? He didn't even know the woman. But he sure as hell wanted to.

Michael's jaw ached as he grit his teeth in frustration. He'd be better off if everyone just left him alone.

A few seconds later the door opened, and Roger ducked inside.

"What happened?" Michael had no patience for preambles tonight.

Roger raised his eyebrows but answered the question without sarcasm for a change. "She wanted to talk with you, but I told her no dice, so she left." He laughed, a sound rusty from disuse. "I think I scared her. Imagine that?"

Michael stifled his disappointment at the ease of her capitulation. "Well, that's the last we'll see of her then."

"Not quite." Roger retrieved the card from his pocket and he extended his hand to Michael. "She left her phone number for you. Said if you call and she can't convince you to work with her, she won't bother you again. Sounds like a deal to me."

After a moment's hesitation Michael took the card and put it into the pocket of his shirt without looking at the number. He turned his back on Roger and cued up the music he needed for the night's session.

Later, as they drove home, Michael leaned his head wearily against the seat and sighed. The card with her phone number had been a haunting presence for the entire evening. The slight weight pressed through the thin material of his shirt as though the small paper were her hand resting upon his chest.

When the car stopped in front of the house Michael went to his rooms, leaving Roger to put away the car. Pulling the phone number from his pocket, he placed the card on his desk and stared at it. He had had the naive hope that an encounter with Roger's intimidating physique and determined air would bring an end to Rachel's pursuit of this duet nonsense.

Now she had left the ball in his court. Could he ignore such an invitation? Should he ignore it? He had to do something—either tell her no once and for all or . . . Or what?

With a groan, Michael crushed the card in his hand and threw it forcefully into the wastebasket.

Hours later, still awake despite a heavy workout session in the gym on the first floor, Michael lay in bed and forced himself to close his eyes. He had to call her and at least tell her there was no chance they would sing together. Then she would be out of his life.

You bet, Gabriel. Sure thing.

Before he could talk himself out of it, Michael retrieved the card and dialed Rachel's number.

"Hello?"

Her voice was husky, sexy with sleep, and Michael glanced quickly at the clock on his nightstand.

Damn, 4 a.m.

He sighed. Maybe she'd tell him to take a hike, and that would be the end of it, nice and easy.

"Hello. This is Michael Gabriel. You asked me to call."

"Michael Gabriel?" Her voice cracked with surprise. "I'm so glad you called. Give me a minute, okay?"

He heard fumbling, then the triple click of a light being turned on.

"Sorry about the time. I'm not used to dealing with people anymore," he explained. "I didn't think."

"No, that's all right. Fine, really." She paused, as though unsure of what to say next.

"You wanted to discuss the movie?" he prompted.

"Well, yes. I think we could have a major hit on our hands if you would only consent to doing the scenes and songs together."

"No!" He hadn't been prepared for this new, more detailed request, and his shock showed in the volume of his denial.

"Why not? I don't understand how you can feel the emotion between the characters when you don't have anyone to work with. I'm going crazy trying to feel something for thin air."

He could hear her frustration, laced down deep with a tinge of something he couldn't quite identify.

"I'm sorry you're having such a rough time of it. But I've been at this for years, and the lack of another actor doesn't bother me. I use my imagination to conjure up the appropriate partner."

The snide little voice inside his head, which sounded suspiciously like Roger of late, reminded him that he was speaking with the object of many of those fantasies.

"I need to know the actor I'm working with

in order to create the mood. You've got to help me."

Michael heard the pleading, the desperation in her voice, and sympathy tugged at him. He didn't like the feeling. He had enough problems of his own without adding hers to his list. Why couldn't he just be left alone to live his life as he chose?

"No, I don't have to help you," he told her shortly.

The silence on the other end of the line pulsed with tension. He could tell she wanted to argue the point further, and he braced himself against the assault.

"I understand you had an accident." Her voice was soft, tentative.

He went still. "Yes."

"That's why you won't see anyone? Because of how you look?"

Among other things, he thought and swallowed, hard. He had no desire to explain about betrayal and guilt and lost innocence.

"I'm sure it's not that bad," she persisted. "I wouldn't mind, truly."

He was silent, his heart increasing in speed as unfamiliar hope tugged at him earnestly. He'd come to his feet at her words, and his eyes met those of his reflection in the mirror on the wall. The scars on his face, as always, reminded him of the secret he held within, a secret he had shared with no one since the day of its birth.

"Impossible," he barked into the phone, slamming the receiver onto the cradle.

Dropping back into the chair, head in his hands, he whispered again, "Impossible."

Chapter Three

Rachel spent every spare minute over the next few days re-reading her letters from Bobby and her collection of newspaper clippings about Michael. She couldn't get past the nagging suspicion that she had missed something important.

In the letters over his last year, Bobby had written of his friendship with Michael Gabriel. The two young men met working as ushers in a New York theater. They had discovered common interests and become fast friends. Rachel saw no hint of any trouble between them until Bobby's final letter arrived at her house the day after her brother's death. In that letter, Bobby wrote that he would never forgive Michael for his betrayal, a betrayal that had destroyed Bobby's career and therefore his life. The words on the paper brimmed over with a hatred Rachel had never suspected could exist in the brother she loved so well.

Oh, she could remember his overwhelming fury at their parents for punishing him when they were children. Rachel shrugged. All kids felt such anger at one point or another, and Bobby had been more stubborn than most. All of his life he had been totally single-minded in his wants, and whenever anyone had attempted to change his attitude he only became more fixated on his purpose. Their parents had tried to stop him from becoming an actor, a profession the simple, religious couple felt inappropriate. They had done everything they could to discourage Bobby—threats, physical punishment, days in his room—nothing had worked. Eventually he had run away to New York to prove them wrong.

Glancing at the copy of the newspaper clipping in her hand, Rachel ground her teeth in frustration. Why on earth would Bobby go on a camping trip with a man he professed to hate? The newspaper story told her nothing beyond the basics released to the press—Michael Gabriel's version of the so-called accident, the police investigation of Michael that had released him from any blame in the death due to the lack of evidence, Michael's medical problems and subsequent retirement. Why did she feel there was more to the story than the press knew or were letting on?

A sudden idea occurred to her. In all the newspaper stories she'd read, one police officer's name had continued to crop up—Jim O'Malley. Though a policeman had spoken to her about her brother, O'Malley had not been that officer. Since he had spearheaded the investigation, perhaps O'Malley could enlighten her on a few points. If he was still with the force. There was only one way to find out. Rachel reached for the phone and dialed.

Fifteen minutes later, after half a dozen aborted attempts and as many conversations with desk clerks, she reached the proper building and learned that Jim O'Malley did indeed still work there. And, fortunately, he was at his desk.

"O'Malley, here. Who's this?"

The voice was smoke-roughened and sounded tired and irritable, but Rachel drew in a deep breath and dove in anyway.

"My name's Rachel Taylor. I'm a . . ." She paused, unsure of how to explain her relationship to Michael. "A colleague of Michael Gabriel."

"Who's he?"

"Three years ago you worked on the case. He had an accident while camping near Toroweap Point. Do you remember him?"

"Three years ago. You're askin' a lot, lady."

"I know, but it's important. He and the man he

was with fell over the edge. Gabriel was hurt and the other man was . . ." She swallowed hard and tried again. "The other man, Robert Matthews, was killed."

"Oh, yeah," O'Malley said slowly. "I remember now. What a mess. Somethin' was strange about that case too. Bothered me for a long time after."

Rachel nodded to herself. Her suspicions were about to be confirmed. "What was strange?"

"Nothin' I could really put my finger on. Just a feeling. You learn to trust your gut after a few years on the force. But I never could prove anything against Gabriel. And without a body we had no evidence. Took us a long time to get down below; it's a rough area. By the time we made it there, the damn animals had drug away whatever was left of him. Found some shredded clothes and blood, nothin' else."

Rachel winced at the description, which could still make her sick to her stomach after three years. Her parents, with their deep religious beliefs, had been especially devastated by the empty casket at the funeral. In an effort to compensate, they had hung pictures of Bobby throughout the funeral home and forced everyone attending to look at each and every one. It was a memory Rachel could have done without.

"You never found out anything more about the case?" she blurted in an attempt to block out the visions of that horrible day.

"No, it was just a feelin' I had that there was somethin' more to this than the usual. That I missed somethin' important."

"Like what?"

"If I knew, I wouldn't have closed the case. It was a feelin' is all. Something went on up there. No one but Gabriel and the dead guy will ever know the truth."

"That's what you think," Rachel muttered.

"What was that?"

"Oh, nothing. Thank you for your help."

Rachel hung up. The phone call had only served to make her frustration grow. She hadn't learned anything new. The conversation had merely increased her desire to learn exactly what had happened on that camping trip three years ago.

The only one left alive who knew was Michael Gabriel.

Nearly a week had gone by since he'd hung up on Rachel. Michael was surprised and, if he was honest, disappointed that she hadn't tried to communicate with him again. Every time his thoughts turned to her he reminded himself that it was by his choice that their contact had ended.

When they arrived at the rear door of the studio he waved Roger back to the car. He was sick of having a baby-sitter. Michael shrugged at his friend's puzzled look. "I know you're dying to read the latest *Sports Illustrated*. I can call you on the car phone if something's up inside."

Roger nodded and retreated to the car without argument. Michael unlocked the door and stepped into the darkened building. After listening closely to determine whether anyone else was about, he hurried to his studio and locked the door behind him. He had just put his finger to the light switch when a voice spoke from across the room.

"I thought you'd never get here."

Michael tensed and jerked his hand away from the wall, leaving the room in complete darkness.

"What the hell are you doing here?" He silently cursed the telltale terror in his voice.

"Waiting for you, of course." Rachel's voice came from the chair near the control panel. "Since you won't see me, I decided to come to you."

"You shouldn't have." He stayed near the door, prepared to run again if she came too close. He willed his body to stop reacting to the scent of her, drifting to him on the air-conditioned breeze. It had been too long since he'd been near a woman, and this wasn't just any woman, but Rachel, the object of his most recent erotic dreams.

"I need to talk to you." Her voice was closer.

"Stay away."

There was an edge to his voice, one he recognized from his days spent doing low-budget action-adventure movies—raw desire and suppressed violence. Rachel must have heard it, too, because her next words came from the relative safety of the chair once again.

"All right, I'll stay over here. But could we have a little light?"

"No." His voice rasped harshly in the stillness of the closed room. "Say what you came to say and leave."

Her breath rushed out through her teeth in a hiss of frustration before she spoke. "I talked with Jim O'Malley today."

Michael had expected another plea for the duet. Her words left his mind grasping for their meaning.

"Who?" he snapped.

"The police officer who investigated your accident. Remember?"

He did, and his heartbeat increased in tempo. "What did he want?"

"He didn't want anything. I called him."

"You what?" He rubbed his suddenly tense forehead with his fingers. "Why?"

"Calm down. I'm on your side." She waited a moment before continuing, and her voice, disembodied in the darkness, sounded oddly cool and peaceful despite the tenor of her words. "Since you wouldn't tell me anything, and Harry was just as useless, I decided to find out about you myself. After reading the accounts of your accident I wanted to know more."

Michael frowned. He didn't like the sound of this. "What for?"

"I had some questions. Why were you investigated so thoroughly? You and this Robert Matthews were just camping, and you had an accident. Why did the police treat you like a murderer?"

Michael remained silent for a long time. What should he tell her? He found it odd she wanted to know about the investigation and not his injuries. Most people, he'd found, were morbidly curious about his face. He decided to answer her questions with a frontal assault—throw her off balance until he could determine what she wanted from him. He had learned early in his career to be wary of women in his profession who wanted something. They could be deadly. "Perhaps they treated me like a murderer because they thought I was a murderer."

Rachel shifted nervously. "Don't tease." Her voice shook.

"Who said I was teasing?" Though he had wanted to unnerve her, he found the fear in her voice fueled his anger. She half believed him, despite the fact that she knew nothing about him. This entire incident made him angry, and anger was an emotion that he had tried to exorcise since he had first seen his forever-scarred face. Anger wouldn't change anything. But sometimes, like now, it felt damn good. Who was she to invade his sanctuary, to, in her own subtle way, investigate him? He had been asked enough questions about the accident to last a lifetime. He didn't need any more from her. "Now," he said, striving to keep the edge from his voice and failing, "why don't you tell me what gives you the right to meddle in my life?"

He could tell by her silence that he'd hit a nerve. Well, good. All this talk about his past and the accident made his mouth dry and his palms damp. No one knew what had really happened that day—no one but him. But for some reason Rachel's questions seemed to strip him bare of all the defenses he'd so carefully erected over the past three years.

"I didn't mean to meddle," she said softly. "I just wanted to know you better. Then, when I started looking into things, my curiosity got the better of me. I'm sorry; I'll leave."

The righteous anger that had been coursing through him fled at her low-voiced apology, and he felt small and petty. Though he knew he should let her go, Michael found he couldn't. If she was so curious she had gone to the trouble of sneaking into his studio to ask him questions, there was no telling what she'd do if he let her leave without giving her some kind of answer. "No, wait. I get defensive whenever anyone asks me about that day. I lost a good friend, and my life was changed forever. I spent a long time recovering from what happened on that trip."

"I can understand that," Rachel agreed.

Michael heard the sympathy in her voice and

flinched. He had never needed or wanted pity, especially from her. He opened his mouth to tell her so, but her voice broke into the darkness between them.

"This Robert Matthews and you were good friends, then?"

"Yes," Michael said slowly, wondering at the slight hint of suspicion he sensed in her voice.

"Hmm."

"What do you mean by that?"

"Well, it's just . . . The papers seemed to think you two had some kind of fight and maybe . . . well . . ." She trailed off.

"Maybe I killed him," Michael finished. "I know what people think. The police thought the same thing; that's why they questioned me."

"And?"

The anger he had felt earlier returned at her continued inquiries. He knew he'd never forget that day, but if he tried very hard he could forget for an hour at a time. After all Rachel's questions he was sure his nightmares would return the next time he tried to sleep. His temper snapped for the first time in years. "What's with you anyway? This is all ancient history. Ancient, painful history I've done everything in my power to forget. Why are you bringing it up?"

The force of his anger brought him forward, and he could feel her hovering in front of him, just out of reach in the darkness. Silence descended upon them. When she finally spoke her voice was so near, he jumped.

"Forgive me. I have no right."

She moved closer, and he backed away until his body came up against the door. He didn't know what he'd do if she touched him. His anger and his lust suddenly fused, making him shake with reaction.

She spoke again, so close he tensed even more, his limbs aching with reaction.

"I'd like to discuss the movie with you again. Will you call me?"

He could smell her perfume, an exotic mix that reminded him of the Far East. He inhaled deeply, fixing the scent in his mind to remember later in the privacy of his lonely rooms. He imagined he could feel her feminine warmth radiating toward him through the darkness, calling to the male instincts within him that he had ignored too long. His body responded to the message.

She took another step closer, and his skin tingled at her proximity. He couldn't help himself. He reached out and allowed his fingertips to caress her, reveling in the softness of her cheek, her hair, her neck. God, it had been so long since he'd touched anyone.

His fingers curled around her upper arms and drew her nearer. Rachel's hands came up against his chest, but she wasn't pushing him away. She swayed toward him, resting her cheek against his shirt. His fingers tangled in her hair and his lips brushed the top of her head. Her shampoo reminded him of cinnamon and spice and hot, steamy sex.

She shivered at his touch, and he waited for her to pull away. Instead she slipped her arms around his waist and leaned into him trustingly. Michael took a moment to savor the realization that she wanted to be in his arms, was, in fact, enjoying herself as much as he, if her soft sigh was any indication. Her generous breasts rubbed against his chest as she fitted herself to him, and he stifled the urge to run his hands down her back to her buttocks to pull her hard against his now painful arousal.

"Will you call me?" Her voice, deep and husky, brought him back to the small, dark room, and he pulled away so abruptly, she stumbled.

What the hell was he playing at? He had given up his right to such pleasure long ago. He would live his life alone, with only his music to comfort him, and try to atone for what he had done. Brushing past her, he walked quickly toward the front of the room.

"Michael?" Rachel's voice quavered uncertainly.

Suddenly he wanted nothing more than to be alone. Her nearness was making him crazy with longing for something that could never be. His mind was fuzzy with desire, but he could still hear the warning bells in his head that had been ringing ever since she'd mentioned Robert Matthews.

He took a deep breath, willing the strain from his voice. "I'll call you next week and we'll talk."

The door opened, and he kept his face turned resolutely from the dim, creeping light of the hallway.

"I'll be waiting," she said, closing the door firmly against the light.

Michael listened to the sound of her footsteps retreating. When he could no longer hear the clip-clop of heels on ceramic tile he stared into the darkness and listened to the heavy beat of his heart.

The phone rang and Rachel, standing right next to it in the kitchen, let out a startled yelp and yanked the receiver clear before the second ring.

"Hello," she said, her voice breathless with anticipation. Maybe it was him.

"Rachel, honey, it's Beth."

Rachel sighed and swallowed the disappointment shooting through her at the sound of her best friend's voice. Then she frowned. What on earth was wrong with her that she would be disappointed to hear from Beth? Such a call usually made her day.

"Hey, kiddo," she returned, forcing enthusiasm into her voice. "Haven't heard from you in awhile."

"I was thinking the same about you. What have you been up to?"

Rachel winced at the though of telling Beth what she was really doing in Phoenix. Not only was Beth her best friend, she had been Bobby's girlfriend.

"I'm a . . . I'm just working," Rachel faltered.

"Too hard, I imagine."

"Well, this is my big chance, Beth. I don't think I could work too hard at it."

"Hmm. I wonder. Maybe I should take a trip out there and see for myself how you're holding up."

"No!" Rachel surprised herself with the vehement response. "Ah, I mean I'm too busy right now to spend time with you. When this movie's done I'll come home, and we can spend some time together."

"Rachel, are you sure you're all right?"

Beth's voice, concerned and somewhat suspicious, caused Rachel to bite her lip. "I'm fine. Just tired. You're right; I am pushing it here. But it'll be worth it. You'll see."

Beth was silent for several seconds. Rachel could almost see her friend's concerned face. They had been close since childhood, but Bobby's death had drawn them even closer.

"Do you still dream of him, Rachel?"

Beth's quiet question caught her unaware, and a bright shard of pain pierced her chest. Rachel sighed. "Yes. All the time. Sometimes I think I see him, or hear him. Then I remember he's gone." She took a deep, shaky breath. "God, Beth, it still hurts like hell."

"I know."

The words, uttered in a choked whisper, brought tears to Rachel's eyes. They had shared many things over a lifetime of friendship. If only they hadn't had to share the loss of a man they loved.

"I hear the pain fades," Rachel ventured when she could speak again.

"That's what I hear. Wonder when."

Rachel smiled, glad to hear the dry humor creep back into Beth's voice. "We'll be all right."

"Someday."

"Yeah, someday," Rachel echoed, and for the first time in the past three years she believed it.

After promising to call more often Rachel said good-bye and hung up. Glancing outside, she saw that the Arizona evening was too beautiful to miss.

Rachel retrieved a bottle of wine from the refrigerator and poured a glass. Carrying it, she slid open the floor-length glass window and stepped onto her patio. The night was clear and warm, brightened by a full moon surrounded by a million tiny pinpoints of light. Sighing as she settled into a lawn chair, Rachel sipped her wine. She swirled the gilded liquid absently around with her tongue before she swallowed, closing her eyes. The memory she had been pushing away since she got home hit her with such force, she nearly gasped.

He had touched her. And with those few moments of contact she knew she would never be the same. He had become a man to her woman, throwing her coolly calculated plans into a jumble of confusion.

Her experience with men was virtually nonexistent. The relationships she'd had rarely extended beyond a free meal in her younger days to her present man-on-the-arm required for those Hollywood functions her agent wanted her to attend. Sex was something she had tried in order to learn what everyone thought was so wonderful. Her limited number of experiments had left her unimpressed.

But tonight, with Michael, had come the rush of desire so often written about in books and portrayed in movies. There in the dark she had wanted nothing more than to pull him down onto the cold tile floor, discarding their clothes until his heated skin met hers. Her mind, in the midst of her first taste of lust, had reasoned that maybe if he just touched her, the ache within would cease. A heated flush crept up her cheeks at the direction of her thoughts.

She wanted to gain his trust, but sleeping with him had never been part of the plan. She had to remember Bobby and her reason for being in Phoenix in the first place.

Rachel groaned and squeezed her eyes tightly shut. Why on earth did it have to be Michael Gabriel who made her feel the forbidden? Or did his being forbidden make him that much more alluring? She had heard of women who were attracted to dangerous men over and over again. She had never understood why. For her, safety and serenity would be the perfect combination in a partner. Yet here she was, pining for a man who could do her nothing but harm, especially if he found out what she was up to.

Rachel opened her eyes and bit her lip with frustration as she remembered the scene earlier in the studio. Her thoughts had been so scrambled, she'd blurted out the first thing that had come to her mind and ruined everything. Michael had shied away from her like a horse meeting up with fire. She had been tempted to follow him in his retreat across the room, but she knew such an action would be a mistake. He was confused and on the run; she had no doubt his promise to call had been nothing more than a ploy to get rid of her. She was desperately afraid she had ruined any trust she might have gained by questioning him about the accident too soon. Now she would have to wait and see what his next move would be before she made any more of her own. She couldn't risk destroying any chance to get close to him by pushing him too far. Instinctively, she knew the waiting would be hell.

She was reminded of all the years she'd waited to get out of small-town Kansas. Then all the days she'd spent waiting for the phone call that would deliver her first part. And, more recently, the years she'd waited to get close to Michael Gabriel. She was thoroughly sick of waiting.

Since she was a small child she'd known she had a gift, that her voice was special. As the years passed and she began to realize the limitations of her life, her desperation had increased. When Bobby had left for New York, intent on making his mark on the stage, she had been happy for him but jealous as well. With her brother gone, their parents had turned all their attention to her. They were determined not to have two children desert them for a world they didn't comprehend. Where Bobby had turned sullen and had rebelled at every turn, Rachel learned to follow their strictures on the surface while dreaming within. She had sat in her room for hours as a teenager, thinking of ways to get to Hollywood, living for the time when she could get away. Instead of pictures depicting the latest movie or soap star pinup, her walls had boasted the faces of Streisand and Julie Andrews, women who had made it to the top with their incredible voices and their acting talents. If wishing counted for anything, Rachel would be their equal one day.

She pressed her fingers to her forehead, attempting to massage away the nagging strain settled there. She pushed herself hard; too hard, her friends would say. With determination she would reach the top one day—but first she had to make a detour for Bobby's sake.

Picking up her glass from the low wrought-iron table, she hoisted it in a salute to the sky, then tossed back the remnants of her wine. She stood, then went very still. Cocking her head in the direction of the house, she listened intently. Was that the phone? As she hurried toward the door, the sound intensified into the distinct ringing of a telephone. Rachel began to run.

Quickly sliding aside the patio door, she cringed when it banged heavily against the frame. Her bare feet slapped against the kitchen floor with irritating loudness until she reached the phone and picked up the receiver in midring.

The sharp click of the line going dead interrupted her greeting.

"I hate that," she exclaimed to the empty room.

A plaintive meow caught Rachel's attention and she turned. Minnie, in her attempt to climb the screen over the kitchen sink, was stuck halfway up the window. The heartrending cries increased in volume when no one came immediately to her rescue.

"I know exactly how you feel, baby," Rachel crooned, hurrying toward her pet. "Exactly."

Michael turned away from the phone with a heavy sigh. He had been trying to talk himself out of calling her all evening. Then, when he finally gave in to the irresistible urge to hear her voice, she wasn't home anyway.

She was probably out on the town with some glowing stud of an athlete or the rising Hollywood star of the month—a man without scars, without shadows in his past and in his mind.

Michael walked over to his bookcases, which stretched the entire length of a wall from floor to ceiling. He hadn't done much reading until three years ago, always preferring sports and outdoor activities to sedentary pursuits. Then he'd discovered a hidden passion for all types of stories. As a result he'd had to build these bookcases to house all the volumes he'd grown to love. Running his finger along their bindings, he closed his eyes and remembered.

He had touched her. That had been a mistake. Before tonight he had known his dreams were pure fantasy. Now there were concrete sensations to enhance his night thoughts. The memories would drive him mad.

The shrill ring of his phone made him jump, then frown in puzzlement. Very few people knew his unlisted number, and those who did wouldn't call after business hours.

He shrugged, then turned from the bookcases and quickly crossed the room to the phone.

"Hello."

His voice was more gruff than he had meant it to be, and the silence greeting the word had him clearing his throat before attempting a friendlier tone.

"Hello? Michael Gabriel here."

"Good," the voice whispered. "I didn't want to speak to your ever-present goon."

Michael frowned. Something was familiar about the voice, though he couldn't place it. The caller spoke so quietly, he was unable to determine if the speaker was male or female, but the menace behind the whisper was clearly evident.

"Who is this?" he asked.

"Someone who knows you very well." Laughter crackled over the wire. "I know all about you."

Michael didn't like the sound of the voice. He liked the odd laughter even less.

"How did you get this number?" he asked calmly, knowing he should find out as much as possible before the caller hung up.

"I have my ways. Ways you couldn't imagine." The laughter came again. "I've been watching you."

"Why?"

"I like to watch you. I've been doing it for a long time now. You'd be amazed at all I know about you. And about Rachel Taylor too."

"Rachel?" Michael didn't like the sound of her name on the caller's lips.

"Yes, Rachel. I want you to stay away from that cute, little singing bimbo. Unless you want something to happen to her. Something bad, Gabriel, very bad."

The whisper crawled up his spine, and he

clutched the unyielding plastic of the phone until his fingers ached.

"Leave her alone." He allowed the anger rushing through him at the thought of Rachel being hurt to seep into his voice.

"Shut up." The voice was matter-of-fact, too confident for comfort. "I give the orders here, not you. Your job is to listen and do exactly as I tell you. You'd better remember that if you want her to remain as pretty as she is."

"What do you want from me?" he shouted.

"The same thing I've always wanted. You. Just you."

Click.

He listened intently for a moment until the dial tone returned, then slammed the phone back into its cradle. The resounding crack did little to calm his mood.

"Son of a bitch," Michael muttered.

"Is that an observation about someone in particular or just a random sentiment?" Roger asked from the doorway.

Michael looked up and scowled. "You. You're supposed to be my bodyguard. Where are you when I need you?"

Roger shrugged, unimpressed by Michael's anger. "You answered the phone before I could get near the thing. I figured your babe was on the line. Who was it?"

Michael stared at the phone, deep in thought.

"Mike?" Roger asked, then walked across the room to put a hand on his boss's shoulder.

When Michael knocked away his arm angrily Roger frowned. "Whoa there, buddy. Who tripped your trigger?"

Michael didn't answer, turning away and striding to the window. He pushed back the curtain and peered into the darkness. Despite the late hour, thousands of lights in the distance outlined the Valley of the Sun—the cities of Phoenix, Scottsdale, and others. But he wasn't concerned with them. His interest lay closer, directly outside the walls that enclosed his home and kept him apart from the rest of the world. He watched for several moments, straining his eyes to detect any shadow of movement.

There was nothing.

Chapter Four

Rachel couldn't sleep. She tossed. She turned. She looked at the glowing red numbers on her digital clock every two minutes. Finally, at 2 a.m., she threw back the covers and got out of bed. If she wasn't going to sleep, she'd clean her kitchen floor—no sense wasting the nervous energy.

After flipping on the lights in the kitchen Rachel opened the cabinet under the sink and pulled out a bucket, a sponge, and some cleanser. While she filled the bucket with hot water, she stared at the darkened window in front of her.

Thoughts of Michael and their embrace continued to swirl in her head. No wonder she couldn't sleep. Why had she gone into his arms?

And once there, why had she stayed? She didn't know the answers to those questions, but she did know that she was in big trouble. She had no business responding to Michael Gabriel's kisses. She might want revenge, but there were some lengths to which she was not willing to go—and sleeping with the enemy was one of them.

He had said he would call her, but she doubted he would. His past three years had been spent locking himself away from the world; just because they had kissed once didn't mean he would allow her access to his thoughts and memories. She sighed, knowing she would have to contact him or risk losing whatever ground she might have gained with the man.

But how? She doubted if she would be able to surprise him again in his own domain after what had occurred earlier. With a frown, she realized she would have to mull over the possibilities during the many sleepless nights to come.

Rachel lifted the bucket of warm, soapy water out of the sink and set it carefully on the white vinyl floor. Then she untied her robe and tossed it onto the counter. Nothing like scrubbing the floor in your underwear at two in the morning to clear a confused head, she thought. Her mother, a firm believer in day dresses and sensible shoes for cleaning, would have a stroke if she could see Rachel now.

A half an hour later, dressed and much calmer and with a clean kitchen floor to boot, Rachel sat at her dining-room table, an untasted cup of tea before her. Minnie, who had taken one look at Rachel scrubbing her heart out in pink briefs, touched a delicate paw to the wet floor and fled, hissing, from the room, now snored peacefully in Rachel's lap.

Rachel smiled as she brought the cup to her lips, pausing to smell the herbal brew before taking a sip. She was pleasantly drowsy; there was no need to drag out the window-washing materials. Her eyes strayed to the floor-length window in front of her just as the tea touched her tongue. She jumped, then swallowed convulsively. The hot liquid burned a path straight to her stomach as her heart thumped painfully in her chest.

Eyes stared back at her from the other side of the glass.

Rachel froze, the cup lifted in midair, her mouth stiff and unyielding. Her mind told her to put down the cup and run for the phone, but her body refused to move. The shadowy figure on the other side of the window continued to watch.

Time slowed as she stared transfixed into the eyes hovering in the darkness. Then, as suddenly as the apparition had appeared, it was gone. She peered at complete blackness.

The crash of the china cup as it shattered on the table woke Minnie, who dug her claws into Rachel's legs as she leapt to the floor. The needlelike pain galvanized Rachel into action. She ran to the window and looked outside. Her eyes strained against the glare of the glass and the darkness of the night. She saw no one. Had she imagined that shadow of a face, those shining eyes?

After a thorough check of the locks on her doors and windows Rachel retreated to the living room and flopped into an overstuffed recliner. Her heart still beat overtime, but she forced her hands to unclench and attempted to slow her breathing. Should she call the police?

Rachel hesitated as she thought over her options. Anyone who might have been outside was long gone by now. And if her tired, overtaxed mind had invented the entire incident, she would do best to keep it to herself. No, she would let this experience go. But in the future, she promised herself, she would be more vigilant. At the first sign of trouble she would definitely call the authorities.

Now that her body had experienced a surge of adrenaline the lethargy she'd worked so hard to attain was a thing of the past. Rachel slowly walked into the bathroom. Since window washing was out of the question, she'd do the next best thing. Kneeling, she pulled white bottles, sponges, and scouring brushes from the cabinet beneath the sink.

* * *

"Whoever it is, Mike, he's one sick son of a bitch. You can't let this pass."

"It was just a phone call," Michael said.

"You should still call the police. Dammit, I'm a lot of things, but I'm no match for a lunatic."

Michael looked sharply at his friend. "Who said anything about a lunatic?"

Roger sighed, rolling his eyes toward the ceiling in exasperation. "Do you think a sane person would make a call like that?"

"I don't know. It could just have been a kid. Or a crank who couldn't sleep, dialing any old number."

"Do you really believe that?"

"I suppose not," Michael agreed reluctantly, then slammed his fist down on the surface of the desk on which he sat. "I don't care about myself. What do I have to lose anymore? But Rachel . . . the threat against her is something else entirely."

"She'll have to be told," Roger ventured.

"Told what? Do you have any idea how crazy this sounds?" Michael asked, his fingers curling inward in frustration. "I couldn't even tell if the person on the other end of the line was male or female. If it's a stalker—and I'm not saying it is—then I'd guess female." Michael shoved his hair away from his eyes impatiently. "No, I'm not going to frighten Rachel. I'll have to keep an eye on her until I know if this is real or just another crazy with a big mouth. People in the business get calls like this all the time. Hell, Rachel probably gets them herself."

Roger stared at him for so long, Michael had to stifle the urge to fidget like a child in church. Finally Roger said, "You're the boss."

Michael nodded, thankful there would be no more discussion of the strange caller. He'd had all he could stand of that topic for one evening.

"I'll find out her practice schedule from Harry and go to the studio at the same time," Michael said. "Then, when she's not working, I'll follow her on the motorcycle. It's easier to maneuver, and she'll never know it's me behind the helmet."

"And who's gonna keep an eye on you?"

"I took care of myself before you came along. I can do it again."

"You could have used me on one occasion I can think of," Roger said with irritating surety as he left the room.

Michael stared at the phone, wondering if he should take Roger's advice and call the police. After a long moment he shook his head. They'd only tell him such calls went with the territory. Public figures gave up their privacy; it was part of the job. Michael knew the law as well as the next actor; the police could do nothing about harassment until the caller crossed the line between threats and action. But he didn't plan to wait until Rachel was another statistic on the "Morning News."

Michael stood up and paced his room, his jaw tense with agitation. She would be fine. He would make sure of it.

Why, then, did he feel a creeping sense of alarm?

The recording studios of Danfield Enterprises slept dark and silent when I entered. Just the way I like them. I often watch him from the shadows while he works, listening to him sing. I do so admire talent. When he leaves I sit in his chair and dream of the day when I can finally look him straight in the eye. His eyes will widen in surprise when he sees me. And I'll smile. While he dies.

Watching is what I do best. No one ever sees me; I've learned to blend into the scenery with ease—one of my many talents. That and ferreting out information. I'm a master at learning what I want—no, need—to know.

I watched Rachel sneak into Gabriel's studio yesterday. The thought of her going near him almost made me scream for her to stop. But I've learned to control myself so much better lately. Once I considered the situation, I had to laugh. I know who she really is.

Gabriel hasn't a clue.

But such juicy information is for later—not quite yet. I'll know when the time has come for my first little bombshell.

The phone call isn't enough of a warning for Gabriel. I know actors get phone calls all the time; he'll most likely write my call off as that of an impulsive fan. But after tonight he'll know better.

I slipped into his practice room when no one else was around and left him a message. Nothing elaborate. Just so he'll understand I can get to him whenever I want.

I left the building undetected, an easy fete to accomplish when you know the secrets I know, and returned to my room. Soon Michael Gabriel will discover another clue in the puzzle he has yet to learn exists. The time has come to take the next step in my elaborate, but perfect, plan.

Michael awoke and saw, from the angle of the sun against his drapes, that he'd slept past noon. He rolled out of bed, thankful he felt better than he should, given the night he'd just spent. He had been unable to fall asleep until dawn, his mind a jumble of voices and images hovering just at the edge of recognition. Those voices and the tickling, nagging suspicion that there was something in the recesses of his memory that he couldn't bring forward made him clench his teeth in frustration. He had ended up with a pounding headache, and when he finally did sleep his dreams had been a repeat of those shifting, teasing images.

Michael spent the day in his usual pursuits: jogging, singing, reading. But the everyday tasks did little to keep his mind from the events of the night before. He took time out in the afternoon to make some calls, learning Rachel's practice schedule and her address.

After darkness descended on the sun-parched city Michael mounted his custom black-and-chrome Harley-Davidson. After securing his helmet he drove to the studio. Roger followed in the Lincoln.

Michael hadn't ridden the bike, purchased with a check from the first movie he'd ever made, since before his accident. The night air on his face felt even better than he remembered. The lights of the city glinted with an icy sheen against the indigo sky. During the day the arid heat of the region baked the life from Phoenix. But at night, when the sun slept, the city breathed deeply in relief and came to life once again.

Upon their arrival, Michael was glad to see the parking lot was empty; Rachel hadn't yet arrived. He and Roger entered the building silently. As usual, the place was deserted, the cleaning crews running on third shift.

"I'm going to get some work done," Michael said. "You can wait in here or go back to the car. Just make sure you let me know when she gets here and when she's ready to leave."

Roger nodded before heading back outside, and Michael entered his practice room.

He sat down in his usual chair. A sheet of notepaper lay on the table in front of him. Idly he picked it up, then frowned at the sight of his name emblazoned in red marker across the top of the sheet. He read the carefully written words; they looked as though someone had taken great pains to produce even, generic letters.

MICHAEL GABRIEL
I KNOW WHAT YOU DID.
YOU'LL HAVE TO PAY.

Michael crumpled the sheet in his fist, the crinkle of the paper grating across his nerves like a dripping faucet.

Who had left the note? And why?

No one knew what he had done. He had never told another living soul. Not even the police, though they'd hounded him unmercifully the entire time he spent recovering in the hospital.

Perhaps the note referred to something else—not that horrible day that haunted his mind every day and night. But if not that, what? He had done nothing else to warrant such a threat. First the phone call and now the note; who was after him and why?

Michael removed the crumpled paper from his fist and smoothed it flat on the table before grabbing the phone and dialing.

"Roger, get in here. Now," he barked into the receiver, then slammed the phone back into the cradle without waiting for a reply.

He stared at the bright red letters on the ivory paper. They reminded him of blood. His blood and . . .

Michael closed his eyes and fought against the memories that flooded him. All of his youthful dreams and ambitions had been crushed by the events of only a few moments. The pain, physical and mental, he'd felt on that long-ago day came back with a force so strong, it was as if the three years between had never existed.

Suddenly Roger smashed into the locked door, and Michael's eyes snapped open.

"Mike?" Roger called from the hallway, then slammed his fist against the door with a resounding thud. "What the hell's going on in there?"

Michael quickly crossed the room and flipped the lock on the door. Roger burst inside, nearly knocking him over. Roger's eyes scanned the room as his body crouched in fighting position.

"Relax. No one's here." Michael sighed. "At least not anymore."

"What did you hurry me in here for, then?"

Michael pointed to the sheet of paper on the table. "That."

Roger frowned. "A piece of paper? You brought me in here and nearly gave me a cardiac thinking you were in trouble to look at a fan letter?"

"I don't think the person who wrote this likes me all that much." Michael walked across the room and picked up the letter. Roger followed and took it from him, his gaze quickly scanning the large, childlike writing.

"Aw, hell," Roger mumbled, then looked up at Michael. "Now what?"

"I don't know." Michael sat down, shaking his head wearily.

"What does this mean? 'I know what you did.' "

Michael shrugged.

Roger stared at him for a moment. "You know, Mike, I can't help you if you don't let me. I get the feeling you know what's going on here. If you do, you'd better tell me so I can protect you."

"It's just a fan with an attitude. I'll be fine. I don't know what else we can do but stay more alert."

"Well, I do: We call the cops. I don't think that phone call last night was a fluke. Especially if the caller took the trouble to break in here and leave you a more efficient message."

"We don't know the caller and the letter writer are the same person."

Roger snorted. "Right. Suddenly, after all these years, two people turn up who have it in for you. I doubt it. And if by some chance that was the case, I'd only be more worried. I'm callin' the cops. Somethin' real strange is going on here and I don't like it."

"Neither do I," Michael muttered.

"Michael?"

They both jumped at the sound of Rachel's voice, followed by a tentative knock on the studio door.

Roger glanced at Michael, who motioned for the bodyguard to talk to her in the hall. As Roger slipped through the door, Michael locked it behind him, staying close to hear their conversation.

"Michael here?" Rachel asked.

"He's working," Roger said coldly. "Want me to tell him something?"

"Yes: to call. I still want to try and persuade him to work with me."

"Good luck. Say, you don't look so good. Are you okay?"

Michael straightened at Roger's words. He hated the thought that she might be ill.

"I'm fine. Just didn't get much sleep last night. You know," Rachel's voice dropped to a conspiratorial level, and Michael strained to hear her next words, "I thought someone was watching me outside my kitchen window. Really shook me up." She laughed, but Michael heard the small shake under the attempt at lightheartedness. "My imagination got the best of me, I guess."

Roger was silent for a heartbeat too long before answering. "Yeah, your imagination. Right. Sure."

"Well . . . aah. Just tell him I came by, and give him my message."

"No problem."

Michael heard Rachel retreat as he waited impatiently for Roger to return.

Damn the man. What is he doing out there?

Michael had just unlocked the door, preparing to open it and yank his friend back into the room, when Roger walked in.

He took one look at Michael's face and raised his eyebrows. "You heard?"

"Of course." Michael sighed, then made his decision. He couldn't allow anything to happen to Rachel because of a mistake he had made. Enough people had been hurt because of him already. "I want you to call the police and then wait for them. I'm going after her."

"You sure?" Roger frowned. "They're gonna want to talk to you."

"Yes," Michael said shortly, the urgency to have Rachel protected a tangible ache. "I'll talk to them tomorrow. Set up a time at the house. Show them the letter; tell them I got a phone call."

"There's something you haven't thought about here, Mike."

"What?" Michael snapped, failing to stifle his impatience. Roger ignored Michael's tone, as though he had spoken as sweetly as a ninety-year-old grandmother.

"The only other person we've seen in the studio at night is Rachel. Maybe she put the letter here."

Michael frowned. "Rachel?"

Roger shrugged. "What better alibi than to trot right over here after we come in and act as though everything's just peachy? I've seen it done a hundred times before."

"That's crazy."

"Exactly," Roger said triumphantly.

Michael turned slowly, Roger's words echoing in his ears as he picked up his helmet and left the room. He reached the parking lot just as Rachel pulled away and hurried to his bike. After following her home at a distance he remained in the shadows of the night, keeping her safe as the questions in his mind raged.

By the time dawn finally broke Michael was more confused than ever. Roger arrived to take watch during the daylight hours and filled him in on what the police had done the night before. A Detective Hamilton would come to the house at noon to speak with Michael.

"What did you tell them?" Michael asked.

"Just what you said: that you found the letter when you came to work and you got a strange call the other night." Roger shifted his shoulders and rolled his neck. "God, I hate cops."

Michael nodded absently, familiar with Roger's feelings on that subject. He continued to watch Rachel's house from their position across the street and down a block. Nothing had moved inside or out that he could see since Rachel had entered the night before.

Darkness was rapidly fading into the heat and light of morning, and Michael retreated to his bike and headed home.

Upon entering his room, he sensed someone had been there while he was gone. Nothing was missing, but he could tell things had been moved and then put back in a slightly different position. He tensed, wondering if the invader of his home was still inside watching him, waiting for a chance to spring. His gaze wandered around the room. He spied a small wrapped package on his desk and frowned. It hadn't been there yesterday.

Michael approached the brightly colored box. Did he dare touch it? Could an explosive be contained in such a small package? Maybe he should call the police and let them handle this. But he couldn't call them for every little thing.

Suddenly irritated at the nervousness flooding him in his own house, he snatched up the package. Nothing started ticking; nothing exploded. He tore the paper from the box to reveal a tiny tin of Gummy Bears embossed with the skyline of Chicago. A small white card fluttered to the desktop. Michael lifted the paper toward him and read the neat script.

I know how much you love these disgusting things, so I got you a present while I was on vacation in the Windy City. Enjoy. Love ya, sweetie. Joyce.

Michael let out the breath he hadn't known he held on a long sigh of relief. Of course. Joyce, his cleaning lady. No wonder things looked like they had been moved and replaced—she'd been dusting. Joyce came in once a week when he was at the studio to clean and do the wash. She often left him little presents when she returned from one of her numerous vacations or visits to her grandchildren.

Joyce was a nurse who had retired to Arizona several years before and cleaned a few houses to keep herself busy. Though Michael had never met her face-to-face, she admired his work. She often left him friendly notes, as well as giving Roger medical tips whenever one of them had a minor illness or ache. He must really be on edge if a present from Joyce had him searching the dark corners of his own house for intruders. He should have known the only person who could have entered the house was Joyce; the security system had still been on when he'd returned. Besides himself and Roger, Joyce was the only one who knew the access code.

Crossing the room to his bed, he stretched out and attempted to sleep. Visions of Rachel rose in his mind. Could she be the one who had made the call and left the note? What Roger said made sense. Everything had been fine until she turned up with her demands to see him and work with him. Wherever he turned lately he ran up against Rachel Taylor. But what possible reason could she have for threatening him? And with something he'd done in the past, no less? He had never met her before. *That* was a meeting he would definitely remember. No, she couldn't be the owner of the voice he had heard on the other end of the telephone line. He would recognize Rachel's voice anywhere. Wouldn't he? He'd been listening to it on tape for several months now. He ought to know her voice no matter how she tried to disguise it.

After a half an hour of allowing his thoughts to tangle around themselves Michael gave up trying to sleep and picked up the phone. Maybe if he heard her voice over the phone again, and really listened, he would be able to convince himself of her innocence—or guilt.

After three rings she answered. "Hello?"

Michael didn't respond for a moment, savoring the clear, sweet pitch of her voice. He sighed in relief. Rachel's voice was too beautiful to become twisted with hate. He *had* to believe that. He *did* believe it.

"Hello?" she asked, the volume of her voice increasing.

"It's Michael."

He could almost see her smile, and his lips curved upward in response.

"I'm so glad you called," she said.

"Roger told me you came by."

"Yes. I'd hoped to persuade you about the duet. Maybe if we sang together a little you'd see what I mean."

Michael closed his eyes, letting himself imagine for just a moment what his life would be like with Rachel Taylor in it. Did he dare take such a chance? Once he had a taste of the real world again he knew he would crave the flavor every day of his life.

"Michael?"

Rachel's questioning tone brought his eyes open. Without conscious thought he began to sing what he had come to think of as "their song," the title song from the movie, into the phone.

Rachel caught her breath as Michael's pure, clear voice came to her over the telephone wires. Closing her eyes, she leaned back against the headboard of her bed. Only one thought remained as she immersed herself in the beauty on the air.

His voice shines like sun on the summer water. I could listen to him forever.

She hoped that was how long he would continue to sing to her. The lyrics telling of love denied, love lost, love found went straight to her heart, and Rachel swallowed against the well of emotions that made drawing a breath of air an awesome chore.

Michael's voice faltered in the middle of the song, and the last lingering note died away.

"Don't stop," Rachel whispered. "Please."

"I don't know why I did that," Michael said, obviously uncomfortable.

"I don't care why; I just don't want you to stop."

"I'd like to hear you sing."

"Meet me at the studio tomorrow night and you can."

Silence met her statement, and Rachel could have cursed her too-bold tongue. Would she ever learn to handle people more carefully? When she wanted something she just went for broke, never thinking that other people might not respond to such tactics. Especially a person like Michael.

"You never give up, do you?" Michael asked.

"Not without a good old college try," Rachel admitted.

"I think you've gone beyond my idea of a college try."

She'd been told that before and still hadn't given up. This time she felt chastened. "Sorry."

"Don't apologize. You wouldn't be you if you didn't follow your dreams. I admire that."

His words reminded her of someone else's dreams—dreams that had been crushed forever by this man. She had to remember that Michael Gabriel wasn't what he seemed. Within his appealing body lay a heart hardened to dreams, a soul filled with avarice. She had allowed herself to be moved by the beauty of his voice, the depth of his talent. She couldn't let that happen again or all her carefully laid plans would be for naught. If she let him, he could very well destroy her as easily as he had destroyed her brother. Rachel took a deep breath and mustered her fleeting willpower.

"I'll be at the studio tomorrow night. Meet me there," she said, putting all the earnestness she could muster into her voice. "We'll sing together once, and if it doesn't work, I won't ever bother you again. I promise."

"I seem to recall your promising something along those lines once before. If I'd just call you and you couldn't convince me, you'd stop."

"Oh, right. Well, I mean it this time."

Michael didn't answer for so long, Rachel wondered if he had hung up. Or maybe she had finally pushed him past the point of endurance.

In the tense silence her voice sounded loud even to her own ears. "I don't care what you look like, Michael. This is business. We can do this. *You* can do this. For the good of the movie."

"For the good of the movie," he said, as though to himself, then continued in a stronger voice. "You're right. That's all this is."

An image flashed through her mind of Michael holding her in the practice room—his fingers in her hair, his lips on hers. The feelings rushing through her then had been anything but impersonal. They had been downright dangerous to everything she believed in, as was the connection she sensed between them. They were alike in many ways—both with their secrets, their desires, their ambitions. There was a part of her that had called out to him from the first, and a part of him that answered.

Rachel pushed the thought away. If they were going to work together, if she was going to accomplish her goal, there would be no repeat performances of their embrace, no matter how much her body might want one.

Michael's voice startled her from her reverie. "All right, Rachel. Tomorrow night. I'll be there."

Rachel was so surprised at his words, she clutched the phone tighter, but she found herself unable to speak. The soft click of Michael breaking the connection made her sit up straight.

"Michael?" she whispered, though she knew he was gone.

She hung up and turned to stare at the picture of Bobby on her nightstand. They had never looked alike, a fact that was much remarked upon in their small corner of Kansas. Bobby had always looked like their mother, while Rachel favored their father. Even at birth, when many babies who later have blond hair are graced with dark locks, Bobby's hair had been nearly white. His eyes were a peculiar shade of gray that changed with the shift of his emotions: the color of a lake at dawn when he was happy—the color of the sky before a storm when he was angry. Rachel had always known when to get out of Bobby's way just by looking into his eyes.

She reached out and touched her finger to his chin.

"Tomorrow night, Bobby," she said, hearing the excitement in her voice. But was she excited because her plans would soon be put into motion and all the years of waiting were finally coming to an end? Or did the prospect of meeting the man who made her feel as no other man ever had make her hands shake with an inner chill? "Tomorrow night," she repeated. "Tomorrow night, it begins."

Though she had hoped to get a decent night's sleep for the first night that week, Rachel spent a second sleepless night cleaning an already spotless house. At the rate she was going, she'd have to hire out as a third-shift maid to find another house to clean.

But her mind had been too full of thoughts of Michael for her to sleep more than a few restless hours. He had said he would come to her, and those words threw her mind into turmoil.

Her plans for revenge had been fine when plotted against a man she didn't know. But these past few days, as she'd inched closer and closer to Michael Gabriel, her resolve had wavered. The sound of his voice, be it speaking or singing, combined with his touch on her body had set off feelings she'd never dreamed existed. How could that be when she'd never even seen the man in the light?

Rachel spent the day in her flower garden. The physical labor of digging, planting, and weeding kept her nervous energy at a manageable level. She found that trying to keep a garden alive against the Arizona elements was a challenge she relished. Back home she had helped her mother in the garden. But growing potatoes, carrots, and turnips had never appealed to her sense of adventure. They had needed the food to survive in those days, and she was adept with the earth as a result of that need. Her mother considered growing plants just for the sake of looking at them a frivolity. Rachel had learned that she enjoyed such frivolity beyond measure.

When early evening arrived she leaned back on her heels, removed her wide-brimmed straw hat, and glanced at her watch.

Six o'clock; time to take a shower. As Rachel walked toward the house, the fluttering in her stomach, which had ebbed during her time outdoors, resumed.

She took pains with her clothes and hair, choosing a flowing violet sundress that she knew complimented her eyes and twisting her thick brunette hair into a French braid. Her skin had always reacted well to the sun, though she tried to keep it from burning. The time she'd spent in Arizona had toned her flesh to a shade between honey and cinnamon.

After a moment's hesitation she opened her makeup case and applied cosmetics, something she usually did only to face the press.

Standing back, Rachel stared critically at herself in the mirror. She'd never be considered beautiful, but she did have nice skin and pretty hair. A reviewer had once written that she possessed exotic eyes. She'd saved that article in her scrapbook.

Working in the garden all day, she had forgotten to eat since breakfast. Her refrigerator revealed a half carton of yogurt, a bagel, and a bottle of wine. Rachel shut the door and sighed. The studio cafeteria would have to do for dinner tonight. After leaving Minnie some food Rachel picked up her purse and jumped into the car.

The parking lot reflected the end of the work day at Danfield Studios. Rachel made her way to the cafeteria, nodding to the few people she met on her way. The kitchen crew were in the midst of cleaning up, but Rachel was able to coax a taco salad out of the cook before he shut down for the night. Taking her meal to a table near the window, Rachel sat down and pulled a paperback mystery out of her purse. She dug into her meal with a sigh of satisfaction: The best food was always food you didn't have to make yourself.

She didn't feel someone watching her until she glanced up from her book to take a sip of coffee. She looked around the room, but no one remained beyond herself and the kitchen crew. As far as she could see they were all occupied with trying to get their work done and get home.

Rachel shrugged. She would have to get used to being stared at eventually. She doubted if Barbara Streisand allowed herself to be put off by it. She smiled to herself. She was a long way from Streisand, but it didn't hurt to be prepared. Rachel laughed softly to herself and returned her attention to her book.

A few moments later the feeling returned. Rachel slapped the book down on the table and glared around the room.

No one watched her. No one was even there.

She stood and took what was left of her meal to the conveyor belt that took all the used dishes into the kitchen. There was no reason to try to finish the salad; she was too on edge to eat.

Walking toward the door, she heard a scuffle, and then a shadow drifted away from the iced glass. Rachel increased her pace, yanking open the door and glancing up one hall and down the other. She frowned. No one was there.

She had thought she'd gotten past the nervousness engendered by the sight of eyes peering through her kitchen window. But obviously not. Perhaps it took a lot longer than she'd realized to get over such an experience.

Walking to her studio, Rachel kept her eyes and ears alert for any further clues. For the first time she didn't enjoy the seclusion of Danfield

Studios after dark. Tonight she wished for some company.

Rachel looked over her shoulder uneasily. Was someone watching her again? Just like the other night? Or was her imagination in overdrive?

She increased her pace and reached her studio quickly. Once inside, Rachel sank into her chair with a deep sigh. Her nerves hadn't been stretched this tight since her last audition.

Pressing her lips together, Rachel forced herself to get down to business. She had to do her best work on this movie while she could. If she succeeded in her plans for Michael Gabriel, this could be her last chance for stardom.

Rachel reached across the control panel and turned on her music. Seconds later, she lost herself in the wonder of the melody, and thoughts of Michael receded for the length of a song.

Chapter Five

Detective David Hamilton, a tall, sallow man with graying blond hair, arrived on Michael's doorstep precisely at noon, pen and notebook in hand. He stayed until two o'clock, asking questions around an unlit cigarette.

"Gotta quit," he explained to Michael. "But I can't seem to think without one in my mouth."

After five minutes with the man Michael had to grip his hands together to keep from snatching the cigarette from the detective's mouth. In Michael's opinion Hamilton thought too much, and none of it was good.

"Mr. Gabriel, since I spoke with your man yesterday I did some research. It seems you were investigated for murder a few years back."

Michael clenched his jaw, all the while trying to keep his face in the same neutral position in which it had been since the questioning began. He had hoped once he was cleared of Robert's murder he would never have to go through an interrogation again. He'd been wrong.

"I was never charged."

"Uh huh." Hamilton flipped his notebook to another page and tried to draw on his dead cigarette. He grimaced, then looked up at Michael. "Murder's pretty serious. Think maybe these threats have something to do with this Robert Matthews?"

"I don't see how. The police found me innocent."

"Well, I wouldn't say that. They didn't have enough evidence to prosecute. That's a long way from innocent in my book."

"And what else does it say in that book of yours, Detective?"

"Not much, I'm afraid. Tried to reach Jim O'Malley and get the records on your case, but he's on vacation. They're working on it for me. Hopefully I'll have the whole story in a week or so."

"And in the meantime?"

"In the meantime we'll have a car patrol the area, put a tap on your phone. Not much else to be done."

"Thanks for all your help, Detective," Michael said as he escorted the man to the front door.

He wasn't able to keep the sarcasm from seeping into his voice.

Hamilton looked at him sharply. "I understand you're working on a movie over at Danfield."

Michael nodded.

"Be a good idea, I imagine, to get some publicity going. Especially since you've been out of the limelight so long."

Michael stared at the detective in amazement. The man thought this was all a publicity stunt. Michael stifled his temper and stared Hamilton in the eye. He refused to respond to the innuendo.

The detective shrugged and walked through the door, then stopped and turned back. "Anything else you want to add before I go?"

Michael had planned to tell the police about the threat to Rachel, but from the first Hamilton's attitude had put him on the defensive. Now he wasn't so sure he should tell the man any more, and he certainly couldn't mention Roger's suspicions of Rachel. The idea that the female lead in a movie was stalking the male lead would be tabloid heaven. Hamilton would never believe Michael and Rachel weren't plotting a publicity stunt if Michael told him that bit of information. Any chance they had to get police cooperation to learn the identity of the caller would be gone.

In answer to the detective's question, Michael slammed the door in David Hamilton's face.

Later that night Michael rode into the parking lot at Danfield Studios. Roger awaited him near the back door.

"What's up?" he asked as he joined his friend.

"No problems. You met with the police?"

"Yeah." Michael grimaced, remembering the uncomfortable interview. "They're trying to contact Jim O'Malley, but he's on vacation."

"Did you tell them about Rachel and the phone call?" Roger asked suspiciously.

"Not Rachel," Michael admitted.

"Why the hell not?" Roger exploded.

"You should have heard the guy, Rog. He thinks this is all a publicity stunt. Right now the police are at least trying to find a suspect. If I tell them the leading lady is involved, we won't get any help at all. Besides, I don't want to scare her if this all turns out to be nothing. We'll watch her as we planned."

"She'll be a lot more scared if she starts getting threats of her own."

"True. I'll tell you what: If I get another call, the police will have it on tape, and then Detective Hamilton will have to believe we're not just pulling a publicity stunt." Michael opened the door to the studio. He paused before he entered and turned back to Roger. "Right now I need you to do something for me."

"What?"

"Give me five minutes, then cut the power."

Roger raised his eyebrows.

"Just do it, Rog. Then wait near her studio until I join you."

"Whatever you say, boss man."

Michael frowned but chose to ignore Roger's taunt as the door closed behind him.

Immediately he heard the strains of a song drifting through the air. Michael followed the sound until he stood outside the door to Rachel's studio. For a few moments he waited, savoring the beauty of her voice, imagining she sang only for him. Opening his eyes, he shook his head. He had come to tell Rachel once and for all that he couldn't sing with her. He had no concrete evidence she was anything but what she professed to be: an actress who wanted him to work with her for the good of the movie. That being the case, he had no reason to allow himself the pleasure of her company, no matter how much he craved it.

One of the lights flickered overhead, and Michael glanced up. He'd better get moving and quit dreaming or the power would be off before he was in position.

Walking quickly down the hall, he opened a door and slipped inside. He saw her immediately through the glass separating the recording studio from the control room. The darkness surrounding him magnified the soft golden light enveloping her from above, as though she rested in a muted spotlight from the gods. She sat at the control panel, her eyes closed as she sang. He watched as her soft red lips opened and closed with the movements of the words, though no sound reached him in the soundproof studio.

He leaned back against the wall and drank in the sight of her. He wanted to reach out and touch the smooth perfection of her cheek, drag his fingers through the confining braid and loosen her hair so he could bury his face in its fresh-scent. He had never had such a strong attraction to another woman, and his reaction to Rachel mystified him. He knew nothing about her, yet his body and heart responded as though they'd been together a lifetime. From the first moment he'd looked at her picture she'd seemed familiar to him. Once he'd met Rachel, he'd sensed a sadness within her that called to an answering emotion within himself.

Michael shifted, uncomfortable with his thoughts and the painfully aroused state of his body. At that moment Rachel opened her eyes. She must have seen him move in the shadows for she stiffened, her eyes widening in surprise before her mouth opened in a silent, frightened *o*. At that moment the power snapped off.

He sensed her fear in the darkness, though he heard nothing. He had to reach her before she ran from what she feared. He didn't relish the idea of chasing her through the darkened, twisting corridors of Danfield Studios. Moving quickly along the wall, Michael reached the door to the control room and pulled it open. The scuffling sounds told him she was scrambling toward the exit to the hall. Her breath came in short, harsh gasps between whimpers of fear. At the sound of the door opening she went still.

"Rachel, it's me. Michael," he said urgently. "Don't be afraid."

"Michael." She exhaled with a whispering sigh. "Thank God." Then she began to laugh, a trifle hysterically, he thought. "I don't know what I thought, but when someone came in and then the lights went off . . ."

"I know. I'm sorry. Please, come back and sit down. We'll talk."

After a moment's hesitation Michael heard Rachel make her way back to her chair. He remained by the door.

"Shouldn't we check on the power?" she asked.

"Later. Right now we need to talk."

"There's nothing wrong with the lights, is there? You did this."

"Not me, exactly."

"Roger, then. I know who pulls his strings, Michael. What I want to know is why. I told you I didn't care what you looked like."

"That's easy to say when you've never seen me."

"Do you think I'm so shallow that I'd be unable to deal with your appearance? I'm interested in your voice, Michael, and that voice is the most beautiful thing I've ever heard."

"Pretty is as pretty does?" he asked.

"Something like that."

She stood up and he stiffened, then relaxed when she remained near the control panel.

"Can't you at least try to sing with me?" she pleaded. "This is my big chance. I need you, Michael."

His hands clenched so tightly they ached as he fought against his desire to give in to her need, his need.

Why had he come here?

"I can't," he ground out between clenched teeth. "I wouldn't know how to deal with someone face-to-face anymore. I don't think you know what you're asking of me."

"We'll work things out. We can take it as slow as you want. Go anywhere you want. I can come to your house. We can work here. I can help you through this. I know I can."

Rachel's voice had risen with her excitement, and Michael felt the energy of her personality combined with the drive of ambition. Fleetingly he remembered himself at the beginning of his career and understood her desires.

"Why is this so important to you?" he asked.

"I've waited my whole life for a chance like this. I can feel that this movie is going to push me over the edge to stardom. I can taste success on the tip of my tongue. You can give it to me, Michael. We can have it together."

"Success isn't all it's cracked up to be. I've been there. You can be on top of the heap today and no one knows your name tomorrow.

This is a vile business, Rachel. A business that eats little girls like you for lunch."

"I know what I'm doing. Trust me."

Trust her? He knew what she was after. His voice, his talent—not him. Could he work with her, knowing she was using him for her own gain, caring only about what he could do for her and not about Michael, the man. He had been down that road with a woman before and had sworn he would never travel it again. But Rachel was nothing like Camilla. Camilla had been with him when he was on his way up. Then, when he'd crashed to the ground, she had taken one look at his ruined face and walked away without a second glance. Rachel had never seen him; she didn't know him at all. Did he dare take her at her word?

Michael crossed the room toward her, faltering a little as the pressing blackness confused him. He cursed under his breath. What had happened to his night vision, carefully honed over the past few years of living in the darkness? Whenever he was near this woman everything around him went off center.

"Here," she said quietly to his left.

He turned sharply, bumping into her. Rachel's hands clutched his arms for balance, and he caught his breath as the warmth of her body melted against him.

"Michael?"

The name whispered past his cheek, stirring his hair, and he groaned, attempting to move away from her. Rachel's fingers tightened, drawing him back.

"Don't," she said, and traced her fingers up his arms. She caressed his shoulders, then laced her hands behind his neck, pulling him downward a few inches. Her lips were so close to his that when she whispered, "Don't go," he felt every nuance of the words.

Her lips met his tentatively at first, as though she were afraid he'd bolt and run. The idea entered his mind but was burned to ashes as the heat from their joined lips extinguished all thought. Michael hesitated only a moment longer before responding.

Hungrily, he parted her lips and delved into her softness. His fingers impatiently yanked the ribbon from her hair and loosened the braid until her tresses swung free to fill his hands just as he'd imagined. The reality far outweighed his dreams.

Though he couldn't see her, he made up for that loss with his searching hands, touching her face gently, tracing her brow, cheeks, and nose. He buried his face in her hair, inhaling the scent. Today it reminded him of evergreens in the Minnesota autumns of his youth. He walked his lips across her neck, memorizing the texture of soft, supple skin where her shoulder joined her collarbone. He smiled against her mouth as her moans of pleasure serenaded the darkness. He had kissed countless woman in the reckless years before his accident, yet never had one touched him so deeply, never had he felt a merging that filled the aching emptiness in his soul.

Michael didn't know how long they stood, mouths searching, tongues tasting. Time slowed in the darkness, and his breath became her breath, their desires mingled.

Rachel unclasped her hands from behind his neck and her palms moved to cradle his face. At the light touch on his scarred cheek, reality intruded, and Michael flinched, pulling away.

"I'm sorry. Did I hurt you?" she whispered.

"No." Michael stepped back, out of her reach. "No one's touched me there since . . ." He faltered, not wanting to talk about his accident when he'd just started to feel human again.

"Since you were hurt?" she prompted.

"Yes." He sighed. He wasn't the same man he'd been three years ago, and it was time he stopped pretending he ever could be again. All anything between them would be was pretending in the dark. He went to the door of the recording studio.

"I'm glad I was the first."

Her voice, just above a whisper, floated to him through the darkness, and a breath of air brushed his face. Michael put his hand up to rest where Rachel had touched him. The scars seemed to burn his fingertips, as painful as the reality of what could never be. He clenched his hand and turned away.

"I'll see that the power is turned back on. Stay here until you can see."

"You're leaving?" Her voice was pitched higher with surprise. "We haven't finished our discussion."

"I think we have. My answer is still no. This doesn't change anything."

"If you believe that, you're a fool, Michael Gabriel."

"You can't bribe me with sex. I've done without it for three years; I can continue to do so."

She gasped at his callous assessment of their relationship, but she didn't crumble into tears. Instead her anger came through to him full-force. "You can insult me all you want; it won't make me give up. I haven't had to sleep with anyone yet to get what I want; I'm not going to start with you. You can't tell me you didn't feel something special between us just now."

"I can't?"

"Don't do this," she cried. "Don't try to cheapen what we felt just because you're afraid."

"I lost any capacity I had for fear long ago."

"You lie," she spat. "You're afraid of me, of what I make you feel. You can't write off what's between us by calling it lust, Michael. We both know there's more than that."

Without answering, Michael turned and exited the room. He half expected her to come after him and force the confrontation she'd been asking for. But she didn't, and seconds later he met Roger.

"You can turn on the power now," Michael said.

"What happened?"

"None of your business. Just turn on the lights and meet me in the morning at her house."

Michael could tell from Roger's silence that his friend didn't appreciate the tone of Michael's voice. But his emotions were too raw at that moment to allow him to deal with any questions. Without further comment Michael left the building and climbed onto his motorcycle. Feeling the need for space, he decided to ride for awhile. According to her schedule, Rachel had several hours of practice to attend to tonight so she would be prepared to record the next day. He would have time to calm down and still return to follow her home.

Michael drove into the desert, his thoughts a whirlwind of confusion. What had he been thinking to allow her to get so close to him?

He ached in all the appropriate places, but the worst pain centered near his heart. He should have put a stop to their association immediately. Now that he'd touched her, tasted her, being without her would be torture.

He had been surprised to hear her say she'd also felt the strong currents between them. Then his mind had whispered that she was an actress, an actress who wanted something from him. These women would go to unheard of lengths to achieve their goals. How far would Rachel go to get what she wanted?

That was the question haunting his mind as he rode down the empty highway. His feelings certainly stemmed from infatuation combined with his cursed abstinence. But could there be something more? Did he dare allow himself to find out?

Michael shook his head. He just didn't know anymore.

He returned to the studio in plenty of time to follow Rachel home, but as his gaze swept the empty parking lot he swallowed hard against the unease suddenly stuck in his throat.

She was gone, and she was all alone.

Though she had tried, Rachel had been unable to work after Michael left. She had finally given up with a frustrated curse. Driving home, she relived the emotional scene between them over and over again.

Where had she gone wrong? What had she done to make him so angry? Just when she thought she had gotten through to him she was right back where she had started. She had no idea what to do next.

What had gotten into her to say those things to him? She was trying to get the man to work with her, to trust her, and instead of reasoning with him she'd kissed him like a courtesan, then thrown challenges in his face.

He'd made her so angry when he'd pulled away, then spoken to her in that icy calm voice while she burned with an ache so deep her body echoed his name. A horrible suspicion had taken root within her. Would she ever be able to assuage such a need with anyone but him? When he'd left she had wanted nothing more than to race after him and beg him to kiss her again. Just once.

Rachel groaned and clutched the steering wheel tighter, watching as her fingers whitened from the strain.

Just once? That would never be enough. She had told him there was more than just lust between them and, God help her, there was. That was what frightened her so deeply. If she was smart she would stay away from him before she destroyed herself with this desire for something that could never be.

Why did she forget all about Bobby whenever she was with Michael? Was she losing her mind? How could she forget that the man she was panting over had held her brother's life in his hands—and then let it go?

When she had planned to ruin Michael Gabriel's career to gain some small measure of revenge for the loss of her brother, she hadn't figured on the questions that would arise once she got near the man. She had tagged him as ambitious, greedy, groping for success by using his nonexistent scars to further a cultivated romantic image. Instead, he seemed to purposely sabotage any chance for stardom by only taking enough roles to live on. Admittedly, he and Roger lived well, but not as well as they could if Michael were truly the man she had thought him to be.

The movie they were working on, for example, was the first large project he'd done since the accident. Though it was the biggest break of her career, for a man of Michael Gabriel's scope the picture was little more than child's play.

But her confusion over his motives was the least of her worries. She found herself more and more attracted to a man she had never seen, a man she had sworn to hate. The few times she had been in his company she had been drawn to him in ways she couldn't comprehend. She felt as though everything she believed was spinning away into a great abyss and only the sound of Michael's voice anchored her to the real world.

Rachel pulled her car into the driveway and shut off the engine, then leaned back in her seat to look at the stars. If only the answers she sought were as easy to spot as those tiny pinpoints of light against the backdrop of the universe.

I was near enough to touch him when he went into Rachel's recording studio, and Gabriel never knew it. Maybe a subtle warning is needed, just to remind him to stay away from her. I'll have to think of the best way to do it.

After he went into her studio I crept close and listened to them talk. Then the silence came, and I knew they were kissing, touching. Fury coursed through me, but I held it in check.

How dare she touch him? Kiss him? Disgusting!

But enough of that. Remembering it only makes me angry, and I had to stay calm and keep to my plans.

They argued and he tore out of the room. I barely had time to get out of the way. But I have so many hiding places there, they'll never catch me. I can follow anyone in those studios and never get caught.

I waited until the goon was out of the way and then hurried outside after Gabriel. He rode off on his motorcycle in the direction of the open road. His goon left soon after, but headed toward their home. Seeing that Gabriel was alone for the first time in years, I was tempted to follow him and finish our business right then. But that would be too easy. He wouldn't suffer enough. And if there is one thing I've dreamed of, it is watching him suffer.

So I let him go and followed her instead.

She went straight home, and that was good, though she sat in her car and stared at the stars so long, I wondered if she planned to sleep outside. Finally she trudged into the house.

I haven't been able to figure out yet what she's up to. But I will. Until then, I don't want her hanging around and messing up what I've planned so perfectly.

It's a joke how Gabriel and his goon hover over her night and day. I laugh at their stupidity while I watch them watch her. Nothing can stop me from doing whatever I want. Whenever I want.

Little Miss Songbird needs a warning to keep her away from him. Just a little warning, I decided. No need to get physical yet when a threat has always worked so well in the past.

So I gave her a threat. And I must say I enjoyed the giving. I think my message came through loud and clear. I even came across an idea for Gabriel's warning. If it works, he'll swear off Rachel Taylor for good.

But there's always the chance they might refuse to listen. If Rachel continues to interfere, and Gabriel doesn't take the hint, I can get as rough as necessary to make them understand.

Michael Gabriel is mine.

Rachel walked into her bedroom and began to undress, her mind still on Michael. When someone grabbed her from behind and shoved her into the walk-in closet she was too surprised to scream. The door slammed shut as she turned. She ran forward and turned the knob; it wouldn't budge.

"Stay away from Michael Gabriel, Miss Songbird. He's mine," said a muffled voice, as though someone was speaking through layers of cloth.

"Who are you?" Rachel asked, struggling against her fear.

"None of your business. Your business is to stay away from Michael Gabriel."

The menace in the voice echoed in the black, closed-in closet, and Rachel shivered. As she moved back from the door, something brushed against her cheek. She gasped and froze, her heart beating faster, painful in its intensity. When the touch did not come again she reached up. Her shaking fingers encountered a shirt or dress hanging level with her face. That must have been the cause of the eerie touch. Straining her eyes against the thick, dark air, she attempted to see a sliver of light, any light, so she could get her bearings within the seemingly infinite blackness. Focusing on the stream of yellow showing under the door, she moved slowly toward it. In an attempt to catch the intruder off guard, she shoved hard and abruptly at the door. She was rewarded with a slight give toward freedom. She leaned into the movement. Despite the element of surprise, the door again slammed shut in her face.

"Stop that," the intruder snapped, punctuating the words with two swift kicks on the other side of the door. Rachel winced from the noise. "You wouldn't like what's waiting for you on this side of the door, Songbird. Now I suggest you take my advice."

"And if I don't?" Rachel couldn't resist asking.

"If you mess with me, you'll wish you were back in Kansas with Toto. Because I'll get you, my pretty, and your little cat too." A high-pitched cackle followed this observation.

Rachel frowned as her unease deepened. Whoever was in her house knew she was from Kansas, a fact Rachel did her best to keep to herself. And how had the intruder known her friends at home often teased her about her affection for the movie *The Wizard of Oz?* They had even nicknamed her Dorothy in high school.

"Who are you? Why are you doing this?" Rachel cried, straining her ears to hear anything that might identify her captor.

Silence greeted her question, and after a moment Rachel sensed that she was alone. She wasted no time leaving the closet and calling the police. While she waited for them to arrive, she methodically checked and rechecked the locks on her doors and windows. It looked to her as if the back door into the kitchen had been the point of entrance.

She felt so cold and alone. Someone had been in her house, and she hadn't even known until it was too late. The sense of violation was one she couldn't seem to shake. Had this person touched her clothes, gone through her desk, read her personal papers? She tried to remember if she'd left anything embarrassing or important in plain view. She was still puzzling over that question when the police arrived.

Rachel spent the next hour going over what had happened during her moments inside the closet.

"I don't know what else to tell you, Detective Hamilton," Rachel said, taking an unwanted sip of lukewarm coffee. "I never saw the person who pushed me into the closet."

"You couldn't tell if it was a man or a woman?" asked the detective, his skepticism evident.

"It was impossible to tell from the voice alone. I didn't see anyone."

Detective Hamilton glanced at the notes he'd taken so far, then sighed. "I wonder if there's some obsessive love-hate thing going on here with Michael Gabriel. Almost classic stalker makeup. You never know what they'll do in the name of love. The papers love this stuff."

Rachel looked up at him in confusion. *What an odd thing to say.* "Detective?" she questioned.

"I find it interesting that you suddenly have these problems." Before she could question what he meant, Hamilton pointed out the floor-length sliding glass door to the patio. "This is where you saw someone watching you the other night?

"Yes. At the time I thought I was imagining things. I couldn't swear anyone was there."

"Uh huh. I suppose not." Detective Hamilton returned to his chair, fixing Rachel with a searching gaze.

"Listen, Detective, I get the impression you don't believe me, and I don't understand why."

"Let's just say I've been having a lot of calls lately from people with problems no one can verify. Looks to me like this would make good publicity for you if it came out."

Rachel's mouth dropped open and she stared at the detective in disbelief. Where she came from the police helped people without question. Her mouth snapped shut with an angry click of her teeth. "I'm sure I don't know what you mean, Detective. I hope I won't have to call the station and talk to someone higher up about getting protection." She smiled at him sweetly. "Or perhaps the press *would* like to talk to me. About the police department."

Hamilton frowned. "I'll leave a squad car outside your house tonight, or maybe you'd like to go stay at a friend's house?"

Rachel hesitated a moment, then nodded. She didn't want to stay in the house alone tonight. "I think I'll check into a hotel for tonight, Detective. I doubt if I'll sleep very well here until I get the locks changed and a dead bolt added."

The phone rang, loud and shrill. Rachel jumped, her heart beating hard and fast in her chest. Excusing herself from the detective, she answered the phone in midring.

"Rachel?" Michael's concerned voice interrupted her greeting.

"Michael, I'd like to know what's going on around here." The words spilled out of Rachel's mouth in a constant stream, her anxiety getting the better of her. "Someone broke into my house and told me to stay away from you. Do you know anything about this?"

Silence greeted her questions, and for a moment she feared Michael had hung up in the middle of her tirade.

"Michael?"

"I'm here. I just don't know what to say. Are you all right?"

"I'm fine. But I seem to have a lot of questions that only you can answer."

Suddenly the phone was snatched from her hand, and Rachel stood by gaping in surprise as Detective Hamilton barked into the phone, "I want some answers, too, Gabriel." He listened for a moment, then said, "I'll be at your house at eight sharp tomorrow morning." Hamilton hung up the phone as Rachel reached to take it from him.

"Didn't he want to talk to me?"

"He didn't mention it," Hamilton returned as he gathered his notebook from the table. "I suspect there's a lot more to this situation than Mr. Gabriel let me in on the other night."

"The other night?" Rachel asked, unease stirring within her.

Hamilton looked at her questioningly, then frowned. "You don't know about the other night?"

Rachel shook her head mutely.

"Gabriel says he received a threatening call. Then he found a threatening note at Danfield."

"We're public figures, Detective. We get strange phone calls and letters all the time."

Hamilton nodded. "I'm sure you do. And if this is a legitimate threat, which I'm not at all convinced of, it's my job to keep you both safe." He moved toward the front door. "I'll be in touch, Miss Taylor. In the meantime, get your locks changed. I'll have a squad car circling the area more frequently for the next few days. If you have any more problems, call me directly." He handed her his card. "I'll have one of my men follow you to the hotel."

Rachel nodded, hurrying to her room to throw some things into an overnight bag. She glanced at the open closet, shivering at the memory of the darkness inside and the fury in the intruder's voice. Something was going on here that was above and beyond the undercurrents being played out between herself and Michael. She had a sudden urge to leave Phoenix and Michael Gabriel and forget her desire for revenge.

Then she turned her head and looked at the picture of her brother on her nightstand—so handsome, so determined, too young to die.

No, she wouldn't break and run before she'd accomplished what she'd set out to do. Someone else might be out to get Michael Gabriel, but she would get there first.

Michael watched from the shadow of the phone booth as Rachel left her house carrying an overnight bag. A uniformed officer greeted her, then followed in his car as Rachel's red Mustang pulled away toward downtown. Michael's gaze rested on Rachel's darkened house. The police had left; Rachel was gone. Though a patrol car would undoubtedly circle the area several times during the rest of the night, Michael should be able to slip past their vigilance since he knew they were there. Now was the time for him to do some investigating to set his mind at ease.

He didn't really believe Rachel was behind the phone call and the note. But since he was here, and she was gone, he should at least make sure, if only to get Roger off his back.

Sure, Mike. You just want to get a look at her underwear drawer.

Michael grimaced at the voice in his mind. "Shut up, Roger," he muttered and firmly tuning out any further comments, then made his way across the backyard. He thanked a day of extreme boredom not long ago and Roger's former cellmate, a professional burglar, for his own expertise at picking locks. Within minutes he let himself into the cool, quiet interior of Rachel Taylor's house.

The place smelled of her: dark, exotic, replete with some spice he couldn't quite name. The decor brought visions of Rachel as well. The furniture was sparse but tasteful, muted whites blending with southwestern pastels, the floors bare, old wood polished to a new shine.

Michael shook his head and pulled himself away from his observations. He wasn't here to rate her interior decorator; he was here to have a look around and get out. But where should he look first for whatever he hoped to find? With a shrug he wandered from room to room.

In the living room he stepped closer to the wall to look at some framed photos above the piano. An elderly couple, looking stiff and uncomfortable, posed for a typical studio photograph. If there'd been a barn in the background and a pitchfork in the foreground, Michael could have been looking at a Grant Wood. The woman had the look of Rachel around the eyes, though he noticed a sadness and despair in their depths that he had seen often enough in his own mirror. This woman had seen much of life, and most of it had not been good. The man had the same haunted eyes, combined with stooped shoulders and weathered skin that told of years of hard work against the elements.

Michael's attention moved slowly to the next picture, an outdoor scene on what looked to be a football field. Several young girls were kneeling on top of each other in a pyramid. He recognized a younger Rachel in the middle level, laughing as she attempted to hold her head up and look at the camera. He bent closer to read the inscription in the corner. *To Dorothy—Always remember, there's no place like home!*

Michael frowned. Dorothy. There was something about that name that rang an unpleasant bell in his mind. Sudden memory dawned and he groaned. Recently, just after he'd started working on the Danfield movie, in fact, he'd received several strange fan letters from a Dorothy Myers. The writer claimed to love him, love his work. She wanted to meet him, had to meet him or she'd die. Strange, but not threatening. He had shown them to Roger, who'd set out to learn what he could. He hadn't been able to trace the writer, and when no further mail from Dorothy arrived Michael had put the incident out of his mind.

His gaze returned to the picture. Just a coincidence, Michael assured himself. Rachel couldn't be *that* Dorothy. What purpose could she have for sending him letters? Michael turned away with a curse. He needed to get on with this. The next order of business was to have a peek at Rachel's desk.

His gaze swept each room as he walked through, finally finding the object of his search in her bedroom. Michael's eyes were drawn to the bed, and in his imagination he saw Rachel beneath the covers, tousled from sleep and sex, with himself beside her.

Michael shook his head and growled a warning under his breath. He wasn't here to ogle her bed, contrary to what a little voice kept whispering to him in his head. He had a reason for being in Rachel's house, and he'd better get to it before morning arrived and Rachel came back.

A thorough search of her desk yielded nothing, as did his search of her dresser. He had just sat down on the bed, intent on looking in her nightstand, when his eyes lit on the picture in the ornate gold frame. His heart sank. He couldn't pass this picture off as a coincidence, as he had the other.

"Robert," Michael whispered, picking up the frame. Cold recognition settled over him as he stared into the eyes of a man three years dead. "What the hell are you doing here?"

Chapter Six

Rachel returned to her house the next morning in time to greet the locksmith. Once the man was happily at work on the doors, Rachel retreated to her room. Since the scare of the previous evening, she'd had an overwhelming urge to talk to her family. Though they didn't see eye-to-eye on many things, her parents were still her parents, and she felt a sudden need to hear a voice from her past.

"Hello."

Rachel took a deep breath at the sound of her mother's voice, noticeably weaker than the last time they had spoken. Forcing herself to sound cheerful, Rachel answered. "Mother? It's Rachel. How are you?"

"Same's usual."

Rachel sighed. It was always like pulling teeth to get her parents to talk on the phone. They considered the telephone a necessary evil. Both she and Bobby had been born to their parents late in life; her mother was now sixty-five and her father seventy-two. The desertion of both their children to the land of show business had confused the down-to-earth, religious Kansas farmers. The loss of their only son had broken their hearts and their health beyond repair. They were people who believed that right was right and justice eventually won out in the end. To have their beliefs proved so ruthlessly wrong had shaken them to the depths of their souls. The increased frailty of her mother's voice strengthened Rachel's waning resolve to seek revenge against Michael Gabriel.

"I'm living in Phoenix, Arizona, Mother."

"Hmm. Still workin' for them heathen movie folks? Didn't your brother's troubles teach you nothin'?"

Rachel flinched but ignored the jolt of pain that shot through her heart. "I'm working on an animated movie. I think you might like it. It's . . ." She struggled to think of a way to describe animation to a woman who had just recently started attending motion pictures. There had never been time in her parents' lives for useless pleasures. "It's like a cartoon."

"A cartoon? You're ruinin' your life for a cartoon?" Her mother's voice took on the most life it had shown in the conversation. "Give up this foolishness, girl. We've already lost one child to that world of sin. Come home."

"I can't, Mother. Things are going so well for me now. Soon I'll have everything I dreamed of."

"Dreams aren't real, Rachel. Home, family, God is real. If you love to sing so much, we need a soloist at the church. You can take over the piano playin' too. Josh Redhall keeps askin' after you. You could be married before the year is out, have a baby next year if you get right to it. Your father and I need grandchildren to fill our emptiness. You're the only one left who can give them to us, child."

Rachel closed her eyes against the pleading in her mother's soft voice. This was the same conversation they had every time they spoke.

"That's not the life I want."

"I don't understand what's wrong with our lives. How could both you and Bobby desert us like this? Your father and I did our best with you both. Your brother was so stubborn, I never could make him mind. Nothing worked. And you—you were always in a dreamworld. Whenever I was talking to you, you weren't listening. Don't think I couldn't tell, because I could. I never understood either of you."

"I'm sorry, Mother. I know I'm not the daughter you wanted. I can't help that. What makes you happy doesn't work for me. That doesn't mean it's wrong."

"It makes you happy to use the great gift the Lord gave you singin' for money, pretending to be people who don't exist. Would have thought you might've learned something from your brother's passin'. I suppose you changed your name, too, just like him. The name Taylor ain't good enough out there?"

"Mother, Bobby explained to you that there was already a Robert Taylor registered with the Actors' Guild. You can't use the same name as anyone else, so he chose his middle name for his last name. He had nothing against the name Taylor."

"Hmm," her mother sighed, ignoring Rachel's explanation as she had ignored it from Bobby. "Heaven only knows what you're doin' on your own in that Godforsaken desert. I don't suppose you've met a nice young man at church."

"No, Mother, I don't have a boyfriend."

She thought fleetingly of Michael Gabriel—his touch, his kiss—but pushed the memory to the back of her mind. If her mother knew she was consorting with the man who had hurt "her Bobby" there would be hell to pay. Her parents had no idea of her plans regarding Michael. They would only tell her that "vengeance is mine sayeth the Lord" and lament about her "being drawn into that man's misbegotten clutches."

Her mother's voice brought Rachel back to the conversation at hand. "Your father's out in the fields. He'll be sorry he missed you."

"I'll talk to him next time, Mother." Rachel felt a rush of relief that she wouldn't have to listen to the similar lack of life in her father's voice. Guilt followed swiftly on the heels of relief. She stifled the urge to give in to that guilt and tell her mother to fetch her father in from the fields. He wouldn't feel any better after talking to her. He would only become as upset as his wife to hear that Rachel wasn't coming home. "Well, I have to get ready for work," she finished lamely.

"When are you coming for a visit, Rachel? We haven't seen you for a year now."

"Maybe when I finish this movie I can get away," she hedged.

Rachel had a fleeting thought that when she finished her work in Phoenix she might very well be out of a job permanently. She gave a mental shrug. She knew what she had to do, even more so now that she had spoken with her mother, and she would do it, whatever the cost to her career.

After promising to call and talk to her father the following week Rachel said good-bye and hung up. She shouldn't have given in to the urge to talk to her parents. Every time she did she only became more depressed, and her guilt increased to epic proportions. She could hope until she was an old woman for their understanding, but she knew that gift would never be hers. The problem was, she understood their point of view all too well. They had lost Bobby and that loss had nearly destroyed them; they were terrified they might lose her too.

As she got ready to go to the studio, Rachel's thoughts turned back to Michael. He had a lot of explaining to do after what had happened last night, but she'd be damned if she would beg him to do it.

Michael had to trust her, to let her in on his secrets. Then she could expose him either for the fake he was or for the monster he professed to be. The media and the public would be happy to carry on with his destruction from there. Right now Rachel needed to get on with her plans for Michael while her anger bubbled near the surface. She couldn't allow herself to be led away from her purpose by the awareness that sang in her blood whenever Michael was near. She would keep the reactions of her treacherous body in check. Lust wouldn't be allowed to rule her mind or her heart any longer.

Rachel knew from experience that she would be unable to sing with any amount of feeling after speaking with her mother. She placed a quick call to the studio and arranged to view the latest animated release from Danfield. It always helped her to get into the mood for work by viewing a completed film. Since the songs and dialogue were always recorded first, and the animation done later, there was no footage of the movie she was working on. It amused her that the animators watched videotapes of her singing and acting so they could incorporate some of her mannerisms into the behavior of the animated heroine. She wondered what they planned to do with Michael's character; he obviously hadn't allowed himself to be videotaped.

When she reached the studio Rachel went straight to the screening room. The movie had been left for her; all she had to do was turn off the lights and turn on the film.

Soon all her problems faded in the wonder of the colors and sounds before her. She was constantly amazed at the great strides animation took with each new film. With the advent of computers and Xerox, the ancient processes of inking the penciled cells and painstakingly drawing frame-by-frame animation were no longer necessary. Still, the animators were stars in their own right, actors of the pen, geniuses with the mystery of art.

The movie she watched was excellent technically, but the film she was working on would be far and away the better of the two. Her mind wandered as she went over the plot of that film, which was somewhere between science fiction and romance. A man from the future and a woman from the past are each transported to the present. They fall in love and learn to cope with the mysteries of the time period and their own differences. When they return to their own eras they do everything possible to triumph over time to be together forever.

Tears stung Rachel's eyes at the thought of the tale of love lost and found. Michael's voice as the hero would make every viewer's heart sing with joy. With his talent, every nuance of emotion the hero felt for the heroine would be revealed. She experienced a familiar shadow of doubt about her own talent. Would she be able to produce the emotion necessary to make the heroine as strong a character as the hero? She hadn't been lying when she told Michael she found it nearly impossible to conjure up the emotions called for in her script. Perhaps if she had ever experienced the depth of love her character had, she would understand. But as things stood, Rachel felt as though she spoke her lines from an emotional abyss.

The movie on the screen in front of her ended, and Rachel sat for a moment in the darkness, trying in vain to remember the story she had just witnessed. When the door to the screening room opened she tensed, then relaxed as she recognized the slow, measured gait of Michael's approach.

"I hoped you'd come," she said as he sat beside her.

"Oh? Why's that, Rachel?"

Rachel frowned, confused at the intensity of his tone. She sensed something new in his voice, a wariness she didn't trust.

"I—ah—wanted to talk to you."

"Is everything all right at your house? You got your locks changed? A dead bolt?"

"Yes. The police think whoever it was came in through my patio doors. I had a new lock put on those too. I'm also getting a security system."

"Good. I don't like to think of what might have happened."

"Me either. Why do you think this person wanted me to stay away from you?"

Rachel heard his body shift, as though he'd shrugged. "I don't know. Hamilton thinks a fan might be obsessing over me. I have gotten some odd letters. . . ."

His voice drifted off expectantly, as though he wanted her to pick up the thread of the conversation.

"Yes?" she asked. "What did they say?"

"Oh, the usual. You know."

"Well, not really. I don't get much fan mail yet. And so far I haven't gotten anything weird. Lucky me."

"It'll come sooner or later. You learn to do what you can and ignore the rest. If you don't you'll make yourself crazy worrying."

"True. Listen, I wanted to talk to you—"

"The movie again?" he interrupted.

"Yes. I've told you; I don't care what you look like, Michael. Your voice is perfection."

"Ah, yes, my voice. Isn't there anything else about me you're interested in?" he whispered. The heat of his body warmed the cool skin of her arm as he leaned closer. "What is it you really want, Rachel?"

Before Rachel could ask what he meant Michael had grasped her by the shoulders and pressed his lips to hers in a kiss that awakened every taut nerve in her body and caused every thought of revenge to leave her head.

She strained toward him, drinking in the taste of him, inhaling the springtime scent of his hair, which fell in a curtain around their faces. The emotions welling up inside her at his kiss were too numerous and too intense to identify. Suddenly she had to touch him or she'd burst. Reaching up, she tangled her fingers in the soft strands of his hair and tugged him closer.

He resisted for a moment, and she had a sudden fear that he meant to leave her. She made a small sound of protest. He stopped pulling away and held himself very still, his mouth hovering over hers as though he were fighting a battle within himself. Then he sighed deeply and relaxed, his mouth softening and melding to hers.

The arm of the chair between them bit into her ribs, and Rachel shifted uncomfortably. Without breaking the warm, moist contact of their lips he reached over and lifted her into his lap.

Her hands went to his chest to steady herself, and she groaned with pleasure at the increased contact, feeling the hard, defined muscles beneath her fingertips. She found the top button of his shirt, popping it from the buttonhole. Several more followed, until she was able to slip her hands beneath the fabric, and flesh met flesh.

He muttered something indistinguishable against her lips, and his hands flexed under her buttocks, pulling her hard against his arousal. His fingers wandered upward, tugging her blouse from her shorts, then delving beneath to trace loving patterns across her stomach and ribs as her breath fluttered in response.

He paused when he realized she wore no bra, but at the urgent clenching of her fingers on his chest he continued his exploration. Seconds later his thumbs grazed her nipples.

Her head fell back at the explosion of sensation that followed Michael's intimate caress. His mouth trailed down her neck to the hollow of her throat where he kissed and nipped at her sensitive skin until she thought she might scream with pleasure. She had never been a woman to feel such passion; had, in fact, wondered if she was cold where most women were hot. Now she couldn't seem to stop the tide of sensations rushing through her. She didn't want to stop them.

An all-consuming ache had centered between her thighs, and she squirmed in an effort to ease the unfamiliar sensation.

"God, Rachel, don't," he groaned, stilling her motions with his hands at her waist. "I can't stand this much longer."

She leaned forward, outlining his mouth with her tongue while she tangled her fingers in the soft, curling hair across his chest. At his harshly indrawn breath she smiled with pleasure at the power coursing through her. She wasn't the only one who was a prisoner of the urges of the body. What she experienced when Michael touched her was a shared emotion. She moved her mouth upward to feather light kisses across his forehead and eyelids. But when she kissed his scarred cheek he stiffened and pushed her away.

"What?" Rachel's head swam with the newness of passion. Confusion flooded her at his withdrawal.

"We'd better stop before this goes any farther."

"Why?"

"I want you, Rachel, more than I've ever wanted anyone or anything in my life. But it wouldn't be fair to you. You don't know me."

"Yes, I do," she insisted. "All I need to know."

"I wonder," he said, as though to himself.

The tingling of unease returned at his tone. She stiffened. "What's that supposed to mean?"

Michael suddenly lifted her from his lap and set her onto her feet next to him. He stood, and she heard him move away from her.

"Dammit, Michael, you're driving me crazy. You can't keep coming to me in the dark, kissing me, touching me, making me want you like this." Her voice broke, and she took a deep breath to steady herself. "I need you."

"For the movie? Or is there something else?"

Rachel froze. He was acting very strange tonight. What was it about his soft questions that had the hair on the back of her neck sizzling a warning?

But the newness of a passion she had never before experienced overrode all other sensations. She gave way to the emotions springing to the surface. Though she knew she would regret her actions in the morning, Rachel stepped forward, her hands reaching out for him and meeting nothing but air. "This has nothing to do with the movie. It's just you and me. Please, Michael, make love with me. I don't want to spend another sleepless night wondering what it could be like between us. I want to know."

Her answer was the soft but final click of the door closing behind him.

I went to my watching place early in the evening to wait for him. But when he arrived he went to the screening room to talk with Rachel instead of to his studio to work. I had to hurry out of my safe place and hover outside the door to hear them. What I heard made me angry. All that kissing is enough to make me sick. Rachel is definitely up to no good. She's been warned, and she's not listening. Perhaps I should let Gabriel in on the secret of Rachel's identity. Maybe that will drive him away. Or maybe I'll have him sent out of town for awhile—that'll cool them off a bit and give me some time to think about Rachel's part in all this. And how to make her stop.

When I'd heard enough I went back to my watching place until they left, careful to get out of the studio before the cleaning crew arrived. I know the comings and goings at Danfield so well, it's nearly automatic for me to come and go at the most opportune times. And if anyone sees me, I have my fake I.D. card on hand to explain my presence.

But I'd prefer to keep out of sight. Just in case I have to get rough with Miss Songbird in the future—and the way things sounded tonight between the two of them, getting rough is a definite possibility—someone might remember my presence and report it to the cops. I can't risk that happening. Not when things are going my way; not after so many years of planning.

I know when to cut my losses and regroup for another day. Tonight is one of those times. If I bide my time, the cops will back off. I watch their useless marked cars circling the blocks around both Gabriel's and Rachel's houses every night. But I know that if everything remains calm for awhile—no threats, no phone calls, no break-ins—the police will have no choice but to pull off the extra surveillance. It's the way of the world and the bureaucracy. No one has the manpower to patrol indefinitely. The police wouldn't have taken this much interest except that Gabriel and Miss Songbird are "stars."

I've waited for years to have Gabriel all to myself—right where I want him. A few more weeks won't matter.

I can be patient if I try very hard.

Michael removed himself from the studio as quickly as possible. Once outside, he moved around the corner of the building to stand where he could watch Rachel's car but not be seen by her when she left. While he waited he recalled the events of the previous day.

Michael had left the house in a semidaze after coming across a picture of the man who had haunted his dreams for the past three years on Rachel Taylor's nightstand. The shock of his discovery had numbed him. He'd almost forgotten to look for the patrol car. Luckily for him, it had just made its slow sweep past Rachel's house when he let himself out her front door. He hurried to the next block and drove back to the security of his own house, his own room. There he went into action, calling a private detective to run a check on Rachel Taylor. By noon he had his answers—and a lot more questions.

The man he had known as Robert Matthews was, in fact, Robert Taylor, Rachel's brother. Michael closed his eyes and leaned his head back against the building, rubbing his fingers across the pain exploding in his forehead at his memories of Robert.

They had met at work, both ushers in a theater, two young men out to prove their worth to the world. Robert was new in New York, and Michael had introduced him to his circle of friends and the few agents he knew. Both their careers began to accelerate, Michael's perhaps a bit more quickly, and they reveled in their youth and talent and success. Now that Michael thought back, Robert had only spoken of his family once. He had sworn to prove to them he would become a megastar. Rob had never mentioned a sister or the fact that he had changed his name. But that wasn't unusual; a lot of people in New York didn't discuss their pasts. Most actors had changed their names.

Michael remembered the day he had been sitting around Rob's apartment, at loose ends. His friend had just gone out to get a pizza when the phone rang. Michael shrugged, then answered it. The message was about an audition for a movie—a movie with a star-making director and a big-time budget. He had heard about the picture and knew it was the part of a lifetime. Michael wrote down the information, then stared for a very long time at the paper in his hand. He knew if he could get the part, his career would be made. He was perfect for the role, too, more so than Rob, he assured himself. But a little voice at the back of his mind had reminded him that Rob needed this part—needed it very badly.

For the past several weeks his friend had been on the edge of destruction—manic with energy, desperate for a role to prove to himself and others that he possessed the talent to stay afloat in the business. Then, just as abruptly, his mood would crash, and he'd spend the day in his darkened apartment. When Rob was in the thrall of a depression Michael avoided him as best he could. When his friend was like that there was something about him that made Michael uneasy, almost as if Michael didn't know him at all. Before he'd gone out for pizza Rob had confided to Michael that if something didn't happen soon, he didn't know what he'd do. When he'd said that Michael had glimpsed something in Rob's eyes that hinted at a desperation Michael couldn't quite understand. Perhaps Rob wasn't as cut out for a career in the business as Michael had thought. Maybe Rob would be happier if he gave up the struggle and found a career more suited to his temperament. Acting was so subjective; the hard knocks could make anyone lose faith in himself.

It was that thought more than anything else that made Michael's decision for him. He got up and left the apartment before Robert returned, hopping the next plane to L.A. and snatching the part for himself.

When he'd returned to New York a week later Robert was waiting at the airport. Before Michael could even get past the gate Rob knocked him to the floor with a well-aimed punch to his jaw.

"I can't believe I trusted you. How could you be so low as to steal the part of a lifetime right out from under me?"

Michael rubbed his sore jaw and looked up at Robert. The world of show business was dog-eat-dog, and Michael knew he had only done what hundreds of others would have in his place. He had told himself just that for the past week—every time he looked in the mirror. Still, he experienced a wave of shame at the behavior that had smashed the trust of Robert Matthews.

"I'm sorry you feel that way, Rob," he said as he got to his feet. "Maybe I can get you an audition for another part in the movie."

"Don't do me any favors, Gabriel. Just watch your back from now on. I won't let you get away with this. I won't let them win. Never. I needed that part," he muttered to himself as he walked away. "It was my last chance to keep alive out here."

Michael's guilt increased, drowning out his excitement over the biggest break of his career. When Robert showed up at his door the next week and made a peace offering in the form of an invitation to go camping in Arizona, Michael had seen the gesture as a way to end his own torment. He agreed, hoping to talk things out with his friend and soothe himself in the process.

The two of them had gotten on a plane for Phoenix the next day. Two days later Robert was dead and Michael lay in a hospital bed, disfigured for life.

Michael never told the police that Robert had tried to kill him. Even when they accused him of killing Robert he kept his mouth shut. Robert was dead, and Michael had been the one to send his friend over the edge of reason with his betrayal. Rob had been desperately searching for a way to justify himself, and Michael had taken that chance away from him. Though he couldn't understand the mental machinations that had been going on in his friend's head those last few minutes of his life, he could at least keep the secret of Robert's final moments to himself—along with the secret questions Michael harbored about his own part in Robert's death.

Now Robert's sister had suddenly turned up in his life, inching her way into his trust and his heart. He had received threatening phone calls and a threatening note. Rachel had a reason to hate him; but did hate rule her mind and actions as they had Rob's? He didn't want to admit it, but Rachel Taylor was now a prime suspect for crazy-of-the-week. He knew he should call the police and tell them all he had found out, but something held him back. Perhaps the way she had kissed him. He didn't think she could fake such a response if she was really out to hurt him. But he had trusted a Taylor once before, and look where that had gotten him. He had learned the hard way not to take chances. One thing he knew for sure: he wouldn't allow himself to be caught off guard again. If Rachel was responsible in any way for what had been going on, he would find out and beat her at her own game.

Rachel came out of the studio, startling Michael from his memories. He could tell by the way she walked that she was angry. Perhaps that was for the best; if he made her angry enough, she might blurt out something that would tell him what she was up to. At the very least it would keep her out of his arms. He didn't know if he could hold her again and not make love to her. And knowing what he did, making love to Rachel Taylor could be a very deadly mistake.

He followed Rachel home, observing nothing out of the ordinary during the night. He would feel pretty foolish if he was watching Rachel to protect her from . . . herself.

When Roger arrived to take the day watch Michael told him what he had learned over the past few days. He also decided the time had come to tell Roger about his past with Robert Matthews. The bodyguard wasn't pleased.

"I thought something was strange about that broad," Roger growled.

Michael winced. "Maybe. But she hasn't done anything yet, so don't get all excited."

"What do you call that phone call and the note?"

"I can't prove she's behind those. Innocent until proven guilty, right?" Michael pressed.

Roger scowled darkly. "I doubt you'll be so hyped up over innocence when you're dead. I can't believe you've never told me before about this Robert Matthews character."

"He was dead, and I didn't want to talk about him. I still don't."

"Uh huh. Well, it looks like his being dead is part of your problem." Roger started to turn away, then swung back for another attack. "And I hope you aren't seriously considering working with the woman. You'll be playing right into her hands if you keep letting her get so close to you."

"It might be the best way to find out what, if anything, she's up to. And she *is* right; the movie will be better if we work together."

"Uh huh," Roger said again. He didn't sound any more agreeable than the last time he'd said it.

Michael ignored him and went home. He needed some time to get used to the idea of Rachel as Robert's sister. Had she come to exact revenge for what she believed he'd done to her brother? When he thought about it, the idea seemed pretty farfetched. She would have had to plan for years. Besides that, no one could predict she'd win the part in the Danfield movie, and if she did, that he'd ever let her near him. She could never have known the strong reaction they would have to each other when they met.

Or perhaps that reaction was all on his part, and Rachel was a better actress than anyone had ever given her credit for. She could have depended on his prolonged celibacy to make him react to her and then worked on that reaction. Michael clenched his fists at the thought of being played for a fool with something so precious. No, he wouldn't believe Rachel was capable of such duplicity until it had been proven.

Despite his personal doubts about her, Rachel was still his co-star, and she had a valid point about their working together. He would have to make a decision about that partnership soon. If he did decide to give her idea a try, he still didn't know if he could look into Rachel's eyes and not allow his guilt over her brother's death to show on his face. He was an actor, but Rob's death was a burden that had tormented him for the past three years. The guilt and confusion had become as much a part of him as the scars marring his face. Besides, just the thought of allowing her to look at him, her gaze wandering over his ruined skin before her eyes clouded with pity, made him clench his teeth in fury. He had been willing to spend the rest of his life alone to atone for his part in Robert's death, but he wasn't willing to subject himself to the pity of others, especially a woman he wanted as badly as he wanted Rachel. That was too much to ask, no matter what he had done.

The phone rang, slicing through the stillness of his room and causing his heart to leap in . . . what? Anticipation, curiosity, dread? Any one or all three, depending upon who was on the other end of the line.

Crossing the room quickly, he picked up the receiver before the second ring.

"Hello, this is Gabriel."

Silence met his words, and the back of his neck prickled.

"Hello," he said more forcefully. "Who is this?"

"Oh, Michael, I'm so glad you answered and not Roger. I'm sorry to call this early, but I have a message for you from Bill."

Michael exhaled the pent-up breath in his lungs. "Hi, Susan. Nice to hear from you again."

He had always liked his agent's partner. She was a capable and friendly woman in her late thirties who had steadily taken on many of her employer's clients over the past few years, though not Michael. Bill Finch had been Michael's agent—and Robert's, too, for that matter, at the beginning of their careers. Michael owed the man a lot for sticking by him during the bad times. Susan had been there, too, and for that he would always be grateful.

"We have a client who would like you to do a commercial voiceover, Michael. You'd need to be in New York for the weekend."

Michael hesitated. He needed time alone over the weekend so he could decide what to do about Rachel. But he wasn't sure the police would be thrilled about him leaving the state.

"I'm afraid I can't, Susan. There's too much going on here with the movie. I'll catch the next one."

"That's too bad. The client asked for you specifically; said he had you in mind when they wrote the jingle. They'll be very disappointed."

"Sorry. See if you can get them to put off the taping for a few weeks. Then I'll be happy to come out."

"If you say so, Michael. Bill won't be too happy. He was counting on that commission."

Michael frowned. It was unlike Bill to care about money. His agency had always been at the top. "Is Bill having a problem with the agency?" he asked.

"No. Well, ah, nothing we can't work out. Just a minimal cash-flow problem right now."

Michael didn't like the sound of that, but he made no further comment.

"Are you sure *you're* all right?" Susan asked. "You don't sound like yourself."

Michael sighed. He had always been able to hide his emotions from others. Acting was as much suppressing emotions as it was portraying them. He must be slipping if Susan could hear his agitation over the phone. But she had known him from the beginning of his career, and she knew him well. She had been especially close to Robert, and Michael had been amazed and gratified when she showed him such support after Rob's death. Susan was one of the few people who truly cared about Michael Gabriel; not his talent or his voice, just him.

"I'm fine, Susan," he said, making sure his voice reflected the assurances of his words. "Thanks for caring about me."

"Of course. You know you're our favorite client."

After he hung up the phone he went to stand at the window, staring out at the early morning sun as a plan of attack formed in his mind.

At loose ends, Rachel wandered around her house all weekend, touching her things, playing with Minnie, trailing her fingers down the keys of her piano. Nothing exorcised the creeping sense of alarm invading her heart. She was in over her head, and she had no idea how to go back to where life was sane and safe once again.

Everything she had been planning since her arrival in Phoenix was within her reach. She only had to follow through with what she believed to be right. Or, at least, what she had believed to be right up until the instant Michael had touched her.

But now that she had gotten close to Michael and learned the depths of his talent, she saw possibilities she had never dreamed of for their movie. The ambition that had driven her all her life had surfaced. Perhaps she should finish the movie, further her career with the performance of a lifetime, and then destroy him afterward.

The thought, which had once given her so much pleasure, seemed suddenly callous and petty. She had seen for herself how Michael's life was since the accident. He lived in darkness—his body as well as his soul. She sensed that he harbored a deeper pain, perhaps something to do with Bobby.

After the accident the police had believed that Michael might have killed Bobby; whether it had been premeditated or in the heat of an argument, no one knew. But in the end they had no proof, and the only witness was Michael himself. Her parents, in their grief, had retreated into silence. Rachel had looked for someone to blame, and she hadn't needed to look far.

But that was before she had met the man and heard for herself the despair in his voice. He was punishing himself for something, and she could bet that something had to do with Bobby's death. And then there was the uncommon and unexplainable sexual attraction between them. She had never felt anything so intense in her life, and she hadn't even seen the man.

Rachel sighed and reached up to touch her cheek where Michael had touched her only days before. She might not have seen him, but she knew how he tasted, how he smelled, how he felt in the darkness. She knew how exquisite his voice sounded as he sang words of beauty and love. She knew how she reacted when he touched her. She was hot. She was cold.

She was scared to death.

She could deal with bitterness, hatred, and revenge. What she couldn't deal with were tenderness, lust, and the yearning for him that stalked her every moment of the day and long into the sleepless nights.

Her mother had always told her to face her fears and they would no longer have the power to frighten her. Well, she was going to take Mother's advice and meet with Michael Gabriel face-to-face. Then she would know if she could follow through with her plans to destroy the only man who had ever made her feel alive.

Chapter Seven

The temperature on Monday reached 110 degrees for the first time that summer. Rachel thought it fitting, since she had felt as if she were on fire since she first awoke that morning. By the time she reached the studio that night her nerves had fried to a thin band of tension between her neck and shoulders. She was ready to explode at the slightest provocation.

She reached Michael's recording studio and, finding the door unlocked, breathed a sigh of relief that he hadn't yet arrived. Stepping inside, she reached for the light.

Someone grabbed her wrist and yanked her into the room, closing the door and locking it behind them. Rachel opened her mouth to scream, even though such an action would gain her nothing. No one else was in the deserted studio; that was why she had always enjoyed coming to Danfield at night.

"Don't."

Rachel immediately relaxed when she recognized Michael's voice. But she yanked her wrist from his grasp, irritated over the unnecessary fear he had caused her.

"Michael, what are you doing in here?" she hissed.

"Waiting for you. We need to talk."

"What about?"

"The movie."

Rachel caught her breath. "Are you going to work with me?"

"Well, I propose a test," he said, moving closer in the darkness, his body bumping against hers and causing a resurgence of the heat that had plagued her all day.

"A-a test," Rachel faltered, backing away in an attempt to focus her mind away from her body's call. She backed into the door and froze. His body was too close to hers. She couldn't open the door and escape. She wondered fleetingly why she was so nervous. But she had never liked being cornered.

"A test," Michael repeated. "We'll sing one song together, tonight. We'll record it and find out how it sounds. Then we'll give it to Harry and see what he says."

"You're going to let me see you?" Rachel asked, standing up straight as her excitement overrode her tension. His hair brushed her face and she found the fresh, clean fragrance calmed her.

"No. We're going to sing. Right here. Right now. In the dark."

"In the dark? How?"

"You know the songs by heart. So do I. You don't need sight to sing, Rachel."

"No. But what about the recording?"

"I can do the recording. Who do you think records my songs and dialogue?"

"I guess I never thought about it. I'm so used to having a studio full of people whenever I record."

"You'll be amazed at how much easier it is alone. When I first started working the way I do now I learned how to operate the control booth so I wouldn't need anyone else."

"What about the union?"

Michael laughed. "This is America, land of anything for a buck. You'll learn that most objections disappear when money's involved. I'm surprised you weren't aware of how I work, Rachel. I would have thought you'd done your research on me."

Rachel frowned, wondering if he could have learned just how extensive her research into Michael Gabriel had been. But he moved away from her without further comment, and she heard him pushing buttons and flipping switches on the control board. Soon small lights on the panel illuminated Michael's silhouette, and Rachel was confident enough to cross the room and stand next to him without fear of falling headlong over a stool.

She reached his side and glanced at him, straining her eyes against the tepid light to catch a glimpse of his face. She observed that the placement of his nose and eyes was correct. Beyond that, nothing. He had planned this well.

Rachel looked away. Her own ulterior motives were starting to make her think everyone else had hidden agendas as well. Still, the thought of her secrets caused her a moment's unease. He had asked if she had done her research on him. Could he know something? What *would* Michael do if he knew who she was and what she planned for him?

"I'll admit that I've read everything I could about you and your accident," Rachel ventured. "I wanted to know who I was dealing with, especially since I hadn't been able to meet you. I don't think that's unreasonable."

"No?" he asked, reaching across her toward another switch.

The back of his arm brushed her breasts. She sucked in her breath on a sharp hiss as heat shot from her nipples to her belly. Without thinking, she took a step backward. Her thighs bumped a stool, and for a second she was falling. Then Michael's hands grasped her upper arms and pulled her against his chest.

She hit the solid wall of muscle with a thud and gasped.

"Be careful," he said, and though his lips moved soothingly against her forehead, the words held a touch of warning.

"I always am," she returned.

"But are you careful enough?" He released her.

Rachel sat down on the stool she had nearly fallen over, puzzling at the double meanings to their conversation. He was different tonight than he had ever been before, but she couldn't quite put her finger on that difference. He had always seemed strong and in control of himself in the darkness, where she floundered around uncertainly. That hadn't changed. But he sounded almost angry when he spoke with her, despite the gentleness of his touch. Had he learned who she really was? The thought made her shiver.

No, that was impossible. Bobby had never told anyone his real name. He had been ashamed of his roots and wanted no one to know he had been raised on "a hick farm in godforsaken Kansas." She had managed to keep the truth of Bobby's name and heritage out of the papers, believing, in her grief, that she was following her brother's wishes.

If Michael knew Robert Matthews's real name had been Robert Taylor, wouldn't he have commented on that fact when he first met her? What purpose would he have for such a deception?

"Ready to start?" Michael's voice came to her from the door to the soundproof studio.

Rachel nodded, still preoccupied with her thoughts. She allowed him to lead her into the other room, seating her on a stool and helping her adjust her headset before he attended to the technicalities.

The clear, crisp notes of the introduction forced her mind from personal concerns to the work at hand. Michael would begin the song, then she would follow with a verse, and they would sing together on the refrain. Lord, she hoped she was up to this.

The second she heard his voice, all other thoughts fled from her mind. She had heard him sing before, but never had she been in the same room as he sang words of love directly into her ears. She didn't want to breathe and risk missing one second of his performance. Closing her eyes for just a moment, she reveled in the texture and tone of the wondrous instrument that was Michael Gabriel's gift to the world.

He took her hand and her eyes snapped open. It was too dark to see anything but the silhouette of his face. Rachel focused on the gleam of Michael's eyes and sang directly to him. The words of love lost and love found came directly from her heart as she sang to the man who had shown her a depth of need within herself of which she had never known herself capable.

As they sang together for the first time, Rachel was struck by the perfect harmony of their voices. She had the sudden thought that they were meant to sing together as birds were meant to fly and fish were meant to swim.

The music reached a crescendo and they moved into the final stanza of the song. Sometime during the piece they had both gotten to their feet and moved toward each other, the emotions portrayed in the lyrics pulling them together. He was seducing her with his voice, drawing her away from her set purpose into a vortex of needs and desires. She tried to stop herself from being pulled in—and couldn't.

As the last note of their combined voices echoed in her ears, the tension between her and Michael stretched tighter than a guitar string. She opened her mouth to congratulate him on his performance, but the words didn't have a chance to form on her lips. Michael's mouth came down hard on hers, and after a moment's debate with herself she kissed him back, her hands reaching up to tangle in his hair. She knocked his headset to the floor and drew him closer.

The kiss went on and on, lips and teeth and tongues meeting and melding. Finally she broke the contact, breathless, and turned away from him to move out of his reach.

"What's wrong?" he asked, his voice sounding as hoarse as her throat felt.

"Nothing. I—ah—I'm sorry about that."

"Oh? Why's that?"

"I shouldn't—I mean, we shouldn't get involved. I told you I wanted to work with you, and I meant that."

"I seem to remember your saying something different the last time we kissed."

Rachel's cheeks flamed at the reminder that she had begged him to make love to her—and he had refused. For once she was thankful for the darkness that shielded her emotions. "I made a mistake. I let myself get carried away. That's never happened to me before."

"You've never been involved with one of your co-stars?"

"No. Never. I don't believe in sleeping around on the set."

"There's a first time for everything, as they say," he said flippantly.

"Not for me."

"Come on, Rachel. I know you feel what's between us as strongly as I. You've admitted as much. How can you ignore it?"

Rachel sighed and leaned her head against the wall. "I don't know. Maybe it's just that I've been alone a long time now."

"And I haven't? I've done without a woman for the last three years. What's happening here isn't a case of pent-up lust."

"How can you be so sure?"

"Because I know what that feels like, and this isn't it."

Since she had no idea what to say Rachel remained silent. She was supposed to be recording songs and dialogue with this man while she became his friend, then gained his trust. She wasn't supposed to be kissing him as if her life depended on it. Though sleeping with him would probably be the quickest and easiest way to gain the trust she sought, she didn't think she could go through with such a plan.

Michael came up behind her and placed his palms against the wall as he aligned his body with hers. Trapped by his warmth and strength, she felt a resurgence of her early unease. She stiffened but didn't try to get away. He murmured to her, soft, calming words meant to soothe away her fears. Instead, tension of a different kind invaded her body. He pushed aside her hair and nuzzled her neck, placing his hands at her hips and pulling her back against the evidence of his arousal. The shock of sensation cascading through her at his every touch proved she was right in one respect: She couldn't distance herself enough from her awareness of this man to coldly seduce him. The strong feelings of hatred she had harbored for Michael Gabriel were turning into feelings just as strong, feelings she couldn't, wouldn't put a name to.

"Is it because of my face?" Michael whispered into her ear.

For a moment Rachel was too caught up in her own inner struggle to understand his question. Then she turned around quickly, bumping into his chest with the force of her movement.

"No! How could you even ask such a thing? I would think a man of your intelligence would realize the truth in the notion that beauty is only skin deep."

"Oh, I do. Believe me. That's only being proven to me more and more every day." He released her and moved away. "You know nothing about what goes on underneath my skin, Rachel, or in my mind, for that matter."

His voice was suddenly so cold and empty, she frowned. Had she missed something while she was preoccupied with her own thoughts?

"What does goes on in your mind, Michael?" She leaned back against the wall, waiting for him to share something of himself with her.

He didn't answer for so long, she started to feel uneasy. Had she pushed him too far again? Asked a question that in some way made him want to run from her?

Then he spoke, so near she jumped. "My mind?" His voice was thick with warning and gooseflesh prickled on her arms. "I don't think you'd like to find out."

Later that night, as Michael threw clothes into a backpack, he remembered the scene with Rachel. They had spoken no more. She had merely looked up at him with wide eyes, muttered an excuse, and left the studio. He'd let her go; they both needed time to regroup.

He had decided to travel to his home in Sedona, a ninety-minute drive from Phoenix, for the weekend. He needed time to think, to decide what he should do about Rachel and the problem of the mystery caller.

Throwing the backpack over his shoulder, Michael left the room. On his way out the back door, the phone rang. It was Roger.

"I thought you were going to come over and watch her tonight."

"Sorry. I'm going to Sedona for a few days. I need to think."

"What about the babe?"

"That's what I need to think about."

"I'll be right home. We can go as soon as I pack a bag."

"Ah, no thanks. I'd rather you kept an eye on Rachel. I need to be alone."

"Alone? I don't think that's such a good idea."

"I'll be fine."

"I have a bad feeling about all this. Something's going to break on this. Soon. I can feel it. I don't like you alone anywhere, especially up there."

"You'll have to live with it. I'll be careful. Won't talk to strangers or let anyone in the house. Okay? If you need me, I'm in Sedona. But I'll be there alone."

Roger didn't answer, the silence on the line fraught with his displeasure. Regret for his sharp tone twisted within Michael. Roger was just doing his job.

"Look." Michael broke the thick silence. "You'll be watching Rachel. If, as you think, she's the one I need to worry about, she won't be able to get near me if you're watching her."

After another moment of silence Roger finally graced him with two final words: "Have fun." Though the tone was anything but pleasant, Michael took the words at face value and hung up without a reply. He slipped from the house.

The night was dark and warm and clear, a perfect Arizona evening. He would take the motorcycle and enjoy the most freedom he'd had in the past three years. Within minutes he had secured his backpack and was driving up the highway toward Sedona.

Rachel went directly home after leaving the studio and spent the next several hours sitting on her porch, staring out at the darkened desert while holding Bobby's picture. She needed to make a decision. Either Michael Gabriel was the monster of her nightmares, capable of hurting anyone to get what he wanted, or he was a man struggling to get on with his life after a devastating accident. To find out the truth she would have to confront him and ask the question that had plagued her for the past three years.

Had Michael Gabriel killed her brother? And if so, why?

Rachel went inside and picked up the phone. She listened to the endless ringing for several seconds before hanging up. Maybe she should go over to his house. She would never sleep tonight if she didn't at least make an attempt to talk to him.

She grabbed her keys and purse from the table in the hall, then jerked open her front door. As she stepped outside, the hot, orange glow of a cigarette flared at the edge of her vision. She turned her head quickly toward the minute light. She could just make out the silhouette of a man leaning against a tree in the neighbor's yard. Her breath caught in her throat.

Someone was watching her.

Rachel reached behind her for the doorknob, hoping to get inside and call the police before he saw her. Fingers clammy, clumsy, she fumbled the attempt.

"Relax, babe. It's just me."

The man moved away from the tree and walked into her yard. The front porch light illuminated an immense form.

"Roger," Rachel gasped, her heart pounding with fear and relief. "What are you doing here?"

"Keeping an eye on you."

"Why?"

"Just following orders. After the weird things that have been happening lately Mike decided you needed looking after."

Rachel frowned. How long had this been going on? It could explain the feeling she'd had of being watched over the past few days. Even if it was for her own good, she found she didn't like the idea of being observed without her knowledge. "Where's Michael?" she asked. "I just tried to call him and he wasn't home."

"He went away for a few days." Roger peered at her closely. "You two have a fight?"

Rachel ignored the question, more concerned with the fact that Michael had gone away. She wanted—no, needed—to see him. Now that she had decided to confront him she wanted to do so before she lost her nerve.

"Where is he?" she demanded.

The big man snorted derisively. "You think I'm gonna tell you that? He wants to be alone. And what Mike wants I make sure he gets. Get the picture?"

She did, and she didn't like it. With a glare at Roger, Rachel turned on her heel and returned to the house. She would have to figure out for herself where Michael had gone.

An idea teased at the back of her mind, but she couldn't bring it forward. Deep in thought, Rachel drifted into her bedroom and pulled out her file folder of clippings on Michael Gabriel. Thirty minutes later she let out a soft exclamation of triumph as she held up an article clipped from *House Beautiful*. The headline read *Hollywood Recluse Buys Home in Sedona Hills*.

Sedona: That's where he was. Close enough for a weekend trip, but far enough away to be isolated. Rachel smiled as she tucked the clipping into her purse. She threw together a bag of clothes. While she changed from her dress into jeans and a blouse, she planned how to reach Michael.

Obviously Roger would be camped outside her house for the evening. But he would never expect her to slip out the back. She could be in Sedona before he even knew she was gone. Crossing the room, Rachel quietly opened her window and lowered herself to the ground outside.

She couldn't take her car or Roger would be on to her in a flash, so she called a cab from a nearby convenience store and directed the driver to drop her at the airport. Once there, it was an easy step to rent a car; soon she was on the highway to Sedona.

Michael would have enjoyed the trip to his house in the Sedona hills if his mind hadn't been so full of questions. At any other time the freedom of the wind in his hair and the air on his face would have energized him to the point of ecstasy. Instead, he arrived at his darkened home bone-weary.

After parking the motorcycle in the garage he dug the house keys from his pocket and unlocked the front door; a moment's fumbling in the hallway and the lights flared to life both inside and out, illuminating a rustic home set into the red rock common to Sedona. From the floor-length windows of the living area the hills overlooking the town were visible in daylight.

Without more than a cursory glance around the ground floor, Michael trudged upstairs and into his bedroom. He threw his bag into a corner and glanced around his sanctuary.

The far corner of the room was also set with windows, this time surrounding an elevated hot tub. Michael's bed rested just inside the doorway, invitingly made up with a hand-quilted American Eagle spread. Undressing quickly, he fell onto the bed with a groan.

He had told himself time and time again not to get involved with Rachel Taylor. Why hadn't he listened to his own warnings? He had never considered himself a stupid man, but now he would have to rethink that opinion.

He knew her body responded to his touch, but for what reason? Did she truly feel the same passion as he, or were all her sighs and whispers part of an elaborate scheme? He knew that lust was no basis for a relationship, and one built on lies was no better.

That was a lesson he had learned the hard way three years before. He and Camilla had been like dogs in heat. As he remembered things now, that was the only reason he had tolerated her. Even Rob, who appreciated beautiful women as much as the next man, had mentioned Camilla's cold heart—though his friend's tone had been somewhat admiring.

Michael smiled wryly at the image of himself as a young man, flush with the power of his own prowess on the screen and in real life. Camilla had been a grasping, conniving actress, intent on what he could give her professionally even over what they shared in the bedroom—and wherever else they could share each other. Still, he had believed with youthful naïveté that she also cared about him as a person.

Then came the accident, and he had changed, physically and mentally, his guilt eating a raw space within his heart. He knew deep down that he had acted out of youth and stupidity, unwittingly pushing Robert past an unseen breaking point. But stupidity was no excuse, and being sorry wouldn't make Robert live again. Nearly every night Michael dreamed of his friend, and in those dreams Robert never forgave him, just as Michael did not forgive himself. He deserved the scars on his face as a reminder of what he had done—and what he had been unable to do.

He hadn't understood what an oddity he'd become to the world until Camilla's visit. She had waltzed into the hospital, accompanied by the reporters his doctors had refused entrance. Gasping at her first sight of his ruined face, shock and revulsion had washed over her perfect features before she fled the room. When she neglected to appear again Michael was relieved. By running she had made it easier for him to sever his ties with the world.

Despite his heavy thoughts, Michael drifted into sleep, only to be awakened several hours later by thunder. The room was black around him, and for a moment he wasn't sure where he was. Then lightning flashed, illuminating familiar objects, and he relaxed before getting up and moving to the window.

In the distance dark clouds tumbled over each other in their headlong rush toward Sedona. He could smell the rain on the tepid air, drawing in the fresh scent. Nothing would suit his mood better than to watch the storm roll in over the hills.

He jerked on a pair of shorts and then, without bothering to don shoes or shirt, let himself into the walled garden off the bedroom. The cool, moist wind whipped at his skin, and he sighed in pleasure as he sat on a low cement bench in the midst of the overgrown and sunburned flowers and shrubs. He should really hire a gardener to keep up the place, but he balked at having anyone but himself enjoy his sanctuary. He felt much freer in the wildness of the outdoors. He had spent too many days without the sun and fresh air, and he had missed their absence acutely. He needed a few days in Sedona to revitalize. He had lost too much of himself while trying to forget one long-ago day.

Michael loved his house and the surrounding town. The peace and serenity soothed him. That was why he'd come here tonight. Yes, he had needed to get away from Rachel, but he had come to Sedona because he knew deep in his soul that the place had the power to heal. Many people interested in New Age enlightenment visited the area to witness the four vortexes—supposed sites where the earth's unseen lines of strength intersect to form powerful energy fields. Michael shook his head at the fanciful turn of his thoughts. He didn't know if he believed that explanation, but he did feel something in these red sandstone hills that he couldn't explain. Still, neither a well-loved house nor a rustic town could soothe away his problems at the moment, no matter how much he might wish for that to happen. He was too confused, too uncertain of what was to come to enjoy his surroundings as fully as he wished.

Leaning back his head, Michael gazed up at the black velvet night and endeavored to keep his mind as blank as the sky above. Unfortunately, the heavens split with shards of hot ice in the same way his mind flashed vivid images of Rachel's face.

Michael gritted his teeth and waited for the storm above and within to pass.

* * *

A sudden burst of lightning opened the sky, and Rachel sighed. She had been watching the storm descend on Sedona for the past half hour. She was close to town, but it looked as though she and the rain might arrive at the same time. Since she didn't know where Michael's house was, she expected she would be trudging around in the thunderous dark while she made inquiries. Would anyone still be awake at this time of night? She might have to get a hotel room and wait until morning to find him—if he was even in Sedona.

She drove into town and saw, at the end of the street, lights shining into the blackness. The restaurant looked like any other shop or house on the street—old, but classy—no neon lights or plastic blinds for this town.

A blast of frigid air conditioning puffed into her face as she entered the diner. The lights hurt her eyes after so long in the dark. Squinting and blinking, she glanced around. The only occupant was the reed-thin elderly woman who stood behind the counter, looking at her curiously.

Rachel figured they didn't get much business at four in the morning. But if that were the case, why were they still open? Exhausted and hungry, Rachel was just thankful to find someone awake in town.

Rachel smiled shyly at the woman and nodded in greeting.

"Hello, dearie, can I help you?"

Rachel sat at the counter, grimacing as pain shot through her lower back, which had stiffened during the drive from Phoenix. "Please. I need some coffee and a hamburger."

"I think you do at that. Coming right up." The woman hurried off.

Rachel didn't know if the hamburger really tasted so good, or if hunger, as her mother always insisted, was truly the best sauce. She ate the sandwich in record time and drained her cup quickly. The waitress came over to give her a refill.

"Are you new in town, dearie?"

"I'm looking for a friend."

"Who's that?"

"Michael Gabriel."

The woman tilted her head to study Rachel. "You say you're a friend?"

Rachel sat up straight, hope flooding her. Might this woman know where Michael lived? No, life wasn't that easy. She wet her lips. "You know where he lives?"

"I might. I've heard the man is a hermit. Sees no one but that monstrous bodyguard."

"He sees me," Rachel said bluntly, although she wasn't sure if Michael would be very happy to see her today.

The waitress's face lit up with a smile. "That's wonderful, dearie. Never met the man myself. But it's a shame what happened to him. Is it true about his face? I heard he retired from the movies because he had some awful disease that ruined his skin."

Rachel's lips thinned at the avid curiosity in the woman's voice. This was what Michael would have had to deal with every day if he went out in public. It was no wonder those horrid tabloids made millions; people loved disaster and scandal.

"No, he doesn't have a disease," Rachel answered coldly. "He was injured, but he's fine now."

The woman blinked at Rachel's tone, then had the grace to flush. "I'm sorry. I don't know why I asked that. None of my business. You say you're a friend of his?"

Rachel nodded.

"Well, good for you. Young man needs to see someone besides that bodyguard character. It's that glad I am to hear he's coming out of his funk."

Funk? Rachel stifled a smile at the word. This woman and her mother must have the same dictionary.

A flash of lightning illuminated the windows, followed by a burst of thunder, and Rachel glanced outside apprehensively. She'd hate to be caught on the street in the coming deluge. "So, do you know where Michael lives?" she pressed.

"Sure thing, dearie. And you'd better hurry if you want to get there safe and dry. Just go to the end of this road. Past the last store there's a small street that heads into the hills. Take that road up, but be careful if it's raining; your car might slide. The house is built into the rock. Beautiful place," she finished.

"Thanks; I appreciate this," Rachel said as she got up and put some money on the counter.

"Don't mention it, dearie. Hope to see you again soon."

Rachel merely waved, anxiety returning at the thought of the reception she might receive from Michael when she appeared at his door uninvited. She'd be lucky if he didn't throw her back down the hill in the rain.

The air was charged with electricity; Rachel could feel the energy play along her skin. Looking up, she watched the storm rolling in over the hills. Silhouetted by lightning, the gray-black clouds stood out against the blue-black sky, their dancelike movement accompanied by the harsh music of thunder on the wind.

She was able to drive up the steep, narrow road without mishap. Then she reached the flat asphalt-covered parking area below the house and saw the only access to the front door was a stone staircase cut into the side of the hill. The house was obscured by trees, but a light winked in the foliage.

She reached the stone staircase just as a slight mist began to fall. The steps were narrow, with no support on either side, and she slipped more than once, banging her shin the final time. Gritting her teeth and rubbing the bruise, she picked herself up and climbed to the top. Michael's house loomed ahead.

The lights were on, and she breathed a sigh of relief. He was home.

Making her way to the door, she pounded as hard as she could. When no one answered she searched around the door frame for a bell.

Nothing.

Rachel pounded again, this time adding her voice to the thuds. Finally, in irritated desperation, she reached for the knob, rattling angrily. The door opened, swinging quietly away from her to reveal the entryway.

Rachel paused, wondering what to do. A burst of lightning directly above her, followed by a torrent of rain against her back, made the decision easier. She stepped into the house and closed the door behind her.

"Michael?" she called, drifting down the hallway and into the living room. There was no sign of him. She glanced quickly into the adjoining kitchen.

Empty.

She began to feel uneasy, and a hundred questions assailed her. Maybe he wasn't here. Maybe the lights were hooked up to timers. Was she in the right house?

At that moment she noticed lights upstairs, and she headed toward the staircase. At the foot of the steps she stopped, a terrifying thought occurring to her. Maybe whoever had threatened Michael had decided to take up residence. Hell, it had happened to David Letterman.

Slowly she crept upward until she stood at the entrance to a bedroom. No one was there. Crossing the room quickly, she glanced into the bathroom.

A slight creaking sound from behind made Rachel whirl, her hands raised defensively even as she flinched, waiting for a blow to fall. Her gaze swept the room, which remained empty, and lit on a door, partially open, leading outside. Rain swept onto the plush forest-green carpet.

Shaking away the fear, Rachel crossed the room, planning to close the door more firmly. She glanced outside and saw a walled garden. Just as she moved to shut the door, lightning flashed and illuminated a man with hair the color of ebony.

Michael.

Rachel stepped into the storm, oblivious to the downpour soaking her to the skin in seconds. Drawn toward the shadowy figure sitting alone in the middle of the overgrown garden, she made her way over the wet ground. Just as she reached him the storm came upon them in earnest, blacking out what was left of the moon and stars and thrusting Sedona into complete darkness.

"Michael?" she whispered, and felt rather than saw him tense.

Without turning, he asked wearily, "Why are you here?"

"I'm sorry I left the other night. You were right. We need to talk."

He didn't answer, continuing to sit in the rain with his head turned away from her.

She went to him then and laid her hands on his bare shoulders. Her first contact with his flesh sent shivers through her that put the electrical storm above them to shame. She could feel the powerful muscles tighten and then relax as she ran her hands down his arms. Leaning forward, she put her cheek against his wet hair; her breasts flattened against his back. The realization came to her that she hadn't come to Sedona to talk; she had come to experience everything this man had shown her she could feel. In the midst of the storm, witnessing the power of an angry universe, only the two of them existed. The world, their problems, the past receded.

Michael's body went still at her touch, and Rachel was afraid he meant to bolt again. She circled her arms around his neck, holding him to her. Lightning blazed, thunder crashed, and the lights in the house behind them went out, painting the very air around them black.

Suddenly he turned, placing his hands on either side of her face, and jerked her toward him to ruthlessly plunder her lips with his own.

Michael pulled her across his lap, hands tugging at her T-shirt. When he had freed the material from the waistband of her jeans his hands skimmed over her damp skin, making Rachel ache with the need to have more. Pulling back for a moment, she yanked her shirt over her head. Dropping it to the ground, Rachel searched Michael's face. She could only see the gleam of his eyes in the darkness. Her head fell back as he bent to kiss her throat.

No words were necessary as their clothes fell away, and soon they lay on the rain-soaked grass, naked and entwined. The scent of the earth rose around them, fresh and damp, along with the slightly acrid sizzle of lightning on the wind. In a remote corner of her mind she thought she should be cold, lying on the wet ground, yet she had never been so warm. What was about to happen between them had been inevitable from the first time she'd heard Michael's voice in the night. They had been leading up to this for weeks, dancing around the attraction, backing off from their need. Instead of extinguishing the inferno they had only served to bank it for a time. Now the fire inside them raged out of control.

The storm around them matched the storm within. The tension inside Rachel built to a painful edge and she pulled Michael to her, urging him inside her warmth.

Michael's harsh breath sounded in her ear as he plunged into her, burying himself deeply in a single thrust, and Rachel dug her nails into his shoulders to keep from screaming at the sensations exploding in her body. *At last,* she thought, *at last.* And the rightness of their lovemaking filled her as fully as Michael did at that moment. She felt whole with him, safe—with herself and the world. She let her hands roam over his back and down to his buttocks, relishing the play of his muscles as they contracted and released. His head dipped lower and his mouth closed over a nipple. His warmth met the cool dampness of her skin, and he suckled her in a rhythm to match the motion of their joined bodies. Her last thought before she lost all sense of herself was that nothing in her life had prepared her for this moment.

She could feel the pressure within her building toward something new and wonderful. Michael moved above her, his breath fast and sweet on her cheek. The sky behind him sparkled and burned, creating a shadow lover. She began to contract around him as she reached up, tangling her fingers in Michael's long, dark hair and bringing him down to kiss her as she murmured his name deep in her throat.

Just when she thought the experience was over Michael turned, bringing her on top of him and showing her that things had only just begun. He brought her to the peak again and this time when she fell—weightless, thoughtless—into the abyss, he followed. Rachel strained her eyes against the night for a glimpse of his face as he reached his climax, but he had closed his eyes and she could see nothing. Spent, she lay her head against Michael's warm, damp chest, rubbing her cheek against the soft matt of hair and listening to the strong, steady beat of his heart. Doubts crowded into her mind, but she pushed them away resolutely as weariness washed over her.

She awoke the next morning in Michael's bed with the sun streaming across her face. Shadowed memories came to her of being carried inside the still-darkened house—wet, but warm and safe in Michael's arms—then a shared shower followed by a soft bed. Stretching languorously, Rachel turned, hoping to see Michael's face in the light for the first time and prove to him that the way he looked was irrelevant to her.

She was alone.

Confused, she sat up, her gaze sweeping the room, then lighting on the empty bathroom.

Where could he be?

Grabbing one of his shirts from where it hung on the bedpost, she thrust her arms into it as she hurried downstairs, searching for the kitchen.

She relaxed when she saw him sitting at the table, his back to her as he drank a cup of coffee. She hadn't realized until that moment, but she'd been afraid he'd left her alone. She had no right to invade his privacy, a privacy he obviously needed right now since he'd left town to obtain it. She also had no desire to examine what had occurred between them the night before. She had sworn she wouldn't sleep with this man to gain his trust. What could she tell her conscience now that she'd woken up in his bed?

"Good morning," she said softly.

She went still as he turned toward her, schooling her features so as not to react in shock no matter what she saw. She didn't want to upset him and ruin the tentative trust they shared.

His long, dark hair swung away from his cheek and her eyes rested on the smooth perfection of his skin. She frowned. Her gaze moved to his nose—smooth, strong, straight—nothing wrong there.

Had she been right then? Were his supposed injuries just a ploy to gain public sympathy and enhance his mysterious image? She had felt the scars with her fingertips in the dark, but maybe they were under the surface and not visible in the light. It had been impossible to tell their extent. He had always yanked away her fingertips before she could truly gauge his injuries.

The thought that Michael Gabriel was a common cheat should make her happy; such knowledge would strengthen her weakening resolve for revenge. But she wasn't happy. The emotion that settled in her breast felt suspiciously like bitter disappointment.

Then he turned fully toward her and revealed the other half of his face, as imperfect as the first had been perfect. Despite her desire to remain impassive she winced at the sight of the thick, puckered scars covering his cheek. His face reminded her of a divided television screen, revealing before and after shots of a Hollywood makeup artist's talent. Her eyes stung with tears when she thought of the pain such an injury must have caused, both to his mind and his body. She felt him staring at her and she met his gaze. His eyes hardened when he saw the tears shimmering on her lashes.

"Seen enough?" he asked flatly.

She ignored his question, instead whispering, "Did it hurt?"

He blinked, surprised, and looked away. "Yes. In every way you can imagine."

"I can imagine quite a bit." She paused, wondering what she could say to take away the hardness in his eyes and the tenseness of his shoulders. She went with the words in her heart. "I'm sorry." And she was surprised to find she truly was.

"Sorry?" He laughed, a short, bitter sound, and fixed her with a cold stare. "You don't know the meaning of the word."

"I know you've suffered. I hate to think of how much. I wish I'd know you when this happened. I wish I could have helped."

"Wishing changes nothing. It only makes reality harder to bear."

"I can't believe that. You survived and rebuilt your life. It might not be the life you dreamed of in the beginning, but I admire you for what you've done."

"You admire me?" He shook his head. "This is unbelievable. Most women would be making silly excuses so they could get the hell out of here as fast as they could."

"I'm not most women. I like to think I'm not so shallow that I care about a person's appearance above what's in his heart and mind."

Michael frowned. "What's in my heart and mind isn't very pretty either. If you saw that, you'd really run." He sighed, a deep, jagged sound that made her heart jump in sympathy. "Maybe you should leave now." He stood and went to stand at the sink, looking away from her out the window.

Rachel experienced a moment of panic. She had tried so hard not to hurt him, and in the end she had. She needed to do something quickly to stop his withdrawal from her. Without thinking, she crossed the room, putting her hand on his shoulder and turning him back to face her. He looked down into her eyes, a puzzled frown marring his brow.

She reached up with both hands, cradling his face between them, and drew him downward. When he was closer she turned his face and kissed the ruined flesh of his cheek.

Michael jerked as her lips touched him. He slowly straightened, staring at her intensely, as though trying to see into her mind. The thought made her uneasy. She shifted her shoulders against the sudden tension as he continued to stare at her with an unreadable expression on his face. After a moment he moved away without a word and sat down at the table.

"Aren't you going to say anything?" Rachel asked in amazement. She had hoped a major milestone had been passed in their relationship, but Michael just went on with business as usual.

Michael glanced over at her. "Want some coffee?"

Rachel released her breath in exasperation. "Not right now. Don't you want to talk . . . about . . ." She waved her hand vaguely in the air. "About . . . you?"

His eyes searched hers, and her discomfort deepened. She was suddenly conscious that she stood in the doorway in nothing but his shirt while he peered at her as though trying to pry open her head and see what was inside. She had always preferred to be fully clothed for confrontations; half-naked people started off at a disadvantage.

Abruptly Michael shifted his gaze and got up to pour her a cup of coffee. "I'd rather not discuss me right now. Believe it or not, this is terribly uncomfortable." He turned around, avoiding her eyes this time, and returned to the table. Tilting his head down to stare into his cup, Michael's hair swung forward to curtain his face. "It's hard enough letting you see me.

I don't think I can deal with talking about the accident as well."

"All right," Rachel agreed and joined him at the table. She didn't think she was up to discussing the accident either. Her nerve endings were raw with the tension of the past few moments, combined with the tension of the past few days.

"You never did say how you found me." Michael sat up and sipped his coffee. The gentle brown shade of his eyes didn't disguise the razor-sharp intelligence of the gaze that observed her over the rim of the cup.

"I guessed."

"Really?"

"I'd read you had a house up here, so when Roger told me you wanted to get away I thought you might come here."

"An awful long drive on a hunch," he observed.

"I have good hunches."

His eyes snapped up to meet hers, and she saw wariness in the brown depths. "Why are you really here, Rachel?"

She stiffened at his tone and remained silent for a moment. When had all the anger and distrust shrouded his eyes?

"I wanted to talk to you. But I can see now you want to be alone." Rachel rose. "I'll get out of your way."

She started to turn away, but Michael grabbed her wrist in a crushing grip. She flinched and looked down at his fingers where they grasped her arm.

"I didn't say I wanted you to go. I just want to know why you're here, Rachel."

His voice was soft, deceptively so. She could feel the tension in the way his fingers tightened on her flesh. She tugged on her arm, hoping he would release her, but he didn't.

"I felt bad about the way I ran out on you the other night," she ventured. "I was being childish and I wanted to explain."

"I can't believe you'd come all the way up here just to explain." He tightened his grip further and she winced. "Why are you really here?"

She bit her lip and tugged on her arm. He released her then, and she had to stifle the urge to run now that she was free. Rubbing her wrist, she glanced toward the front of the house and the door. She took a step away, out of his reach. Her wrist tingled and she shook it to try to revive the circulation. He was a different person this morning from the attentive, gentle lover of last night. She had no idea how to deal with him.

"Why, Rachel?" he prodded.

Suddenly all subterfuge became too much for her. She was so tired of secrets and lies and deceptions. He was so close, so intense. She couldn't think straight.

Rachel blurted out the words she had been hiding in her heart since the day before—or maybe even longer. "I wanted to be with you.

Is that such a crime?" She moved across the room to lean against the counter. She needed to put some physical distance between them since her emotional distance was a thing of the past. "Do I have to spell it out for you, or can you decipher this for yourself? I wanted you."

Michael raised his eyebrows. "Me? I don't think so. I think you're hiding something, Rachel. You have been from the beginning, and I want to know what."

Her breath froze in her lungs. "I don't know what you're talking about," she choked out.

Michael stood up and moved toward her. The look in his eyes frightened her. He meant to have the truth right now, and she didn't have the strength to resist his will. The guilt that had been hovering at the fringes of her mind since she'd awoken in Michael's bed overflowed the tight bonds she had placed over it. With a sob, she spun away from him, avoiding the hand that snaked out to stop her.

Then she was running, running through the house, tripping in her haste, then dragging herself upward and onward and out the front door. She had been frightened of him before, but never like this. Those other times she had never been certain if the threat she heard in his voice was real or a product of her own imagination. But this time she had seen the anger in his eyes, the suspicion on his face. She wanted nothing more than to get as far away from him as possible, from what he had made her feel, from what he could make her feel if they only had the chance. But if there was one thing she knew in all of this madness, it was that they didn't have a chance—not one.

Chapter Eight

Where had they gone?

The question pounded in my head throughout the night as though printed on a sign in neon.

I was watching the house, but I never saw Miss Songbird fly the coop. Even that goon, Roger, was confused.

I went to Gabriel's and discovered him gone, as well. It's so unlike me to make a mistake like this and lose them both. I was getting so close to the realization of all my hopes and plans, my excitement made me slip up. Such a thing won't happen again.

Once morning came it took me very little time to learn the truth. In fact, I'm quite proud of my detective skills. If I was on the police force in Arizona, I'd be behind bars right now. But I'm dealing with public service drones who have no more brains than the average dog. And I—I am brilliant.

But my brilliance did not prevent Michael and Rachel from getting away. Right now they are probably rutting like animals in Gabriel's Sedona hideaway.

I am staying in an antiseptic hotel room. Each hour I fight against the anger consuming me. It hasn't been this bad for a very long time. I promise myself, I will take care of them both in due time. Then the rage will disappear forever.

When I first got here I couldn't control my fury. I picked up a shoe and smashed every bit of glass in the room into tinkling, glittering shards. Then I destroyed whatever glass I had in my suitcase. Soon the room reeked of a mixture of unidentifiable scents, overlaid by cheap whiskey. But even that wasn't enough.

I had to use the knife.

It didn't take me long; the pillows and mattress lay in shreds strewn across the floor. Still my anger raged.

Not until every piece of cloth had been shredded, every breakable smashed and everything else thrown against the unyielding wall did I feel some measure of control. I surveyed the room with approval. It's been a long time since I've vented my anger so completely.

I pick my hotels well. The tenants know better than to ask questions about noise. I doubt if any of them even heard a disturbance, so deep are they in the practice of their own vices.

I left my room, smiling the smile of the content. Getting into my car, I drove out of town, then stopped at a phone booth along the highway.

Quickly I dialed a number and waited for a response.

"I've got information." I listened, then rolled my eyes with exasperation. I am tired of dealing with morons. "Of course it's reliable. Aren't I always?"

I tapped my toe impatiently while my contact spoke. If these people hadn't proved themselves so useful in the past, I'd never deal with their type.

"Michael Gabriel and Rachel Taylor are staying at his house in Sedona. If you hurry over there you can get some exclusive pictures of the two of them before anyone else even knows they're an item."

I listened again, then bit my lip as the anger threatened to rise beyond my control.

"Listen, you idiot, there haven't been any photos of him for nearly three years. Can you imagine how may people are dying to get a glimpse of Michael Gabriel as he is now? People will be banging down your doors to get a recent picture of him once his new movie's out. And what about her? She's a little no-name. You'll probably have the first pictures of her available to the press."

I hang up, knowing my point had been well taken. Sometimes you have to explain things to these imbeciles. But once they understand, they do the job.

That ought to fix Rachel and her loverboy for a while. They must learn I am not to be trifled with.

Michael caught Rachel before she ran three feet from the house. When he looked down into her face and saw that he had actually frightened her he muttered an oath and pulled her to him, smoothing her tousled hair away from her face with his palm.

She stiffened and tried to pull away, but he held on. Finally she gentled, relaxing against his chest. He kissed her brow. How was he ever going to get her to trust him enough to admit the truth?

A strange whirring noise from the shrubbery made him raise his head. He saw nothing, but unease flooded him at being out in the open. Though he had told Roger he would be safe in Sedona, that he would be careful, he hadn't been. His mind was too filled with Rachel to think of safety. But now that she was with him she was in danger as well. He couldn't be as lax with her safety as he'd been with his own.

"Let's go inside," he said. After a slight hesitation she nodded, allowing him to lead her back into the house.

Rachel's face was streaked with tears, and she sniffled along with a soft hiccough between each breath. The sound set Michael's teeth on edge, a constant reminder that he had made her cry. He was angry with himself, and so his voice came out sharper than he had intended.

"Take a shower and get dressed. Then we're going for a ride."

She stared at him for a long moment, and he had the impression that she wanted to blurt out something to him right there and then. He waited, hope rising within him. Then she nodded and turned to run upstairs.

Michael sighed in disappointment. When he'd looked into her wide turquoise eyes he had wanted to tell her he knew who she was. But after what had happened between them the night before he needed her to trust him enough to tell him the truth on her own. Since they were so close to the scene of his and Robert's accident, perhaps a visit to the North Rim of the Grand Canyon would help Rachel open up.

Michael went back into the kitchen and refilled his coffee cup though he didn't feel like drinking. He hadn't been back to that area since he'd left it in an ambulance. Oh, he'd seen the Canyon in his dreams often enough, but dreams weren't the same as standing at the rim and looking at the place where his life had nearly ended. Could he do that without falling apart? The time had come to find out.

The phone rang, ending his discourse with himself. Michael crossed the room to answer it.

"Mike." Roger's usually taciturn voice had a decidedly harried edge. "I lost her."

"I found her," Michael said dryly.

"She's there with you? And you didn't call me. What the hell are you trying to prove? If she's as crazy as I think she is, you should be dead right now."

"Well, I'm not, so that shoots a pretty big hole in your theory, doesn't it?"

"I'll be there in a couple of hours," Roger said.

"No."

"What do you mean, 'no?' I'm your bodyguard. I'm supposed to be with you, protecting you. Remember?"

"I'll be fine. We're going to take a little trip to Toroweap Point."

"Are you nuts? Do you want her to push you over like her brother did?"

"I doubt she'll do that, Rog."

"Why do you trust her? What is it with you two?"

Michael sighed. "I honestly don't know. But I have to find out the truth. Maybe this is the way to do it."

"Do you want to die?"

"No, but I need to find out if living without her is worth the trouble."

"I don't like the sound of that."

"Neither do I," Michael muttered.

"If I don't hear from you tonight, I'm coming up there."

"If it'll make you feel better, I'll call you after we're done there."

"You damn straight better."

Michael smiled and hung up the phone. It felt good to have someone care about him. Maybe that was what was at the root of his feelings for Rachel. She had come along when he needed someone, even though he hadn't known it at the time. She had wormed her way past the defenses he'd erected, and before he knew it he counted on seeing her. When he'd learned who she was and what she might be up to, it had been too late to make a difference.

"I hope you don't mind," Rachel said from the doorway, "but I borrowed one of your shirts."

Michael turned. She looked incredibly young. Barefoot, she had rolled up her jeans at the cuffs and she wore one of his white cotton shirts. The tails tied at her waist exposed a small sliver of flesh above the loose waistband of her pants. She'd braided her hair and secured it at the nape of her neck. Devoid of makeup and slightly pink from the shower, her face was as alluring as he'd dreamed it could be.

Michael bit back a groan at the response of his body. He had better control himself. Last night had been incredibly stupid on his part; though he couldn't regret it. Until he had some answers, he shouldn't give in to temptation again.

But what a temptation.

"No, that's fine. It looks better on you anyway."

"I brought clothes, but I was in such a hurry, I forgot it's colder up here than in the valley."

"It'll be even colder on the bike. I thought we'd take a ride to the Grand Canyon."

She stiffened. "Why?"

"I haven't been back to the scene of my accident since it happened." He shrugged. "I feel a sudden urge to see the place again."

Rachel watched him warily. "I don't think I want to see that."

"Why not? You've been curious from the first about me and my accident. If I can look at the place, surely you can."

She lifted her chin a bit at the challenge in his words and looked him straight in the eye. "Fine. Let's get it over with."

He gave a short nod. "I'll get the bike. I hope you brought some good walking shoes. It's a hike once we get to the point."

Rachel nodded. "I didn't know how far I'd have to walk to get to your house, so I wore my best hiking shoes." She turned and headed to the front of the house to retrieve the ankle-high boots.

The trip took them the rest of the morning. Michael drove with Rachel's arms loosely circling his waist. He hated to admit how much pleasure her slightest touch gave him.

They reached the remote camping area shortly after noon. Though it was summer and the area should have been busier than the last time he'd been there, in autumn, no one else was about. The heat of midday must have driven most tourists into restaurants and gift shops for the afternoon.

They removed their helmets, and Michael glanced at Rachel. She stared toward the canyon, her face a set mask. He experienced a twinge of guilt. Should he have brought her here?

"Let's get this over with," Rachel said again, still gazing at the Canyon.

"Listen, if you don't like heights or something, you should have said so. You don't have to look."

"No. I don't mind heights. Let's go."

She strode off without looking back, and after only a moment's hesitation Michael followed.

He had forgotten the beauty. Or maybe he had never known. When he had come here with Rob they hadn't even set up camp before . . .

Michael looked at Rachel. She glared at the vast expanse of reddish rock with the same stony expression on her face that had been there since he'd first mentioned coming to the Canyon.

"Rachel," he said softly.

She started. "Hmm?" She didn't look at him.

"I'm going to go closer. I want to see the ledge where I fell."

He left her where she was and crossed the distance to the edge. There was a railing now that hadn't been there before—probably installed as a result of Rob's death. Michael leaned over the barrier and gazed into the abyss.

The Colorado River was a black, snakelike streak at the bottom of the canyon. He craned his neck but couldn't see the ledge. A glance back at Rachel revealed that she still stood several yards away, her gaze fixed on him, her face pale.

Michael turned back and climbed up on the guardrail. He swung a leg over the top. His heart accelerated as he leaned farther out over the edge.

There it was: the ledge that had saved his life.

No. He leaned a little farther, hooking his leg over the railing. There were two ledges, one a few feet below the other. Michael frowned. He didn't remember that. Well, it didn't really matter. He had obviously fallen on the topmost ledge.

To tell the truth, he couldn't remember much about his surroundings that day. A lot of what had happened and what had been said was a garbled mess in his mind. He remembered the worst, though.

He remembered Rob's screams.

Someone grabbed his leg and pulled. Michael's balance teetered precariously. His arms waved for purchase. For a moment he thought he was going over again. He took a deep breath in preparation for the fall.

Then she caught his hand. He sat down abruptly on top of the safety railing. A short grunt of pain escaped him.

"What do you think you're doing up there?" Rachel shouted, yanking on his hand.

Michael's balance tilted again, this time toward solid ground. He swung his leg up and over the rail. Then he jumped down to the earth, landing next to Rachel with a thump.

Her eyes were wide, bright pools in her stark face. Michael frowned. For just a second, when he'd been off balance, he'd thought she meant to push him over. But now, looking into her frightened face, that idea seemed ludicrous.

"I told you I was going to look at the ledge where I fell."

"You didn't say you were going to hang half-way out over the Canyon. If you were doing that, it's no wonder you fell over the last time."

Michael hesitated only a moment before answering. "I was pushed over."

Rachel inhaled sharply. "I don't believe you."

"Why wouldn't you believe me, Rachel?" Michael pressed.

"I . . . ah . . . I just find it hard to believe that anyone would do something like that."

"You didn't know Rob."

Rachel's lips tightened, and Michael hoped he'd struck a nerve. That she might open up to him. Then she glanced over and saw him watching her. She flushed.

"No, I guess not. Why don't you tell me what happened?"

Michael stared at her. She wasn't responding as he'd hoped she would to the scene of the accident. Michael shrugged, considering her request. He hadn't talked in great detail about what had really happened that day to anyone. He'd told Roger the basics, but Rachel had a right to know the whole truth. Maybe if he told her, she would reciprocate with truths of her own.

Michael reached out and took her hand. Startled, she glanced up at him. When her eyes met his she quickly looked away. He drew her forward, against her will, until she stood next to him at the railing.

"We went over right here." Michael pointed to a spot directly in front of them. "We both hit the ledge. I didn't know it at the time, but I broke an arm and a leg in the fall. Rob landed on top of me, but the force of the fall sent him over the edge. He grabbed my leg and nearly dragged me over too." Michael reached up and traced his cheek, remembering. "That's how my face got scraped. Then I grabbed something—I still don't know what, a root, a crevice—and held on. I tried to pull Rob back up with my leg. But I just couldn't do it. He couldn't keep holding on, and he fell. Then I blacked out."

But not before I heard him scream, Michael thought. *The scream I hear every night just after I fall asleep.*

He heard the scream again, and though he knew the sound was only in his mind, he reacted anyway. His breath came in painful rasps, as though he'd just run a mile in the arid heat. Talking about the accident had strained him more than he would have thought.

Michael looked at Rachel and immediately straightened, alarm washing over him at the increased paleness of her face. He could see the tiny blue veins against the stark white skin of her temples. Where he was breathing heavily, she was so still, he became afraid she had stopped breathing completely. Her eyes were staring, fixed on the Colorado River miles below.

Michael reached out and touched her elbow. Her skin was icy cold. He put his arm around her shoulders and tried to draw her closer to his warmth. She didn't resist, but her body was stiff. The only way to make her move would be to force her. Michael didn't want to do that yet. He had made a mistake telling her like this. But it was too late to take back the words that had hurt her—even if they were the truth.

"He fell," she whispered.

"Yes."

"So far. That must have been horrible."

"I'm sure it was."

A solitary tear glistened at the corner of her eye. Michael watched in fascination as it wavered and finally fell onto her ivory cheek.

"Rachel?" he said, trying again to take her into his arms.

This time she came to him. Michael wrapped his arms around her back and held her as the sobs shook her body. Had she ever cried for her brother?

He had broken through her defenses, but he didn't feel proud of himself. If he questioned her now, he was certain she would admit everything. But Michael didn't have the heart to do anything but hold her.

"Hey, is she all right?"

A voice came from behind them, and Rachel went rigid in his arms. Michael kept her shielded with his body as he turned to face the speaker.

A young man, obviously hiking from the looks of his boots and backpack, hovered a few feet away. He met Michael's eyes curiously; then his gaze shifted to Michael's scarred cheek and he frowned.

Michael tried to ignore the irritation sweeping over him. No one had seen him for so many years, he'd forgotten how most people reacted to the sight of his scarred face.

"We're fine," Michael said, allowing a degree of coolness to seep into his voice. Just because he was an oddity didn't mean he had to stand for being stared at.

The young man returned his gaze to Michael's eyes, then glanced over at Rachel pointedly.

"She's upset. She'll be fine in a minute."

"I'd like to hear that from her, mister."

Michael clenched his jaw. Why did he have to run into a knight in shining armor today? Just because the damsel's distress was wetting his shirt clean through didn't mean she needed rescuing.

"Rachel," Michael prompted, "tell the nice man you're fine so he'll go away."

Rachel sniffled—once, twice. Then she cleared her throat and raised her red-rimmed gaze to his. She blinked, then frowned.

"I'm not fine. I doubt if I'll ever be fine again."

She pushed away from him and strode toward the motorcycle. Michael sighed and rolled his eyes skyward. He started after her.

"What did you do to her?" the young man demanded.

"Mind your own damn business."

The kid grabbed Michael's arm as he went by. "I asked what you did to her."

Michael looked down at the hand restraining him and counted slowly to ten; then he looked up into the young gallant's eyes. "I killed her brother," Michael whispered, and smiled thinly when the other man's eyes widened in shock. Michael jerked his head toward the Canyon. "Right there. He went over. Want to see how it happened?"

The kid looked at Michael a moment longer, then released him with a nervous laugh. "Hey, mister, you had me goin' there for a minute." He glanced over at Rachel, waiting by the bike. "You're right. None of my business. I just hate to see a woman cry, ya know?"

Michael nodded slowly. "I know." He turned away, but something made him swing back. "Hey, kid."

"Yeah?"

"Stay away from the edge. It's a killer."

Rachel watched as Michael spoke softly to the young man. She couldn't hear what they said. She didn't really care. Listening to what had occurred during the final minutes of her brother's life had upset her more than she had ever dreamed.

And there was more to come. Michael hadn't told her what had occurred in the moments before he and Bobby had gone over the edge. She had a feeling that tale would be just as difficult to hear, especially given the state of her feelings for Michael. She no longer knew what to believe. What she did know was that she'd heard enough about her brother's death and seen enough of the Grand Canyon for one day. She needed a glass of wine, or two, and some sleep.

When Michael joined her he didn't ask any questions, just handed her a helmet and climbed on the bike. The return trip to his house was accomplished in the same silence as the trip to the Canyon.

They entered the house just as night fell. Rachel followed Michael into the living room and plopped into a chair that faced a wall of windows. She stared out at the siena sky and wondered what on earth to say to him.

The clink of ice being dropped into a glass drew her attention away from the unfolding night. Michael was behind the bar pouring himself a drink. He noticed her look.

"I don't drink much, but I think today calls for a few. How about you?"

Rachel nodded. "Whatever you have that's white and dry."

A few moments later he handed her a crystal glass of golden liquid, then moved away to lean against the window.

"I haven't been back there since the accident," he said. "I didn't know how much it would bother me, seeing the place again." He let out his breath in a long, heavy sigh. "It's not as though I don't see it every night in my dreams."

Rachel nodded. She'd dreamed too. But before today she'd never had any concrete memories to go with those imaginings. She didn't doubt that as early as tonight she'd dream of Bobby's fall exactly as Michael had described it.

Michael laughed suddenly, though the sound held no humor. "That kid: You should have seen his face when he looked at me. It's been so long since I let anyone see me, I'd forgotten how it feels to have someone flinch away from you because of how you look."

"Oh, Michael," Rachel began and started to get up.

"No." He waved her back. "I don't want your pity. I don't want anyone's. With the advances in plastic surgery, there are very few people walking around these days with scars like mine. I know I'm an oddity. That doesn't make being this way any easier. Luckily, there are those who take the time to look past the scars on my face and find me. People like you, Rachel."

Surprise flashed through her at his words. Then she smiled. He was right. She had only seen his face for the first time that morning, but she was already accustomed to it. Perhaps that was because she'd gotten to know him first without the benefit of sight. What she felt for him, confusing as those feelings were in the shadow of Bobby's death, had nothing to do with how he looked and everything to do with the essence of Michael Gabriel.

Images of the previous night flitted through her mind. She had probably made a big mistake, but she couldn't regret what they'd shared. Now she at least understood what she'd been missing all these years. Until last night she had believed herself some kind of sexual freak. Now she knew she had simply never met the right man. Or perhaps she should make that the *wrong* man.

Because if Michael Gabriel was anything, he was certainly the wrong man to make her body tingle and her heart sing.

"Rachel?"

Michael had turned away from the window and was staring at her. Many of the things she was thinking were reflected in his eyes. He was as uncertain as she. And he didn't even know the truth. What would he do if he knew who she was?

Rachel stood abruptly. "I'll see what I can make for dinner."

"No. I'll do that."

"Please. I've invaded your house; the least I can do is cook. Why don't you get changed?" She nodded at his dust-covered clothes. "I'll call you when I'm ready."

Michael stared at her for a long moment. Then, as if he understood her sudden need for space, he nodded and left the room. She soon heard the shower start upstairs and made her way to the kitchen.

Suddenly angry with herself, she yanked open the refrigerator and peered inside. Someone must have stocked the kitchen, or Michael had ordered groceries; a wide array of choices met her eyes. Rachel decided on salad and turkey sandwiches. She wasn't up to turning on the stove tonight.

As she took the food out of the refrigerator and placed it on the counter, her mind turned to what Michael had said at the Canyon. The story he had told her was plausible. But did she believe him? According to Bobby, Michael was the cause of all his problems. The police had investigated Michael for murder; they must have had something more to go on than what Michael had told her. She had to find out more, and the best way to do that was to question Michael.

Tomorrow. Tomorrow was soon enough to learn what she needed to know. Tonight they would just relax. Maybe after dinner and some neutral conversation Michael would tell her without being prompted.

Arms encircled her waist and a warm mouth pressed a kiss to her neck. Rachel let out a little shriek and dropped the knife she'd been using to chop carrots.

"Michael, you scared me to death."

"Who'd you think it was?"

"Never sneak up on a woman holding a knife."

"Good point," he murmured against her skin. "I'll try and remember that next time."

He smelled of soap and damp, warm man, and Rachel's body responded immediately. Against her better judgment, she leaned against him. Her eyes drifted closed as he continued to move his lips in tantalizing patterns across the back of her neck.

He untied the shirt she'd knotted at her waist. The material was loose, and he slipped his hands inside, stroking his long, supple fingers across her stomach and making forays below the waistband of her jeans. When his hands slid up to cup her breasts, unfettered and aching for his touch, she moaned deep in her throat, startling herself with the longing of the sound.

His fingers were clever, playing across her taut nipples, making them harder and more responsive with his every stroke. She arched back against him, offering more of herself for his touch. He whispered her name before turning her to face him and taking her mouth with his.

If she'd had any thought of resisting, she no longer recalled it once his tongue met hers. He wore only a towel, which fell to the floor when he reached between them and yanked her shirt open. The buttons sprayed onto the floor next to the towel, but she barely heard them.

She needed to feel Michael's skin against hers, to feel life within life after agonizing over death for so long. Michael was the only man who had ever made her want this way. Though it might be wrong, though it might be crazy, she had to have him at that moment or shatter into a million painful shards.

"Now," she whispered against his mouth.

He nodded and yanked off her jeans and panties with impatient fingers.

Rachel glanced around the room helplessly. Where?

Michael leaned back against the counter and lifted her, settling her legs over his hips. His hardness probed at her, and suddenly she understood. Tightening her buttocks, she raised herself slightly and took him inside.

"That's it, baby," Michael urged. "Oh, Rachel, I needed you so much."

Grasping her hips, he showed her the rhythm. Rachel had never known such exquisite tension. Though she wanted to make the pleasure last, her body took over and she tightened around him. He went very still. Then he pulled her even more firmly against him, and his release came in time with her own. He kissed her again, drinking his name from her lips.

When it was over Rachel's legs slid down Michael's flanks and her feet hit the floor with a muffled thud. She leaned against him as he pushed her now unbraided hair back from her face.

"I swore that wasn't going to happen again," Michael said softly.

"Hmm?" Rachel murmured, still in the thrall of spent passion. Then his words penetrated. "Why not?"

"I—ah. Aw, hell, Rachel, I didn't even ask if you were protected. I'm sorry, but I'm just not good at this anymore."

"Could have fooled me," Rachel said dryly, pushing away from him.

He caught her hand and yanked her back. "I've never cared about anyone the way I care about you, Rachel. I can't seem to keep my hands off you when you're near. When you're not all I do is think about you."

She nodded in understanding. That about summed up her own problem.

"I should have asked you last night about birth control. Once is stupid. Twice is moronic."

"It's all right, Michael. I've got that covered."

He stared at her a moment, then nodded. Rachel breathed a sigh of relief at the end of the discussion. She wasn't a virgin, but her experience with these situations was pretty slim. She found such talk embarrassing while standing naked in the kitchen.

"I . . . ah . . . think I'll take a shower before we eat," she ventured.

Michael nodded. "Help yourself. I'll finish here."

Rachel smiled at him gratefully, picked up her clothes, and fled the room.

Michael watched her go, admiring the view. He turned to finish dinner as the phone rang.

"Hello?" he answered.

"Michael? I'm so glad I found you."

The voice was breathless, harried, but he recognized it nevertheless.

"Susan? What's the matter?"

"There's been an accident with one of the tapes. Danfield needs you to come back to town right away and re-do your solo."

"Now? Are you sure? Can't it wait until Monday?"

"No, I'm sorry. Time's too short right now."

Michael sighed. He had been hoping to spend the weekend working things out with Rachel. Instead they would have to head back to Phoenix in the morning.

"All right. I'll head back in the morning," he conceded.

"Thanks, Michael."

There was a pause, and Michael waited for her to continue, glancing at the ceiling and wondering how much time he had to chat before Rachel returned. He could still hear the water running in the shower, but he wanted to get off the phone. "Was there something else, Susan?" he prompted.

"Well, ah, yes. I don't know how to tell you this, but I really think you should know."

"Yes?"

"It's about Ms. Taylor. I was doing some research for publicity and I came across some information about her family. She had a brother who was an actor also. . . ." Her voice trailed off uneasily. "It was Robert, Michael. Her brother was Robert."

Michael sighed. Susan and Robert had been close. He'd often wondered if something was going on between them, though Susan had been nearly ten years older than his friend. But Rob had never said, and Michael had never asked.

"I know all about Rachel being Robert's sister, Susan. I appreciate your telling me, though."

"You already know?" she asked, her surprise evident.

She sounded doubtful, concerned. But Michael was in no mood to explain anything to her—especially since he didn't understand himself what was going on with Rachel.

"I'll see you at the premiere, Susan," he said absently, and hung up before she said goodbye.

He cocked his head, listening intently. The shower was off. He'd better get moving.

Michael finished putting the cold meal together and set the table. Rachel still hadn't come downstairs. After waiting a few more moments he went upstairs. A cursory glance around the room told him the story.

She was gone.

Chapter Nine

He knew who I was all along.

The thought kept running through her head with varying degrees of astonishment, anger and trepidation during the return drive to Phoenix.

At her house the lights were still blazing, just as she'd left them. Had it only been last night? Rachel was pleased to discover that Roger no longer haunted her frontyard. He must have figured out she was gone and left. She wondered momentarily what had tipped him off, then decided she really didn't care. As long as he was gone, she was thrilled.

Entering the house, she dropped her bag in the front hall with a thud and, after flicking off all the lights, went directly to her room. She threw herself onto the bed and rested her head on her folded arms. Minnie jumped up next to her and proceeded to purr and rub against her head in a bid for attention. Rachel patted the kitten once, then shoved her away, earning a sheathed-claw rebuke in return.

He knew who she was. How long had he known? What did he plan to do with that knowledge?

Why had he kissed her, caressed her, made love to her if he knew she wasn't who she said she was? Did he have a secret agenda of his own? Or did he feel the same irresistible longings as she?

Rachel turned over onto her back and stared at the ceiling. There was always the chance he was a much better actor than she had ever dreamed. He could be out for his own brand of revenge, and she had played right into his hands.

Stupid, stupid, stupid.

She had told herself time and again that she wouldn't sleep with him to get his trust. But what if Michael Gabriel had no such scruples? She choked back an involuntary sob. Then what they had shared had meant nothing—at least to him.

She didn't know what to do. She didn't think she could face him, knowing he might be laughing at her behind those beautiful brown eyes. And what of her own plans for revenge? She had been doubting for a long time if she could follow through on them. Now it would be nearly impossible to put anything over on Michael. Maybe her best bet would be to cut her losses and leave. Then she would never have to face him again.

The thought, which should have soothed her, instead only served to bring further tears to her eyes.

The doorbell rang. Rachel sat up abruptly, swiping at her eyes.

Who on earth?

Could Michael have come after her so quickly? She hadn't considered that he might follow her and force a confrontation. Maybe she should just ignore the bell.

As if in answer, whoever was outside began to pound on the door. Rachel sighed and made her way to the front hall.

With a heavy heart she yanked open the door.

The color drained from her face at the sight of the person standing on her doorstep.

"Beth," she whispered.

Michael wasted no time packing his bag and returning to town. She must have heard him on the phone to Susan. If so, she knew he was aware of her identity. The question was, what did she plan to do now that her secret was out?

He was still deep in thought when he reached his house. Stepping inside, he immediately sensed he wasn't alone.

As silently as he could, he set his bag aside and moved stealthily through the lower floor. Dawn had just broken, showering the house with an eerie half-light. Unused to being up and about at this time of day, Michael paused as shadows he had never noticed before danced in the corners.

A slight shuffle from the living room turned his feet in that direction. He crept along the wall, wondering how anyone had gotten past the security system and into the house. It was too early in the day for Joyce to have arrived.

A shadow moved behind him. Michael instinctively bent and turned, lowering his shoulder and ramming it up into the stomach of the person to his rear. The shock reverberated along Michael's arm as he made contact with rock-hard muscle.

"Oof . . ." the shadow exclaimed, and a puff of exhaled breath stirred Michael's hair. "I give, Mike, I give," Roger croaked.

"Sorry." Michael straightened, then frowned at his friend. "What are you doing here?"

Roger rubbed his stomach and glanced at Michael with wounded eyes. "I live here, unless, of course, you've decided to fire me."

"I thought you were going to watch Rachel's, see if anyone tried anything while she was gone."

"I came home for a shower and a change of clothes. Looks like she's back home, though, huh? I guess I'd better get back over there pronto."

"I want to talk to you a minute first. The police are still patrolling there. She should be all right for a while."

Roger growled, a sound of pure irritation. "Well, not exactly."

Michael, who had been in the process of walking into the living room, stopped and returned to the hall. "Not exactly what?"

"The police aren't exactly patrolling past Rachel's. At least, not any more than the usual. I got a call from Detective Hamilton. Since there haven't been any more incidents they can't spare the manpower to keep up the extra protection. I get the feeling they aren't taking this too seriously. Hamilton suggested, if we're still concerned, we hire a private security team."

"What do you think?" Michael asked.

"I take it, since you're back safe and sound, Rachel isn't after your skin. But we'd better stay on our toes. You never know what's in a crazy person's mind. Oh, I wanted to tell you—I had Hamilton check out Joyce."

"Joyce? Have you finally blown a fuse, Rog?" Michael asked, exasperated with his friend's suspicions. "She's a sweet little old lady who leaves me candy. Why don't you turn in the pool service and the gardener, too?"

"I did. But Joyce fits the profile Hamilton gave us; at least more than anyone else. She leaves you presents and notes. She idolizes you."

"Did they find anything on her?" Michael asked, reluctant to hear the answer.

Roger grimaced. "Not yet. But that doesn't mean they won't. I've told Joyce not to come to work until I call her again."

Michael just shook his head. They'd be knee deep in dirty socks by the time Joyce got back.

"Hamilton did uncover one interesting bit of information though," Roger ventured.

Michael raised his eyebrows but said nothing.

Roger continued. "I remembered your mentioning a woman named Camilla, once, and not very fondly. Hamilton ran her down." He looked at Michael closely. "Did you know she's doing dinner theater in Phoenix this summer?"

Michael frowned, waiting for the flash of pain that usually accompanied any mention of Camilla. Nothing came. "No. Should I?"

"Well, Hamilton went and talked to her, and she's got an alibi for the nights in question. She's been on stage."

"She could have hired someone."

"Same point I made. But she has no motive. According to her, and several of your old acquaintances, she dumped you, not the other way around. She isn't the scorned lover."

"No," Michael said quietly. "That wasn't her role. Where's she working?"

"Some little club downtown." Roger's brow creased as he tried to remember the name;

then he snapped his fingers as it came to him. "Melody Lanes."

"Call there and get her number, then get back to Rachel's. I'll be over after I shower."

"No."

Michael had turned to start upstairs, but he froze at Roger's softly spoken negation. Slowly he looked over his shoulder.

"What was that?"

"I said, 'no.' Now that the cops have given up, whoever this is will come after you. That's what they've been waiting for. If it's Rachel, all you need is to be sitting in her front yard when she decides the time has come for some gunplay."

"If Rachel wanted to hurt me, she would have done it already."

"Maybe she has a different plan. Crazies don't need a reason for what they do, Mike."

"Someone sneaked into her house and threatened her. What about that?"

"She could have made it up."

Michael sighed; there was no arguing with Roger once he made up his mind. "All right. Just for a minute, let's say it isn't Rachel who's after me." Roger nodded. "Rachel's been threatened, too. What if whoever this is goes after her first?"

"Won't happen," Roger said flatly.

"Why's that?"

"If Hamilton's right, and this is some obsessive thing, Rachel's just an irritation. Probably jealousy behind the threats to her. If you two stay apart, there won't be any reason to hurt Rachel. No one knows you two were together yesterday."

Michael thought for a moment, then nodded his agreement. "Since you're going to be stubborn you can hire a security team and get them over to Rachel's."

"Fair enough. I have a friend who owns one. I'll give him a call right now."

"Convenient," Michael muttered. "How long do you think it'll take before I get another call or perhaps a visit?"

"Soon. Whoever it was had to back off because of the police interest. I'm sure that wasn't in the plan. Now that the police have gone about their business our friend will be anxious to get back on track. The nervous make mistakes."

"Just so you don't make any."

"Not me, buddy. This is more than just a job; it's an adventure."

Michael rolled his eyes heavenward at Roger's usual humor and retreated upstairs. Shortly thereafter, the bodyguard buzzed him on the intercom with Camilla's unlisted home phone number. Michael dialed quickly before he could talk himself out of it. He had no desire to talk to Camilla, but he found it odd that she had turned up in Phoenix at the same time he had. Though Hamilton had questioned her, Michael wondered if she might reveal something more to him. He listened patiently as her phone rang several times. Just as he was about to hang up, she answered, and he knew immediately he'd woken her. Camilla's voice had always been deep and hoarse after sleep, and if he didn't know that quirk, he would be hard put to determine if the voice was male or female.

"Camilla. It's Michael."

She didn't answer, and Michael knew she was debating whether to hang up on him. Several seconds later she rasped, "What do you want?"

"The police told me you were in town," he ventured.

"I haven't had to deal with the police since the last time I saw you. Now here we are in the same town after all these years, and the police show up at my door. Go figure."

He heard the bitterness in her voice, and it puzzled him. "Why are you so angry? You kicked me when I was down, if I remember our relationship correctly."

"We could have ridden to the top together. But now I'm forced to do dinner theater in the midst of a desert while you have the lead in a Danfield production."

"That's not my fault, Camilla."

She sighed, though the sound came over the telephone wire as something akin to a sob. "I know. But I can't help how I feel. I could have had it all if I'd only had the courage to stay with you. Or if I'd gone with Rob when he asked, maybe he and I—"

"Rob? What about Rob?"

"Robert Matthews. When you and I were together he was always after me to leave you, to go with him. He promised me we'd be stars, but I wouldn't listen. I believed in you. He used to get so angry when I'd say that."

"I didn't know you two even knew each other."

"We did," she said shortly. "Forget him. He never lived up to his promises anyway. But you and me, Michael, we could have been big time. Hepburn and Tracy. Newman and Woodward. Nothing would have stopped us."

"You don't know that."

"Yes, I do. I've got the talent; all I needed was a break. And you would have been that break. I never would have let you hide yourself away the way you have." She paused, as though a thought had just occurred to her. "You know, with the right PR we could make your face work for you. Disabilities are in now. We'd make a fortune. Michael, we were good together once. Now that you're better and back to work, things could be the way they were. No, they could be better."

Michael winced at the hopeful, grasping tone. "I'm afraid not, Camilla," he said gently.

"Why not? You haven't seen me lately, Michael. I look better than I did before; I've had surgery. Remember how you always loved my br—"

"No, Camilla," Michael said firmly and hung up the phone. "Everything changes, yet some people remain the same," he muttered, running a hand through his hair.

If Camilla didn't have the alibi of a crowded theater full of people, he'd have serious doubts about her. She had always been ambitious, and now she sounded desperate. That was one woman he would never trust. Her kind had soured him on all women for years. In fact, his enforced celibacy hadn't bothered him overmuch until recently. All he'd had to do was remember Camilla and his frustration had eased. Until Rachel had come into his life. Then all the old desires had returned full force, and even Camilla's memory hadn't been strong enough to send them back into hiding. Even though Rachel had come to him under false pretenses, she had done so out of loyalty to her brother. He had to admire that.

Michael spent the rest of the day going over the song he needed to re-record that evening. Several times he thought of calling Rachel, but something always came up to prevent him from doing so. In a way he didn't mind. What they had to discuss wasn't meant for a phone conversation.

The taping went well, and he contacted Harry the next morning to let the producer know the problem had been corrected.

"What problem?" Harry yelled.

Michael held the phone at arm's length to avoid damage to his eardrum from the volume of Harry's shout. "Calm down," he said into a lull. "I thought you'd be happy I raced home to fix things."

"What? No one told me anything was wrong. Am I the producer or not? Shouldn't I be informed when something happens? Tell me, Michael, is that too much to ask?"

"I'm sure it's not, Harry. I just did what I was told. I'll call my agent and get back to you."

While dialing Bill's number in Hollywood, Michael impatiently tapped his fingers on the desk. It was bad enough he'd had to run home before the weekend was over, though he would have anyway once Rachel left. But the cost of the re-recording would send Harry over the edge.

Finally a voice answered on the other end of the line. "Susan?" Michael asked. "I'm glad you're there."

"Michael. I've been trying to call you. I'm so sorry. I made a mistake about the taping. I don't know how I could have been so stupid. It wasn't your tape that was ruined, it was another of our client's. I read the message wrong."

"Harry's going to pitch a fit."

"I know. Just tell him to yell at me. I deserve it. Can you ever forgive me?"

Michael sighed. He didn't have the heart to yell at Susan; she was so eager to please.

"There's nothing to forgive.. We all make mistakes. Maybe the second time through was better and Harry will end up praising you instead of cursing."

"I doubt it." She paused, as though listening to something else. "Michael, my other line's buzzing. I'll talk to you later."

Michael hung up, frowning. It was unlike Susan to make such a mistake. Perhaps she had taken on too much with her new responsibilities. He shrugged, then picked up the phone to dial Rachel. He listened to her answering machine and bit back his frustration before hanging up. He had assumed she would come home after leaving Sedona, but perhaps that wasn't the case. He wondered where she could be.

She undoubtedly wanted to avoid him, and he would let her for a while; give her some time to get used to the idea that he knew who she was.

Still, after the break-in at her house he'd feel better if he knew where she was. He'd give her one more day; then he would find Rachel Taylor—whether she wanted to be found or not.

"Aren't you going to invite me in?"

Beth stood on the porch, suitcase in hand, a question in her eyes. Rachel hadn't seen her best friend since Bobby's funeral three years before. Beth looked the same—tall, athletic, with light brown hair and sun-kissed skin—perhaps there were a few lines around her eyes that hadn't been there before, and she was definitely thinner. Rachel had always thought her friend looked more like she belonged on a California volleyball team than teaching phys ed to Kansas teens.

"Hey, Dorothy, set down your balloon and let the scarecrow in."

Rachel blinked and let out a shaky laugh. She hadn't heard their old nicknames in years. "What are you doing here, Beth?"

"I told you I thought I should come for a visit."

"And I said I was too busy."

"Since when do I listen to you?" Beth shouldered her way into the house and dropped her suitcase with a thud. Without a backward glance she continued on into the kitchen. By the time Rachel caught up, Beth was already starting a pot of coffee.

"So, if you're so busy, what are you doing home in the middle of the day?" Beth turned away from the coffeepot and flopped into a kitchen chair.

Rachel stood in the doorway without answering. Beth's appearance had really thrown her. She couldn't seem to grasp the fact that her friend was in her kitchen, expecting to sit down and chat. Rachel was still reeling from the events of the past two nights. Her thoughts were filled with Michael.

She caught her breath. *Dear God, Michael.*

If Beth found out what she'd been doing with Michael Gabriel, it would be the end of their friendship. Her friend would feel duty bound to inform Rachel's parents that their daughter had gone off the deep end.

"Rachel?"

Rachel focused on Beth and attempted a smile. "Hmm?"

"I've asked you several questions since I got here and you just keep staring into space and chewing your lip. I know that means you're hiding something."

Rachel clenched her teeth to keep from chewing her lip even harder. She had to get rid of Beth. The woman knew her too well. There would be no hiding anything from her once she got it in her mind that there was a secret to be ferreted out.

"I'm fine." Rachel crossed the room and sat across from her friend. "Just tired. I . . . ah . . . just got back from a trip."

"Business?"

"You could say that."

Beth raised her eyebrows and looked about to question Rachel's statement. Rachel jumped to her feet and walked to the counter. "Coffee's ready," she announced, and kept herself busy with the mugs and creamer for several minutes.

When she returned to the table she was in control again. She was an actress; she would *act* like she was fine. If she had any talent at all, she could make Beth believe it.

"I'm afraid you've come at the worst possible time, Beth." Rachel handed her a mug and smiled casually. "The movie has to be done within the next month. I'll be at the studio nearly every day recording, and I'll have to rehearse in the evenings. We won't have any time together."

Beth shrugged and took a sip of her coffee. She studied Rachel over the rim of the cup as though she had suddenly grown another nose in the center of her forehead. "I didn't have anything better to do. Summer recreation's been cut from the budget, so I'm free as a bird until school starts again. If you're so busy, you could use me around to help. I can be your housekeeper for the two weeks I'm here."

Rachel bit back a groan at the mention of two weeks.

Beth looked around the kitchen, her sharp eyes taking in every detail of the immaculate room. Then she returned her piercing blue gaze to Rachel's face. "Looks like you've been on a cleaning jag. Sure there's nothing you want to tell me?"

Rachel shook her head and shrugged, feigning innocence. But Beth wasn't buying her act. Her friend knew as well as anyone that Rachel cleaned when she was nervous. Add to that the chewed-up condition of Rachel's lips, and Beth didn't have to look very far to determine that there was a problem.

The phone rang and Rachel jumped, spilling hot coffee over the side of the cup and onto her fingers. She swore and, ignoring the phone, crossed the room to get a paper towel.

"Do you want me to get it?" Beth asked.

"No! I mean, let the machine answer. I don't want to talk to anyone right now."

Rachel had a feeling the caller was Michael, and she didn't want to talk to him with Beth listening in. The machine picked up the call in the bedroom, and Rachel relaxed. She returned her attention to the spilled coffee.

"Has someone been bothering you, Rachel?"

"No." She looked up to meet Beth's concerned gaze. "Why would you ask that?"

"You're so jumpy. You don't want to answer the phone. You went out of town, but won't say where. I get the impression you're hiding. I read all the time about these obsessed fans and I worry. You're not being stalked, are you?"

"Hardly, Beth. I'm not much of a star yet. I doubt if a handful of people even know I exist. I'm sure no one's obsessing over me." Rachel remembered the cold, muffled voice speaking to her through the door of her bedroom and the threats Michael had received. No, no one was obsessing over her, but someone other than herself seemed to be obsessing over Michael Gabriel. The thought made her shiver, and she got up to warm her coffee.

"Oh, what a sweetheart," Beth exclaimed, and Rachel turned to see what had brought the softness into her friend's voice.

Minnie sat on Beth's lap, purring and cuddling away.

"Traitor," Rachel murmured with a fond smile.

"You didn't tell me you'd gotten a kitten."

Rachel shrugged. "I was lonely in the house all by myself. I'm used to having a roommate to share costs. This is the first time I've been able to afford a place of my own."

Beth rubbed under Minnie's chin, and the kitten closed her eyes in ecstasy. Beth chuckled, then looked up at Rachel. Her expression sobered. "Your parents are worried about you, Rachel."

"Did they send you here?"

"Not really. I wanted to come, and they asked me to make sure you were all right. To see if I could convince you to come back with me."

"Aw, Beth," Rachel groaned.

"I know, I know. You're finally living your dream. I understand. But I want to be sure you're happy—that this is what you really want. You're not just doing this because of Bobby?"

Rachel caught her breath. "Doing what?"

Beth frowned at her as though she'd lost her mind. "Acting. What did you think I meant?"

"Oh, acting, of course. What else?" Rachel let out the breath she'd been holding. For a minute there she'd thought Beth knew about Michael.

"How long have you known me, Scarecrow? Have I ever wanted anything else?"

"No." Beth sighed and looked out the window at the garden. "No, you haven't. I can understand wanting something that bad. Though for me it wasn't a career, it was someone."

Rachel's heart gave a painful thump. *Bobby.*

Beth had loved him since the first moment she'd seen him—the day Rachel had brought Beth home from first grade for a sleep-over. Bobby had been in the eighth grade—strong, healthy, handsome, an outgoing child in a quiet community. Everyone knew Bobby Taylor.

"Beth," Rachel began, still uncertain how to handle her friend's pain.

Beth turned from the window and waved away Rachel's concern. "No. Forget it. I have to get over him sometime. He's gone and I'm alive—though at times I wish I wasn't."

"What?" Rachel squeaked. "Beth, you can't be serious."

"No. Not anymore. But right after he died . . ." She shrugged one shoulder. "You can't understand what it's like, Rachel. You've never loved anyone like that. I hope you do someday. It's wonderful."

"Doesn't sound wonderful."

Beth smiled and closed her eyes. Her face took on a faraway expression as she continued to stroke Minnie absently. The kitten in her lap purred on, even though she had long since fallen asleep. "He was everything to me," Beth said. "I had such dreams for us. I imagined our wedding, our first home, our first child. I knew he had dreams of his own, and I respected them. But I always believed he'd come back for me when he was ready."

Rachel raised her eyebrows, but Beth, eyes still closed as she remembered, didn't see the skepticism. When Bobby had gone off to New York Rachel had often wondered how serious he was about Beth. Her brother had been focused on his career to the exclusion of all else. He'd written Beth, though not very often, and he'd visited even less frequently.

"I'm sure everything would have worked out eventually," Rachel murmured, hoping to ease her friend's pain.

Beth's eyes opened, bright with unshed tears. She blinked a few times and her lips turned up in a shaky smile. "He never meant to hurt me. I know that. Bobby was just Bobby. You know, brighter than the rest of us. A shining star."

"I know." Rachel reached over and took Beth's hand, squeezing it slightly in support.

"I'd feel better somehow if that man had been punished."

Rachel went very still. "Man?"

Beth withdrew her hand and stood up quickly. She paced the kitchen in short angry strides. "Michael Gabriel. The one who killed him."

Rachel surprised herself by saying, "We don't know that, Beth."

"I know it. All that crap about an accident—you and I both know Gabriel killed him. Bobby wrote me about him. He wrote you too. That man was out to get him. And he got away with it. It's a disgrace."

Rachel didn't answer. The silence between them thickened as Beth waited for her agreement. Somehow Rachel couldn't bring herself to give it.

The phone rang again, startling them with its shrill siren call. Beth moved forward to pick up the receiver, but Rachel got there ahead of her and smiled apologetically as she practically snatched it from her friend's hand.

"Rachel." The volume of Harry's voice made her wince. "Change of schedule. We need to finish the recording on this movie in two weeks. Be at the studio tonight to record."

"Harry, wait!" Rachel shouted before he could hang up.

"What's the matter?"

"What about . . ." She glanced at Beth, who was watching and listening avidly, then turned around to face the wall. "My co-star. Will he be there?"

"Not tonight. The recording the two of you did was spectacular. We'll use it in the movie. But he's still saying 'no' to doing any more. Is there something going on between the two of you that I should know about, girl?"

"No, nothing you need to know about. I'll be there tonight," she said absently and hung up.

Though she should be glad she didn't have to face Michael so soon, she wasn't. A pressure had begun to build inside her, a desire to know the whole truth. To commit herself to an act one way or another. She had never been a person who wavered in her resolve. All the wavering she'd done lately was making her ill.

Her head had started to ache the moment she'd seen Beth on the doorstep. Now that ache had turned into a full-blown pain shooting directly from her eyes into her brain.

"I've got to lay down awhile," she said as she hung up the phone. "I have to go in to work tonight. For some reason they've cut our time in half. The movie has to be finished in two weeks." Rachel moaned at the thought. "This is going to be a nightmare."

Beth looked as though she wanted to ask questions, but after one glance at Rachel's face she relented. "Of course. Go." Beth shooed her toward the bedroom. "I'll take care of things here. Don't worry about me. We can finish talking later."

Rachel bit back a groan at the thought. She felt as though her entire world was crashing down about her, and she was being buried amid the rubble of memories and passions.

She hated Michael. She wanted Michael.

Michael killed Bobby. Bobby tried to kill Michael.

Rachel reached her room and shut the door. Throwing herself down on the bed, she cradled her throbbing head in her ice-cold fingers.

Faces swirled in front of her eyes, merging and mingling—Michael, Bobby, Beth, Mother, Father.

Her life was a mess. Things had seemed so simple before she'd met Michael Gabriel. It was easy to hate a shadow, to pass judgment on a person you knew nothing about. But fate had thrown her a startling curve. The sexual attraction that had flared between the two of them from their first touch in the dark had confused her at every turn. And Michael was so different from the man she had believed him to be. She had always admired his talent; one couldn't be an artist and not admire beauty. But it was Michael's inner strength that she had come to respect. He had turned his back on what could have been a stunning career in order to punish himself for her brother's death. Most men would be glad they hadn't gone to jail, but Michael had entered a prison of his own design.

Rachel sighed as memories of Michael's lips on her skin invaded her thoughts. Making love with Michael had been a major mistake. Her only excuse for the lapse in judgment was that she couldn't think clearly when he was near. Her body responded to his, and now it seemed as though her heart would follow as well.

By the time she had to leave for the studio, Rachel had been able to calm herself, and the headache was under control. She found Beth on the patio, sipping wine and reading a mystery novel.

"I have to go to the studio now. I won't be back until late."

Beth nodded. "Don't worry about me. This is the best vacation I've had in years. A warm wind, excellent wine, and a good book. I'll be in heaven."

"Don't wait up."

"I won't."

Beth turned back to her book, and after a moment's hesitation Rachel left. The idea of leaving Beth alone made her uneasy. But her friend should be safe. Nothing untoward had happened since the night of the break-in. The few times she'd felt as though she was being watched had been explained once she'd found Roger haunting her frontyard. Though she hadn't seen him when she left, Rachel assumed the bodyguard still hovered somewhere in the area. The prickling sensation of being watched had returned when she'd come back from Sedona.

The recording went well, though Rachel found it odd to work with a roomful of people after the last session she'd spent with Michael. Now that she'd worked both ways, she could see why Michael insisted upon being alone. Creatively, there was a lot to be said for isolation.

By the time she left, Rachel's headache had returned full force. She had always dreaded returning home to an empty house, but now that she had a house guest, she prayed Beth had gone to bed. She wanted nothing more than to be alone.

The front-porch light blazed, but the rest of the house was dark when Rachel arrived. She breathed a sigh of relief. Tomorrow would be time enough to deal with Beth again. Tomorrow, when her head didn't pound in a singsong pattern the words "Michael-Bobby-Michael-Bobby."

She let herself in at the front door and almost immediately tripped over a heavy object on the floor. Minnie emitted an ear-piercing shriek when Rachel stumbled into her. The sound of thudding cat paws retreated toward the kitchen. Reaching for the wall switch, Rachel flicked on the light and glanced down at her feet.

"Beth," she gasped, and went to her knees beside her friend.

"I'm all right," Beth groaned and attempted to sit up.

"Stay right there. Are you hurt? What happened?"

"I—I don't remember."

Ignoring Rachel's protests, Beth got to her feet. Rachel helped her friend into the living room and seated her on the sofa before going about the room to turn on all the lights. Then Rachel sat down next to Beth.

"Try to remember what happened," she urged.

"Everything seems so fuzzy, like it happened to someone else, and I just watched." Beth rubbed her eyes with the back of her hand." "I made a sandwich and was going to come in here and watch TV."

Beth frowned and peered at the large window in front of them. Rachel followed her gaze.

"There." Beth pointed out the window. "I sat down and looked outside." She turned to Rachel with wide, frightened eyes. "There was someone standing in the window watching me. I screamed and jumped up. Then I ran out into the hall and slipped. The next thing I knew, you were home."

"Did you hit your head?" Rachel felt for a bump but could find nothing.

"I don't think so. I feel fine now. Shouldn't we call the police?"

Rachel sighed. She should have warned Beth about Roger, but she hadn't known what to say to explain a bodyguard in her frontyard. Still, if she'd told her friend something, Beth wouldn't have become frightened out of her wits at the sight of the man.

The doorbell rang, startling them both. Rachel got up.

"Don't," Beth said, grabbing her hand. "You don't know who it is."

"I'll just take a look." Rachel disengaged her fingers from her friend's clasp.

She bent to look through the peephole and gave a sigh—half irritation and half relief—before she yanked open the door.

"Roger," she hissed, "you scared my friend to death. If you're going to insist on lurking around my house, please do it right. I would have thought someone with your talents could do a better job than looking in the front window. You're going to get arrested for a Peeping Tom if you keep it up."

Roger didn't answer, just stepped inside and closed the door. He reached into his pocket, but before he could speak his attention focused behind Rachel.

"Who's that?" Beth asked from the doorway to the living room.

Rachel turned. Beth stared at Roger, a fascinated look on her face. Rachel glanced back at Roger. His face sported the same look. *Interesting.*

"This is . . ." Rachel trailed off. How was she going to explain Roger?

"Roger Smith," Roger supplied with a nod at Beth.

"Smith?" Rachel repeated incredulously. "You've got to be kidding."

"Nope. That's my name. Who's your friend?"

"Beth Albright, from my hometown."

The two continued to stare at each other, and Rachel finally stepped between them. She had to get rid of Roger before the name Michael Gabriel entered the conversation.

"Did you want to talk to me, Roger?"

"Ah, no. I just found this on the porch when I was walking around the house. Thought you might have dropped it."

He pulled a worn paperback book from his pocket and held it out to Rachel. The overhead light illuminated the title—*Macbeth.*

Beth let out a pained gasp and snatched the book from Roger's fingers.

"What is it?" Rachel cried.

"This book." She looked into Rachel's face, her eyes dark pools of confusion. "It's Bobby's."

Chapter Ten

"What do you mean, it's Bobby's?" Rachel asked. "It's a book like a hundred others, Beth."

"No." Beth shook her head in quick, jerky movements. "I gave him this book. You know how much he loved the play. He always wanted to star in it on the big screen. I gave him this the night he left." She opened the book and began flipping through the pages, frowning. "It's not here," she mumbled and continued to flip the pages, now somewhat frantically.

Rachel glanced at Roger, who was watching Beth with great interest. He saw her watching him and shrugged. Rachel turned back to her friend. "What are you looking for?"

"I wrote on the first page. I wrote, 'Here's to a

life of stunning success. I'll love you for always. Beth.' I wrote it right here." She stabbed at a page with her finger. "But it's not here. Why isn't it here?"

"Let me see." Rachel gently took the paperback from Beth. She glanced inside: None of the pages had been written on, so far as she could see. Rachel pulled the book open farther and saw that the first page had been torn out. "The first page is gone, Beth."

"See?"

"That doesn't mean anything. It's just a coincidence. Someone dropped the book, maybe on the street, and someone else found it and brought it to the door thinking it was mine."

"No. I'd know this book anywhere. It's his."

Rachel sighed. There was obviously no reasoning with Beth right then. She turned to Roger.

"Thanks for your help, but I'll take care of things from here." Stepping around him, she opened the door.

For a moment Rachel thought he might argue. She tensed. Roger saw the movement, and the corners of his lips tilted upward. With a final glance at Beth he nodded and walked to the door.

"Your friend going to be all right?" he asked softly.

Rachel nodded. "I'll take care of her."

"She looks pretty worked up to me." Roger glanced at Beth again, his gaze lingering for a few seconds. When he looked back at Rachel she raised her eyebrows. The big man twitched his shoulders in a self-conscious gesture. "I just hate to see her so upset."

"She'll be fine," Rachel said. She began to wonder if she'd ever get the man out of her house.

"What's all this about the book being your brother's?"

Rachel looked at him sharply. So Michael had informed Roger of her identity. Why was she surprised? Michael Gabriel owed her no loyalty, especially after the way she had run away from him.

Roger must have seen the anger flare in her eyes. He raised his shoulders and spread his big hands. "It's my job to protect him, babe. Even if I have to protect him from you."

"Rachel?"

Beth's voice froze Rachel's angry retort. Without another word she shut the door in Roger's face and turned to her friend.

"Come on," Rachel said, slipping her arm through Beth's. "Let's make some tea and talk about this."

Ten minutes later they sat at the table, untasted herbal tea before them.

"I hate tea," Beth said.

"Sorry. I thought you could use something to calm you down."

"I'm perfectly calm."

Rachel decided to let that statement pass.

Beth looked anything but calm. Her fingers clutched her teacup reflexively, and she stared intently at the tattered paperback book in the middle of the table. Rachel was shocked to see her usually stalwart friend so shaken over the appearance of a book. "Look, Beth, even if that book *is* Bobby's, and there's no way to prove it is, what does that mean?"

Rachel flinched at the pain in her friend's eyes. "I don't know." Beth's shoulders slumped. "Nothing, I guess. It's just . . . Seeing something of his brought him back so clearly. I hoped . . ."

Rachel sighed. She knew what Beth had hoped. Rachel had hoped for the same thing for a long time—that somewhere out in the world her brother still lived. That he would come back someday, and everything would be the way it once was. She had heard such a belief was common when you lost a loved one suddenly.

Rachel took a deep breath and let it out on a slow, wavering hiss. "He's gone, Beth. You've got to stop thinking he'll come back. You've got to get on with your life. Maybe you should think about moving away from home. There have to be a lot of memories for you there."

Beth nodded. "That's part of the reason I wanted to come here—to get away. Everywhere I go back home reminds me of him. What we did, where we went." She covered her eyes with her palm and her lip quivered. "I see someone and I think it's him and I run after him. When I get close I realize it's not Bobby—that it will never be Bobby again—and I feel like a fool. Sometimes I think I'm going insane."

"No, you're not. It's just grief. It makes you crazy sometimes. You think things. You do things."

Beth took her hand away from her eyes and blinked hard. "My parents worry about me. They try not to show it, but I know they do. They come over a lot, call every night. The teachers at school have even started to check up on me. They ask me to do things constantly, as if keeping me busy will make me forget him. I thought if I came here it would be better. Then Roger brought in that damn book, and all those feelings came back."

Rachel remained silent. There was nothing she could say; her friend would have to work through her feelings on her own. All Rachel could do was be there for Beth, and listen. She had been in the same situation—still was, in many ways.

Beth shook her head as though to clear away the memories. Rachel could tell her friend was still upset but trying her best to hide it. Beth fixed Rachel with a speculative look. "Who's the guy anyway?"

"Huh?" Rachel's heart lurched, and she stared at Beth in shock. She couldn't be talking about . . . No, there was no way she could know about Michael. "What guy?"

"Roger."

"Oh." Rachel breathed more easily. "He's a . . . a . . . an acquaintance."

"And what's he doing looking in the windows and walking around the house at this time of night?"

Rachel hesitated. How much should she tell Beth? From the looks of her friend, not much. Though she was attempting to carry on a normal conversation, Rachel could see Beth's hands were shaking slightly, and her face was pale and strained. Beth had enough problems of her own to deal with.

"There's been a little trouble, and Roger's helping me out by keeping an eye on things when he can."

"What kind of trouble?" Beth frowned. "You never said anything about trouble. Is that why you didn't want me to come out here?"

"Partly. There's just been a few threats—nothing serious. The police weren't very concerned, so you shouldn't be. They think it's just a fan."

"You've been threatened?" Beth's voice was deadly calm.

Rachel tensed. When Beth went all still and calm like that, an explosion wasn't far behind.

"Just once."

"Just once," Beth repeated. "Do your parents know about this?"

"Are you nuts?"

"Are you?"

Rachel made an impatient sound and stood up. She grabbed the teacups, now filled with lukewarm tea, and carried them to the sink. She dumped the contents down the drain with extra force, grimacing when the liquid splashed over the side of the counter and onto the spotless floor.

"It's nothing, Beth," she said as she cleaned up the spill. "You don't understand what the business is like. Weird things happen all the time, and you have to learn to ignore them. There's nothing the police can do until an illegal action is taken."

"What about these new stalking laws I keep hearing about?"

Rachel returned the dishcloth to the sink, then shrugged. "One threat doesn't constitute a stalker. And we have no idea who this is. Forget about it, Beth. It'll all blow over soon enough."

"I won't forget about it." Beth's lips were tight with anger. "If something happens to you, do you know what that'll do to your parents? Do you?"

"Yes, I think I have an idea."

"They'll die, Rachel. Just flat-out die. What is wrong with you? Are you just like Bobby? So blinded by ambition you can't see anything else?"

"Oh, Beth," Rachel said helplessly and started toward her friend.

"No!" Beth waved her back and stood. "I never

said anything to your brother. He got so angry if I ever mentioned that he might not make it, or that there were other things he could do with his life and still be happy. Sometimes he went a bit overboard in his determination to prove your parents wrong. I know they tried their best with him, and they thought they were doing the right thing by trying to force him to chose another profession. But in the end I think they only made him want to be an actor too much." She let out a short, harsh sigh. "You know I could have cared less what he did for a living as long as we were together. I backed down from telling him the truth when he needed to hear it. But I'm not going to back down from telling you. Being a star isn't worth risking your life for, Rachel. There are people who love you." Beth walked to the kitchen door, then turned back and fixed Rachel with a bleak stare. "Love can be everything, if you'll only let it."

"Where've you been?" Michael asked Roger as the big man entered the house.

"Waiting for the security team at Rachel's like you told me to."

"Were they late?"

"No. There was a little problem."

Michael was immediately on the alert. "Is she all right?"

Roger nodded. "She's got a friend staying there. Tall, athletic, cute."

"That's a problem?"

"No. Though this friend, Beth's her name, is a little on the edge if you ask me. She was Robert's girlfriend, which explains a lot."

"Robert's girlfriend?" Michael frowned and turned away. He walked into the living room and perched on the arm of a chair. "From home?"

"That's the impression I got," Roger answered from the doorway.

"Odd. He never told me about a girlfriend."

"Should I have her checked out?"

"If she just arrived, she can't be responsible for what's going on."

"She just arrived at Rachel's. Who's to say she hasn't been around for awhile. And if she's Taylor's old girlfriend, I'm sure she has no use for you."

"True. See what you can find out."

When Roger didn't immediately leave, Michael looked at him curiously. "Was there something else?"

"Yeah." Roger quickly told Michael about the incident with the paperback book. "Kind of weird, hey?"

"Yes. I wonder what it means."

"Like I said, this Beth's a little on the edge. She went dead white at the sight of the book. Kept insisting it was Robert's, even when Rachel told her how unlikely that was. Rachel didn't seem to know anything about the book."

"The more I think about this, the less I like it. You'd better see what you can find out about

Beth's whereabouts over the past few weeks."

Roger nodded and left the room.

Michael stayed where he was. He didn't like the idea of Rachel being alone with this woman. There was no telling who the stalker could be. Until he knew who was after him and why, anyone was suspect.

Before he could change his mind Michael crossed the room and picked up the phone. He punched in Rachel's number. She answered on the second ring.

"I just wanted to make sure you were all right," he said without bothering to return her greeting.

She didn't answer. Obviously she didn't want her friend to know who she was talking to.

"Rachel? Don't hang up. I know you're angry because I didn't tell you I knew who you were. We've both been hiding things. We have to talk."

"That's impossible for me right now. Harry has me working overtime to finish the movie."

"Me too."

"And I have a guest."

"I heard."

"Then you can understand my problem."

"Yes. Your brother's girlfriend. You don't want her to know what's been going on between us."

She sighed. "No."

"I'm not ashamed of us, Rachel. I didn't mean for anything to happen. But now that it has, I won't say I'm sorry. I'm not. I want you again right now. I don't care who you are."

"Don't," she whispered. "Please."

He clenched his teeth to keep himself from saying more. "All right. But you know we can't leave things as they are. I want to see you. Soon. When's she leaving?"

"In a few weeks."

"This won't wait that long."

"What do you expect me to do?"

"Come to my house."

"I can't."

"If you don't, I'll have to come there."

"No! I . . . all right. Tomorrow."

With that final word—half-whisper, half-sob—the line went dead.

My plans are coming along well. Soon, very soon, it will all be over.

The police have given up, as I knew they would. Now it's just Roger between me and Gabriel. I know how to deal with Roger.

I must admit, I almost got caught tonight. I went to Rachel's to check on her and looked in the window. Instead of Rachel, another woman's face appeared. The sight of her shocked me so much, I stood in front of the window a few seconds too long. She saw me and let out a shriek. I think she scared me as much as I scared her. I got out of there as quickly as I could. A very lucky thing too. As I left, I saw Rachel pull into her driveway. Roger was right on her tail, as usual.

Rachel. She's been such a problem. But she's angry at Gabriel now. Her little friend from home should fuel that anger. The poor, pathetic waif will make Rachel remember all the pain of their loss. Never trust a man, my mother always said. They'll destroy you if you let them. Mother was always right in that statement, if not others.

After tomorrow I don't think Rachel or Gabriel will ever want to speak to each other again. I've aimed for the area where the betrayal will hit him the hardest. If all goes according to plan, he'll hate her. At the least, I'll have planted the seed of distrust between the two of them.

It's a shame, really. I think they might truly love each other. Or they could, if they let themselves.

Too bad. Gabriel has a date with destiny.

Destiny and death.

Despite her weariness, Rachel found herself wandering through the house in the quiet hours before the birth of dawn. She sat at the piano and trailed her fingers down the keys, taking care not to make a sound. If she played, the music might soothe her. But she didn't want to wake Beth. Her friend had looked so wan and drained as she'd hurried off to bed. Rachel had looked in on her on one of her circuits around the house and had seen Beth sleeping peacefully with Minnie curled around her head. Rachel didn't have the heart to disturb her, especially for something so elusive as her own rest.

A soft thump against her front door made Rachel whirl toward the sound. Her gaze flicked to the front window, but she had drawn the drapes against the eyes she continued to feel watching her.

Slowly she got up from the piano bench and moved toward the door. No further sound came; cautiously, she peered through the peephole set into the door. She could see no one on her front porch. Drawing aside the small curtain shielding a long window next to the door, she glanced out. The yard and street beyond were equally bare. What, then, had been the cause of the thump?

With a sigh of aggravation, Rachel flipped the dead bolt and jerked open the door. On top of her welcome mat lay the latest edition of a national tabloid.

She frowned. She didn't have a subscription to that sleazy newspaper. Why was it on her porch?

A sudden chill settled over her, and she looked out at the silent street once again. That odd sensation of being watched returned. She had a bad feeling she wouldn't like what she found when she unrolled the paper.

Kneeling down, Rachel snatched the tabloid

from the mat and backed into her house. She slammed the door and drove home the lock with a sharp smack. Taking a deep breath, she unrolled the paper.

"Damn," Rachel muttered. She sank to the floor, heedless of the fact that she sat on the cool tile parquet of the entryway.

The photograph occupied three quarters of the front page. She remembered the moment well. She had run from him in nothing but his shirt. He had caught her, smoothing her hair back from her face and kissing her forehead. With her legs and feet bare, and Michael's chest in the same condition, it didn't take a rocket scientist to figure out what they had been doing only hours before. Her gaze moved up to the headline, and she flinched as she read, BEAUTY AND THE BEAST IN THEIR SEDONA HIDEAWAY! Beneath the picture the reader was directed to turn to page four for a complete story. Rachel turned.

She was in big trouble.

Her entire life, as well as Michael's, was outlined in the story. Someone had definitely done his homework and spent a lot of time on the article. There was a picture of her and Bobby as children, the farm, her parents. The same attention to detail had been taken with Michael's family, his early life in Minnesota and subsequent rising stardom in New York. A small mention was made of a movie role he had gotten right before the accident, a role that was certain to gain him great renown: the role he'd stolen from her brother. Then came a reiteration of Michael and Robert Matthews' friendship, Robert's death, and the subsequent investigation of Michael's role in his friend's death. A sidebar explained the keloids, with several photographs showing the skin condition at its worst. They had even found out about the threats to Michael and Rachel. The paper made much of the fact that the authorities believed Michael and Rachel were groping for publicity and had subsequently dismissed the case. The article ended with a final question, posed under a recent publicity photo of Rachel.

Does she really love him, or is it just revenge?

The phone rang, loud and shrill in the quiet of dawn, and Rachel jumped. She considered allowing her machine to pick up the call. But it was probably Michael on the line, and she got to her feet. She wanted to explain to him. Glancing down at the tabloid still clutched in her hand, Rachel frowned. She hadn't done this.

She reached the phone on the third ring and yanked it from the cradle.

"Rachel?" a voice demanded before she could speak.

Rachel froze; her chest ached. She couldn't breathe. Was this what it felt like to have a heart attack? After a few second's struggle she found her voice.

"Mother. Is something wrong? Is Father all right?"

"I'm surprised you could ask such a thing, young lady. How do you think we are? I'm sitting here right now looking at a picture of you with that . . . that . . . *actor*. The article says this is the man who hurt my Bobby. What do you have to say for yourself?"

Rachel sighed and closed her eyes. How on earth had her parents seen the tabloid that quickly? Unless . . . someone had sent one to them in the same way one had been delivered to her. But why?

"Rachel?" Her mother's voice came over the wire, shrill and loud. "You'd better answer me."

Rachel had a hard time reconciling the angry, forceful voice on the other end of the line with the broken shell of a woman her mother had become since Bobby's death. It seemed that anger did amazing things for grief.

"I don't know what to tell you, Mother. This isn't what it looks like."

"And what do you think it looks like? Like you spent the night in that man's bed? Traipsing around out of doors in nothing but his shirt—what were you thinking? Didn't you know who he was? Is that it?"

"No, Mother," Rachel said wearily, rubbing at the headache starting behind her eyes. "I knew who he was when I took the part in the movie."

"What?" her mother choked, then coughed, then plowed right back in. "That Hollywood lifestyle has ruined you just as it ruined my boy. Or maybe that man has ruined you both. I want you home on the next plane, Rachel."

"I can't do that," Rachel said quietly.

"What do you mean?" Her mother's voice lost some of its anger, and Rachel tried not to wince at the pleading in her tone. "I lost one child to that evil man; I can't stand by and lose another."

"Mother, he's not evil. There's so much you don't know. That you don't understand."

"I understand all I need to understand. Come home. Now." She took a deep breath and let it out on a sob. "If you don't, don't come home at all."

"Mother, you don't mean that," Rachel began, only to break off when she heard the click of the connection being severed.

"Great," she muttered. "Now what am I going to do?"

She returned her attention to the tabloid, frowning as she read the article again.

Michael had known who she was almost from the very beginning. That meant when he had made love to her he had known he was making love to the sister of the man he knew as Robert Matthews. Michael had been playing with her all along, teasing her, putting her off balance.

But for what purpose? Was the brilliant, caring man she had glimpsed through the bitterness merely a charade to gain her trust as she had tried to gain his? Why?

A sudden thought occurred to her, and she dropped the paper as though its touch had burned.

Could Michael have alerted the tabloids to their whereabouts with the express intention of getting a cover story? The publicity would be stupendous. And it would bring him back into the public eye in the part of a desirable male. People would forget about his years as a recluse; women would look at his scars as dashing if he cultivated the image of a lover. Then, when their movie was a hit, his return to the limelight would be assured.

Rachel shook her head picking up the paper. She couldn't believe someone could be so cold-blooded. A laugh, slightly hysterical in tone, escaped her lips. Rachel put her fingers up to stop any more sound from escaping. She was a fine one to talk about cold-bloodedness. She had plotted Michael's downfall for years on end.

"Who was on the phone?"

Beth's voice from the doorway made Rachel gasp and whirl. The tabloid flew from her fingers and landed on the floor between them. Beth bent to pick it up.

"No! Leave it," Rachel cried.

But Beth had already seen the picture, and

she ignored Rachel's plea. Slowly Beth straightened, the paper in her hand. Frowning, she opened the newspaper to the appropriate page. Her face whitened as she read.

Rachel remained silent. There was nothing she could do now to prevent the inevitable.

Beth looked up. "Is this true?"

"Hardly. You know how those papers are, Beth. Very little is the truth."

"This is you on the cover. You *are* kissing this man. Are you telling me he isn't Michael Gabriel?"

"No. It's him."

Beth stared at her for a moment as though waiting for Rachel to continue. When she didn't Beth threw the paper onto the kitchen table and took three steps forward. "Quit stalling. What were you doing with him?"

Rachel sighed and looked away.

"Don't do that," Beth said, deadly calm once again. "I want to look into your eyes when you tell me how you could be with the man who killed your brother. Dammit, Rachel, you loved Bobby, too."

Rachel looked into her friend's eyes. "Yes, I did love him. I adored him. That's how I got into this."

Beth's eyes took on a suspicious gleam. "What are you up to?"

"Oh, Beth." Rachel's voice broke. She had wanted for so long to talk to someone about the confusion raging within her. But would

Beth understand? She would have to hope so, because the time was past when she could keep such new and bewildering feelings to herself.

"I've spent the past three years trying to get close to Michael. I had a lot of grand dreams of revenge. Of making him pay for hurting Bobby. But, as you read in the article, Michael doesn't see anyone. He's scarred. Not just physically, but emotionally."

"I thought you said none of that was true?" Beth pointed at the tabloid.

"Well, Michael *is* scarred. But I think he's kept himself out of the public eye because of his guilt over what happened at the canyon. He's punishing himself more than I could ever punish him. He said Bobby tried to push him over." Beth made a small sound of denial, but Rachel continued. "He told me it was an accident that they both fell. Michael tried to save Bobby, but he was too badly hurt to keep him from falling."

"You believe that?

"At first I didn't. But now I'm not so sure."

"If he didn't hurt Bobby, then why did the police investigate him?"

"I don't know. He started to explain things, and I got upset and wouldn't listen. Then when I found out he knew who I was—"

"Hold on," Beth interrupted. "You didn't tell him who you were?"

"No. How could I? He never would have let me near him if he'd known who I really was.

So I lied and connived and cheated my way into his trust. I told myself I was doing it for Bobby, but the more I got to know Michael, the harder it was to deceive him." Rachel glanced at Beth. She had been afraid her friend would rant and rave once she found out what Rachel had been up to. Instead, Beth merely stared at her expectantly, as if waiting for Rachel to continue. "I haven't talked to Michael—except for a minute on the phone—since I came back to town. The feelings I have for him are all mixed up. I hated him for so long. Then, when I met him, there was something between us I couldn't stop."

"You slept with him." Beth's voice didn't hold a trace of condemnation, only resignation.

Rachel nodded. "I felt like I betrayed everything I believed in and everyone I loved. But even though I felt that way, I couldn't stop myself from being with him again. Even after he took me to the canyon and showed me where Bobby died. He tried to tell me what happened. Even then I couldn't stop myself from wanting him."

Beth nodded. "Sometimes we can't help who we love."

"Love?" Rachel's head snapped up. "I don't know about that, Beth. Maybe a bad case of lust."

"Time will tell. Lust burns itself out pretty quickly."

"You don't hate me?"

Beth shrugged and sat down on the edge of the table. "I won't say I'm happy, but I'm not going to judge you. Friends don't judge; they give advice if they're asked, and sometimes even if they aren't. Then they support your decision, whatever that decision may be. I wish you had asked me for advice before you started this scheme."

"I didn't want to upset you any more than you already were."

"You've been plotting revenge against this guy ever since Bobby died?"

"Pretty stupid, huh?"

"Not really. I had some ideas along those lines myself. I just didn't know how to go about it. I figured I'd only make myself feel worse by dwelling on it."

"You got that right. I haven't felt this awful since the funeral."

"Ouch. That's bad." Beth was quiet for a few seconds as she thought, then she looked up at Rachel with a frown. "Do you think Michael might be behind the threat?"

Rachel blinked. "Why?"

"If you were scared enough, you wouldn't be able to concentrate on what you planned to do to him."

"I don't think so, Beth. He's had threats too."

"Are you sure? Maybe he just said he did to throw off the police."

"Detective Hamilton thinks we're both out to get publicity."

"See?"

"I know. I thought the same thing before, but now I wonder. Michael's spent the last three years trying to stay out of the spotlight. Why would he suddenly try to get back in?"

"I don't know. Maybe you should ask him."

Rachel nodded slowly. "Maybe I should."

Chapter Eleven

Michael lay back in the bubbling, heated water, willing himself to relax. But every time he closed his eyes he saw that damned newspaper, and he wanted to smash something, anything—preferably something made of glass.

How the hell had this happened? He had been on the phone with his lawyer and the publisher of the tabloid all day—ever since he'd discovered the rag on his front doorstep early that morning. He wanted to know who had leaked the story. As usual, freedom of the press won out, and he had no recourse. Especially since everything written in the story was essentially true.

Had Rachel been the one to tell all? The anonymous source cited in the text knew an awful lot about both of them. But would she subject herself to that type of publicity? He didn't know.

That was the crux of the matter, really. He just didn't know her well enough to decide. When they'd made love he'd felt as though he was breaking through the invisible barriers she had kept between them since they first met. He had thought she was about to tell him the truth about herself that morning. Then she had heard him on the phone and left before he could explain. The next thing he knew, his face was plastered on the front page of a national tabloid.

Coincidence? He found that hard to believe.

Either way, the damage was done. His privacy would be a thing of the past come tomorrow morning, when the paper hit the stands. There would be reporters hounding his every move, probably camping out on his street in the hopes of getting an interview or a photograph. He had spent the past three years constructing a wall around himself, trying to make the press forget he existed. He'd thought he had succeeded—Only to have everything ruined with a single strike.

Well, he wasn't going to allow this to pass. He had been duped by a Taylor once in his life, and he didn't relish living through it again. If Rachel was responsible for this latest disaster, she would be very sorry she had ever met Michael Gabriel.

* * *

Rachel hadn't thought beyond getting to Michael's house. But as she pulled onto his street she realized she might have some difficulty getting in to see him. A high wall surrounded his home, complete with a wrought-iron security gate.

She parked on the street and walked up to the entrance, planning to buzz the house and ask for admittance. But as she neared the gate she noticed it stood ajar. She frowned, reaching out a tentative finger to push it open farther, half expecting to get a jolt of electricity for her curiosity. Instead, the well-oiled gate swung open without a sound.

The grounds were dark, eerily shadowed by the moonlight filtering through the trees. She looked around her suspiciously, wondering why Michael would go to the trouble of having a security gate and then leave it open. Glancing up at the house, she noticed the windows were dark as well.

He wasn't home.

She shrugged and walked up to the front door. As long as she'd come this far, she'd make certain no one was there. At the very least she should tell Roger the gate was open. Rachel took hold of the brass door knocker, but as she lifted it, the door swung open as soundlessly as the gate had done minutes before.

The hallway was black; not a sound or a movement greeted her entrance. Her unease increased. Something wasn't right here.

"Michael?" she called, her voice echoing at her as it bounced off the high ceiling of the entryway. "Roger?"

No one answered, but she sensed she wasn't alone. She cast a wishful glance back at the open door. She could run, but her car was a lot farther away than the phone. If someone was here, they could catch her as easily between the house and the gates. Taking a deep breath, she continued down the hallway, watching the shadows for any sign of movement.

She fumbled along the wall until she encountered a light switch. Pressing it, she blinked against the sudden flare of light. The hallway was empty.

A sound behind her made her whirl, heart thudding. Only emptiness met her searching eyes. Another noise, like the creak of a stair, drifted to her from the front of the house. She followed the sound back to the long, curving staircase that led upward to the second level. Craning her neck, she attempted to see if someone was coming downstairs, but the staircase disappeared into the shadows halfway up.

She saw a light switch at the base of the staircase and went toward it eagerly. Light flared at her touch, and she craned her neck to see up the winding staircase.

Nothing. No one.

Quietly, lightly, she hurried upward. She didn't stop until she reached the landing.

Water gurgled and bubbled farther down the hall. Mist drifted from a partially open door, and she moved toward it.

When she reached the doorway Rachel pushed gently and the door swung open. A wave of steam brushed her face. She peered through the mist. Her breath caught.

Had she been somehow transported to a tropical paradise?

Muted lights illuminated a room engulfed in plant life of every imaginable shade of green. Only enough light flowed forth to allow for reflections in the tall windows surrounding the sunken whirlpool. The bath itself was surrounded with greenery, making any inhabitant invisible to Rachel from her vantage point. Lulled by the humid warmth and swirling water, she stepped into the room.

A splash from the tub made her jump. She sensed rather than saw someone moving toward her. Michael appeared in her line of vision. He rose from the whirlpool, naked, like a pagan god of the sea searching for his goddess.

Rachel stared at the glistening droplets of heated water rolling down his smooth flesh. Their eyes met. Her breath caught in her throat at the desire she read in his gaze.

He didn't speak, but continued to move toward her. She froze, as still as a rabbit caught fast in the beam of oncoming headlights. She couldn't move. She didn't want to. The entire situation had taken on a dreamlike quality. She wondered if she had fallen asleep in her car and would soon awaken, cold and alone. Then Michael reached her. He slowly lowered his head to capture her lips with his. If she was dreaming, Rachel hoped she never woke up.

His hair swung forward, long and damp, curtaining their faces as she melted into his embrace. Before she knew what was happening her clothes pooled on the floor at their feet, and Michael lifted her into his arms.

Her head fell back against his shoulder, and she cuddled against his broad, bare chest. For a moment remembrance flickered. She had come here to confront him, not to make love. She tried to bring to mind all the questions she needed to ask him, but all thought fled when he sank with her into the water, water as heated and turbulent as her emotions.

The churning liquid added a dimension to their loving she couldn't have imagined in her most erotic dreams. Limbs moved more slowly in the water, hands and fingers slid more sensuously over wet flesh. The heat of the water added to the heat within her to create a languid tension that threatened to make her scream with the need for release.

She brushed her fingers down Michael's scarred cheek. When he stiffened she murmured soothing words in his ear. She told him that his scars only made him more special to her. That she didn't even notice them. When she looked into his eyes, she saw only a man she desired above all others.

When Michael finally slid inside her she buried her face against his shoulder, then kissed his damp neck with a fervor of which she hadn't believed herself capable.

They climaxed together, hands clasped and mouths searching. As the tidal wave receded, they slid deeper into the welcoming warmth surrounding them and held each other in drowsy contentment.

With a return to awareness Rachel's questions surfaced, as well. Though she hated to bring the world into their sanctuary, it had to be done.

"Did you see the picture?" she whispered softly.

He tensed, and her question was answered. A well of distrust opened between them, as deep and hollow as the ache inside her.

Without a word Michael climbed out and extended his hand to help her. Suddenly the thought of all that had passed between them, what she had done and said, made her self-conscious. Though she accepted his hand, she dropped it as soon as her feet reached solid ground. Large white towels lay on a chair nearby and she snatched one, wrapping it around herself firmly as Michael did the same. They stared at each other for a moment, then Michael sighed.

"Pick up your clothes and come with me."

He turned and left the room, not waiting to see if she would follow. His voice had been cold, distant. Rachel's cheeks flamed. Had what passed between them only moments before meant so little to him that he could turn away from her with such ease? Were all men able to separate the passion of the body from the passion of the heart without a second thought? She hated being so naive.

Rachel bent down and yanked her clothes and shoes to her chest, then walked into the hallway. Michael stood outside a room several doors away, waiting for her.

When she drew even with him he pushed open the door and stood back, motioning for her to enter. With a wary glance at his shuttered face she did.

Once she was inside, Michael followed her and closed the door firmly behind them. She glanced around the large area curiously. These were obviously Michael's rooms, furnished with a masculine touch. They stood in a small sitting room, complete with a desk, couch, and several chairs. Through another open doorway across the room, his bed was clearly visible. Rachel turned away and met Michael's hooded stare.

"Why did you bring me here?" she asked.

"We need to talk," he said, and indicated that she should take a chair.

Rachel hesitated a moment, looking down at the towel that was her only covering. "I think I'd prefer to talk when I'm fully clothed."

Michael shrugged and indicated the bathroom door behind her. "Suit yourself. I'll be waiting."

Rachel hurried away from him, stepping through the door and locking it behind her. The glare of the electric lights on the white tile made her flinch, a shard of pain penetrating behind her eye, but she ignored it and hastened into her clothes. A glance into the mirror showed her flushed cheeks and swollen red lips; her hair was damp and disheveled. She looked like a woman who had been loved thoroughly and well, which, of course, was the truth. A wave of self-loathing washed over her. What kind of woman was she that she couldn't be in a room with Michael for a minute before she was in his arms? From the very beginning he had seduced her. His beautiful voice, his haunted eyes drew her away from her original purpose.

She grimaced at her reflection, stuck out her tongue childishly, then threw ice-cold water on her face until the becoming color had disappeared. A search of her dress pocket produced a rubber band, and she slicked her hair away from her face into a severe ponytail. The painful tugging on Rachel's scalp awakened her from the dangerous languor that had pervaded her limbs as soon as Michael touched her next to the whirlpool. With a nod to herself, she turned from the mirror and unlocked the door.

Michael sat where she had left him, though he had pulled on a pair of shorts and discarded the towel. *Thank God for small favors,* Rachel thought as she took a chair as far away from him as possible. She had to be able to think clearly from this point on.

"Why did you do it, Rachel?" he asked softly.

She stared at him, nonplussed, uncertain of which *it* he was referring to. When a minute went by and she continued to stare at him without speaking he swore softly and stood, then paced the floor in front of her.

"I know who you are. But then, you're already aware of that, aren't you?"

Rachel nodded mutely, unnerved by the suppressed violence in his manner.

"What I want to know is why? Oh, I know why you kept insisting we work together, why you took this part in the first place. You were bent on exacting some sort of revenge for your brother. I can understand that, even admire you for it. I'd probably have done the same thing in your place. What I can't understand is why you let me touch you. Or was that part of your plan too?"

The pain in his voice was evident and echoed so closely the agony in her own heart that she also stood, crossing the room and placing herself in the path of his pacing. He drew up short only inches from her, looking down at her face, searching her eyes for an answer.

"No," she said on a whisper. "That wasn't part of my plan."

"And I'm supposed to believe you? When

you've done nothing but lie to me from the beginning. What did your brother tell you anyway?" he demanded.

"Not much. We wrote each other, and he told me about you and what you did to him. How you stole the part. He was angry, but I thought he'd get over it. When he said you two were going on a trip, and he was coming to visit me afterward, I figured you had worked things out. It made sense; I couldn't see Bobby staying angry over a part. Then another letter came the day after he died. He told me to look to you if anything happened to him."

Michael frowned. "He's the one who tried to kill me. Why would he tell you that?"

"I don't know. I only know that he did, and he's dead. The police investigated you for murder." She shrugged. "I . . . we . . . my parents and I . . . we needed someone . . . anyone to blame."

"And I was elected," Michael said flatly, turning away and walking back across the room to sit on the edge of his desk.

"Yes."

He sighed. "I had no reason to kill him, Rachel. I'd already stolen the part of a lifetime out from under him, and I wouldn't have killed for it anyway. I hadn't realized how on the edge he was or I never would have betrayed his trust that way." Michael looked directly into her eyes. "I was young and ambitious and I wanted that part."

Rachel shook her head, confused. "You're saying that Bobby tried to kill you over that part? There was nothing else? I can't believe it. He wouldn't be so stupid."

"No, I don't think it was just the part, though I'm not sure what else he believed I did to him." Michael stared past her, as if seeing again what had happened the day of Bobby's death. "I thought he had come around, that he understood how things were in the business. I hoped we could be friends again." Michael looked at her earnestly. "Whatever else you might believe, Rachel, I cared about Rob. He was my friend. I've never forgiven myself for what I did. For what happened."

"I know."

He paid no attention to her low-voiced comment. It was as if he hadn't heard it, and he continued with his remembrances. "When we got to the canyon he changed. There was a wildness in him I'd never seen before. He wouldn't listen to me. I can't explain it, but it was as if he'd gone crazy for a moment. Why else would he do what he did?"

"And you've lived all these years in the shadows, punishing yourself."

Michael turned away with a frown, but he didn't answer her.

"I'm right, aren't I?" she persisted.

Michael ignored her question and Rachel crossed the room, putting a hand on his shoulder and forcing him to turn around and face her.

"Aren't I?" she asked again.

Instead of answering her question, Michael stared into Rachel's eyes. But she didn't think he saw her. His mind had returned to that day three years gone.

"I've never been able to decide if Rob died thinking I killed him," he muttered.

"What?" His words shocked her. "Why would he think that?"

The words tumbled from his mouth, as though he was trying to convince her, or himself, of their truth. "He was holding on to my leg, begging me to help him. I pulled my leg back. I was just trying to pull him up. But I couldn't let go of the root with my hands, or we both would have fallen. So I pulled with my leg, and then he fell." Michael's gaze finally focused on her face, and he blinked, as though surprised to find Rachel in front of him. "Whenever I dream of Robert," he whispered hoarsely, "I dream that he died believing I was pulling my leg away from him so that he'd fall. Not that I was trying to save him."

"That's only your dreams talking. I'm sure he knew you did everything you could."

"Did I? Everything happened so fast; I couldn't think. But since then I've often wondered if I'd worried less about saving myself, I might have saved him."

"It's human nature to preserve your own life."

"Nice nature."

"You've been punishing yourself all these years, living in the shadows because of your doubts."

Michael turned away from her again, and she could no longer see his anguished face when he answered her. "I like the shadows. They suit me." He was silent for a few moments, and when he turned back to her she was surprised at the coldness in his eyes, eyes that had only moments before been filled with the heat of his memories. "I'm tired of talking about the past. I want to know about the present, Rachel. Tell me about the newspaper. How did they find out where we were?"

"I didn't tell them. I'd thought that maybe you . . ." She drifted off when she realized how ludicrous her earlier suspicions sounded in the light of his recent revelations.

"I don't think so." He turned away from her and crossed the room to stand at the window.

"If you knew who I was all along, why did you let me near you?"

Michael shrugged but continued to stare out the window. "I didn't know at first. Then I wanted to find out what you were up to. I figured if you were responsible for those phone calls and the note, I was better off being near you than letting you come up behind me when I wasn't looking."

Rachel gasped. "You thought I might be behind that? How could you?"

"Why not?" he said flatly. "My life was going

along perfectly—quiet, peaceful, just the way I wanted it. Then you show up and all hell breaks loose. What was I supposed to think?"

Rachel walked the two steps necessary to bring her up behind him; then she grabbed his arm and forced him to face her once again. "You thought I might be the person stalking you. Yet you let me near you, you made love to me, you allowed me to sleep next to you when all the time I could have been planning to stick a knife in your back?"

"That about sums it up," he agreed.

Rachel curled her hand into a fist and slammed it against his chest. "Damn you. How could you place yourself in that kind of danger? You had no idea what I was capable of. It *could* have been me." She was shocked to realize her eyes had filled with tears. "It could . . ." Her voice caught, and she swallowed deeply before speaking again. "It could have been me."

He stared at her in confusion, then reached out a long, callused finger to catch the single tear sliding over her lips. "Why the tears, Rachel? Isn't this what you wanted? My privacy, the one thing that means something to me, is at an end. It will take me years to return to the quiet life I want. I'm sure you wanted to destroy me even more thoroughly, but you have to realize that if you do anything more to me now, your career will suffer as well. Are you willing to risk it? Even for your precious brother?"

The mocking chill of his voice galvanized her into action as nothing else could. She had hoped they could come to some sort of understanding—put all the lies and the hate and the deceptions behind them and perhaps start anew. But she could see now that they had gone too far for that.

Quietly she turned away. She wouldn't let him see how much he'd hurt her. If she had nothing else, she at least had some small remnant of her pride left. Without another word she left him, the hollow ache inside making her wonder if she had lost the other half of her soul—the half she had never known existed until the moment of its loss.

I watched Rachel leave the house holding back her tears. A sad sight. But good for me. By the look on her face Miss Songbird will not be back.

I considered going upstairs and finishing everything right then. No, I told myself. Too soon. Too easy. After what I had witnessed, he must be made to suffer for his indiscretion. I told him to leave her alone. He didn't listen.

I was nearly in the same room with Gabriel after so many years of watching. Then Rachel showed up, and I had to hide. But not so far away that I couldn't hear what was going on through the open door nearby. It doesn't take much to imagine the rest.

How dare he fornicate with her? I warned him to stay away from that girl. No one is taking my threats seriously enough. But that will be the case no longer.

I slipped from the house and through the shadows. The security gate still hung open, and I reached my car with ease. It's amazing what money can buy—silence, safety, security codes. When I got back to the hotel room I picked up my phone and called him.

"Found your goon yet?" I stifled a laugh at the memory of how easy it had been to sneak into the house and give Roger a helping hand down the stairs.

"Roger?" Gabriel asked. "What have you done with him?"

"He's fine. He'll just have a few aches and pains. Nothing a big, strong goon like him can't handle. Look in the basement if you want him back. By the way, did you like the present on your doorstep? Pretty clever of me, wouldn't you say?"

He was silent for a moment, and I could almost see him thinking, realizing I was the one who had ended his privacy. "You told them where we were? What about the story? You gave them that information?"

"Someone had to."

"How do you know so much about me? About Rachel?"

"You'll find out soon enough, lover boy."

"Why did you do it?"

"A warning. I told you to leave Miss Songbird alone. She's not for you. Then I find out

you took her to Sedona." My voice started to shake, and I had to take a deep breath to calm down. Once I did, I had a wonderful idea. I could make him squirm for a while longer as I watched, enjoying every second. I deserve more entertainment after all I've been through. "I'll give you two weeks. If you can prove to me you've gotten her out of your life, I'll let her live. Don't you understand by now that I see everything, I know everything? I even know that you just had her again in your whirlpool."

"Who the hell are you?" he shouted. "Why can't you just leave me alone?"

"Never, Gabriel. Not until the very end."

Never, Gabriel.

The words echoed in his head as he ran downstairs to the basement. Roger was there as promised, sore and angry but not too much worse for the wear.

"What happened?" Michael asked as he helped his friend upstairs and onto a chair in the kitchen.

Roger shrugged, wincing as he did so and putting his hand up to massage his neck. "I heard something in the basement. I opened the door to check and someone shoved me. The next thing I knew, I heard you coming down the stairs. Are you all right?"

"Fine. I wonder how long our friend was lurking around the house." Michael frowned. "Come to think of it, how did anyone get in?

Rachel was here, too, and if you were out cold, the security system should have gone off."

"I'll have to check it. I put the thing on, just like always. Did you see anyone in the house or outside?"

"No. But someone saw me—and Rachel. I just got a call to inform me we were being watched while we . . . uh, well, we were . . ." He faltered.

"Yeah, I get the picture. Rachel was here? And she's gone now?" He looked at Michael for confirmation. "Well, she could easily have pushed me, gone upstairs to be with you, then left and called you to cover her tracks."

Michael shook his head. "You have a devious mind, Rog."

"That's my job. And whoever is calling you and following you has an equally devious mind, maybe even more so. This has got to stop."

"I think that's the plan," Michael muttered, then continued at Roger's glare: "I was told I wouldn't be left alone until the end. I got the impression the end was near."

"That's it then," Roger said, standing. "I'm calling the cops and letting Hamilton know what happened. He can beef up security again. This time I have a lump on my head to prove we aren't pulling a publicity stunt. And you aren't going near Rachel Taylor until this is settled."

Roger looked at him as though he expected an argument. Michael merely nodded and left the kitchen, drifting absently down the hallway to the living room. He sat down at the piano, but he had no desire to play.

For the past three years he hadn't given much thought to life; he had merely existed. But suddenly, when his life might be ended by sources unknown, he was starting to realize what a precious gift he had been given. He could easily be as dead as Rob. Would that make him any happier?

He had wallowed in self-pity and guilt long enough. What he had done to Robert Matthews he had done stupidly, with no thought for anyone's feelings but his own. That was the curse of youth and arrogance. But he was older now, and not so arrogant. He knew the value of life—and he was beginning to understand the value of love.

He had told himself he was allowing Rachel near him to keep an eye on her, but that wasn't the complete truth. He wanted her near him because he desired her. She stirred longings in him he thought he had buried long ago under mountains of guilt and uncertainty. He had convinced himself he didn't deserve a normal life because he was no good—the scars on his face reflecting the unworthiness of his soul. Because he had deprived Robert of any chance for a career, love, a family, he didn't deserve those things either. But he didn't have to continue to serve penance for something he had set in motion unwittingly. He would mourn Robert's death and his part in it until his own dying day, but he had been given a second chance at life and he knew he had to live it to its fullest or commit the ultimate arrogance of throwing God's gift back in his face.

And by some strange quirk of fate, Rachel Taylor was the woman with whom he wanted to spend the rest of his life. Perhaps that was justice. He would spend the rest of his life making her happy, and maybe he could atone for the loss of Robert in some small way.

He knew he had a hold over her body. But the passion that sparked to flames whenever they touched could turn her against him easier than bringing her to him. He understood now why she had run from him earlier. She hated herself for what had happened between them. She couldn't stop herself from wanting him, but she could punish herself for her weakness. He understood guilt and punishment very well. If he didn't step very carefully, Rachel would end up punishing them both for something they could not control.

There was also the added problem of the stalker. Michael would have to keep a distance from Rachel until the matter was resolved. He would not put her in any more danger than he already had.

The doorbell rang, and Michael moved into the hallway to answer it. Roger was there ahead of him, and Michael nodded as Detective Hamilton stepped inside.

"Gabriel, I hear you had an unwanted visitor today."

Michael motioned for the detective to follow him into the living room. He spent several minutes filling Hamilton in on what had occurred and the phone call that had followed. Roger had checked the security system and found nothing amiss. Whoever had entered the house knew the security code. That fact made Michael very uneasy. He couldn't fathom how anyone could have learned such a secret.

"This is one weird cookie," Hamilton observed. "I don't like admitting I'm stumped. I've checked into everyone who might be harboring a grudge for you, male and female. The only person in Phoenix now who has a reason to hate you and has no alibi for the times in question is . . ." He glanced up at Michael with a thoughtful look. "Miss Taylor."

Roger snorted, and Michael sent him a silencing glare.

"She's not involved," Michael said firmly.

"Oh, how do you figure?" Hamilton countered. "I find it pretty odd that I had to learn on my own that she's the sister of the guy who you supposedly murdered."

"I didn't murder anyone," Michael said through his teeth.

"Oh, yeah, right. And Miss Taylor believes that, too, I assume."

"I don't know what she believes. But she's

had plenty of chances to kill me, and she's done nothing."

"Maybe she's waiting for the perfect time. Who knows with an insane mind? She might want to kill you on the night of a full moon."

"I doubt that, Detective," Michael said.

"Well, stay away from her anyway." Hamilton stood "I'll reinstate the extra patrols until we clear this up."

Michael thanked detective and returned to his seat at the piano while Roger showed the man to the door.

"What do you think?" Roger asked when he returned to the room.

"I don't know, Rog. I have no clue who could be doing this. I'm sick of trying to figure it out. I wish we could just be done with it."

"You may not like the way it ends up," Roger said.

"I'm sure I won't." Michael rose and moved across the room to a small cabinet built in the wall. Squatting down, he opened the door to reveal a small safe. Tumbling the dial, he soon had it open and removed a .38 caliber pistol.

"Where'd you get that?" Roger asked as he came up behind Michael.

"I bought it before I hired you. When I got out of the hospital I was a bit paranoid, with all the people hanging around trying to get near me, see me, interview me. It was stupid, I admit." Michael held out the gun for Roger's inspection. "It's never been used. I just felt better knowing it was around."

"Did you ever learn how to use the thing? I mean really use it? Not just play around?" Roger declined to take the gun from Michael's outstretched hand.

"I never fired it even for practice," Michael said, examining the smooth barrel in fascination.

Roger sighed. "Give me the gun, Mike."

Michael looked up at him in surprise. "You're not supposed to have one. You're on probation."

"At least I know how to use the thing. You might shoot off your foot," he glanced at Michael with a raised eyebrow, "or something else you might need."

Michael hesitated, then shook his head. "I don't think so. I'll just keep this with me for a few weeks."

Roger looked as though he wanted to argue, but a glance at Michael's set face dissuaded him.

Roger shrugged and reached to pull a well-creased paper from his back pocket. He handed it to Michael. "Remember this?"

Opening the paper, Michael glanced at the spidery handwriting, then down at the signature on the bottom.

Dorothy.

He had a sudden flash of memory—standing in Rachel's home, absently reading a dedication on a framed photo.

To Dorothy, There's no place like home.

He'd asked Roger to check out the letters and then, with everything else happening, forgotten about them.

"Mike?"

"Yeah. Did you find out anything about these?"

"Nothing new. The postmarks on the envelopes we checked out when we first got the letters. They were from all over. The handwriting . . ." He shrugged. "It's not Rachel's, but that doesn't mean she didn't send the letters. Anyone could have written them for her."

"None of this makes any sense, Rog."

"Life doesn't make sense. That's a lesson I learned early. But I have a feeling that real soon we're gonna learn more about Rachel Taylor and our friendly neighborhood phone caller than we ever wanted to know."

Rachel entered her house and hurried to the kitchen, where she dropped the newspaper into the trash.

"Good riddance," she muttered, feeling better for disposing of the offensive story.

Beth was nowhere in sight; still asleep, no doubt. Rachel glanced out the back window. The sun had just begun to rise. She should be the one sleeping; she had to work in a few hours. Despite the siren call of rest, Rachel took a moment to watch the sun flame to life in the distance. She rarely got to observe such a sight anymore, and she was surprised to find she missed it. When she'd left her parent's farm she'd sworn never to look at another sunrise. Now she understood the peace her father had found every morning, working in the fields as the new day was born.

Minnie wound around her ankles, nearly tripping her, and Rachel absently picked up the kitten before sitting in the nearest chair.

"I've got a big problem, girl," she said, stroking the kitten under the throat, enjoying the calming vibration of her purr. "I think I've gone and fallen in love with him. How did that happen? I tried so hard to keep my perspective, to remember Bobby. But you should have seen Michael's face when he talked about the accident—I can't believe he could hurt anyone. But if Michael's telling the truth, then my brother lied. Why would he do that?"

Rachel sighed. She wouldn't be able to discover an answer to that question now that Bobby was gone. She would have to decide for herself what to believe. She had come to Phoenix to avenge her brother and instead she had fallen in love with the man she was supposed to be punishing. Once she had believed no punishment great enough for the loss of her brother. Now she knew that nothing could assuage her grief over Bobby's death. She had to let him go and get on with her life—a life that would be nothing without Michael Gabriel in it. But would he still want her?

She remembered Michael's parting words to her the last time they had been together and flinched. He thought she meant to hurt him.

She couldn't blame the man for that; he was right. She had meant to. The kindest thing she could do for him would be to fade quietly from his life. Her presence had only increased the anger of the person stalking him, and Michael would be much better off without the constant reminder of Robert in the person of his sister.

Rachel stood and clenched her hands in determination. The least she could do for Michael after all he had been through at the hands of the Taylors was give him a chance for a new life.

Free of her and memories of Bobby.

Chapter Twelve

The past two weeks had been a party in hell.

Rachel stared at herself in the mirror, disgusted with the purple circles under her red-rimmed eyes and the lackluster appearance of her hair and skin.

"Welcome to my nightmare," she said to herself.

She had spent the past fourteen days finishing the movie. Not only had her work schedule exhausted her, but memories of Michael kept her awake when she should have been resting for the next day's session. Michael's voice, the voice she had fallen in love with before she had even met the man, haunted her every moment of the day and night. She remembered their lovemaking in vivid, excruciating detail. She was terrified to turn on the news lest she hear he'd been killed by a love-crazed fan.

Having Beth around hadn't helped, either. Though Rachel had told her friend about Michael, she didn't feel she could continue to throw his name in Beth's face. There was only so much she could expect Bobby's girlfriend to take.

Harry was in orbit with happiness over the sound track, despite Michael's steadfast refusal to work with Rachel any more. They had finished what remained of their parts separately, just as they had begun before they met. The producer wanted public appearances, interviews on "Oprah" and "The Tonight Show." His enthusiasm only made Rachel's mood sink lower. She doubted Michael would agree, and if he did, she didn't think she could stand to be near him and know that they couldn't be together.

She lived on coffee, crackers, and short naps, dropping several pounds. She had been tempted to call Michael several times but had stopped herself with her hand on the phone. She wouldn't go back on the promise she had made to herself to leave him alone.

On several occasions, when she was awake at night, alone in her room with the darkness and the silence, she could sense someone watching her, waiting for a chance to get close for a final stroke. When daylight came she was able to tell herself that such were the imaginings of the guilt-ridden.

Besides her own conscience, reporters hounded her day and night. She'd had her phone number changed several times, but they always ferreted out the new one, and she'd finally given up. She ignored all their questions, wore dark sunglasses against the flashing lights, and continued with the motions of her life.

Rachel sighed and turned away from her reflection. She didn't have to see Michael again if she didn't want to. Harry could rage and scream all he wanted, but in the end the choice was hers.

Rachel returned to her bedroom and climbed back under the covers. There was no reason to get up, so she wouldn't. She tugged the sheets over her head and closed her tired eyes. Michael's face swam into view and despite her best intentions tears flowed down her cheeks.

"I wish whoever this is would just do whatever they mean to do and get it over with," Michael grumbled over his coffee.

"Something's got to happen soon," Roger said. "It's been two weeks."

"Feels more like two years."

The past two weeks had been the worst of Michael's life—no mean feat, considering what he'd been through in the past three years. He felt stretched to the breaking point—poised on the edge and ready to explode at the slightest flicker of a flame. Since the movie was completed, he had nothing with which to occupy his time. Normally he would have taken on another project immediately. As things stood, Michael didn't feel he could start anything new until he settled his life.

He continued to employ the security team to watch over Rachel, though he rode his motorcycle over to her house every evening, standing across the street and watching as she paced the night away behind the curtains. He was glad to see her friend had stayed with her; Rachel wasn't totally alone.

Did visions of the two of them together haunt her sleep as they haunted his? Or was it guilt and remorse that disturbed her rest?

Heaven knew he hadn't slept well since Rachel left his bed. If only he could have confronted her with their problems right away, instead of putting her out of his life. He was certain they could have worked through everything and made a life together. Still, he'd do the same thing over again to ensure her safety. There'd been no more threats on her life, no more notes in the studio or presents on the doorstep. He had made good on his end of the infernal bargain; now it was up to the mystical caller to make good on the other and terminate the suspense once and for all.

An insistent knocking awoke Rachel from her first heavy sleep in two weeks. Groaning, she turned onto her stomach and pulled a pillow over her head.

The pounding only increased in volume.

Rachel sat up and threw the pillow across the room. "All right, all right," she shouted. "I'll take a shower and be there in a minute, Beth."

The irritating sound immediately stopped, and Rachel fell backward on the bed. She should have known she wouldn't be able to get away with hiding in her room—not with Beth around to roust her out.

Finally coming awake, Rachel saw her room was dark. Glancing at the windows, she frowned. Though her curtains were drawn, she could swear it was night. She turned to the clock on her nightstand. 10 p.m. She had slept the day away. She couldn't believe Beth had let her languish this long.

A shower did wonders for her mood. The sleep hadn't hurt either. Maybe they should go out for a while. She could take Beth somewhere for a late dinner, if they could manage to ditch the press. Her poor friend hadn't had much of a vacation, watching Rachel mope.

Donning her favorite sundress, white cotton with tiny violets sprinkled across the full skirt, Rachel slipped into her white sandals and unlocked her door. She trailed through the house, calling to her friend.

Reaching the kitchen, she frowned. Beth wasn't in the house.

She peered outside. It was too dark to determine if Beth had gone into the garden. Flipping the switch next to the patio doors, Rachel flooded the backyard with light. She opened the sliding glass and stepped onto the patio. Immediately the shutter of a camera clicked, and Rachel pressed her lips together in irritation.

"Beth?" she called.

"Miss Taylor, can you give a statement?"

Rachel ignored the voice from the other side of her fence and stepped back into the house, turning the outside lights off when she entered. Then, with an angry jerk on the cord, Rachel closed the curtains over the glass doors, shutting out the eyes of the world.

Something odd was going on. Why would Beth knock on her door and then leave without telling her? Unless she'd decided to go out while Rachel was in the shower. Rachel looked around the kitchen for a note.

There. On the refrigerator.

She crossed the room and removed the slip of paper from beneath a unicorn magnet.

Where do you keep your car keys? the note read.

Rachel smiled. This was a game she and Beth had played as kids. Each note was a riddle. When you solved the riddle, you found the next note, and so on until you reached the prize at the end of the puzzle.

Leaving the kitchen behind, Rachel sought

out her purse. She found it on the hall table, as usual. Searching inside, she came up with her car keys. Another slip of paper was stuck to them. It read: *What do you drive?*

Rachel picked up her purse, pocketed the keys, and made her way to her car through the reporters and photographers. After getting several flashbulbs in the face she wished she'd donned her sunglasses, despite the darkness of the evening.

Before she looked for the next clue she backed out of the driveway and sped up the street. Several blocks away, she pulled to the side of the road and took the third slip of paper off her dashboard.

Where do you work?

"Pretty easy, Beth," Rachel muttered as she put her car into gear. "You're slipping in your old age."

Danfield Studios slept deserted. Saturday night: not even die-hards like herself were working tonight.

Rachel parked in her usual spot and walked to the back door. Her sandals echoed on the pavement, emphasizing her isolation and sending a slight chill up the back of her neck.

Why on earth had Beth come here? Rachel looked around the empty parking lot. Hers was the only car. How had Beth gotten to the studio, and how had she gotten inside?

Unease crept up on her as she stood in the open. With trembling hands, Rachel searched out her key to the back door. Just as she inserted it into the lock, the now familiar tingle of being watched came over her. She twisted the key to the right, giving a sigh of relief when the lock clicked. Without looking back, Rachel opened the door and stepped inside.

Darkness. Stale, cold, processed air.

"Beth?"

No answer.

Slowly Rachel walked toward her practice room. She would just check in there, and then she would call home. Perhaps she had misunderstood the clues.

Rachel reached her room and opened the door. Immediately the sound of labored breathing cracked the silence. She froze on the threshold, her heart speeding painfully with fear.

Flee or fight, her mind screamed.

She took one step backward. Then she bit down hard on her lip and reached around the doorframe to flick on the light switch.

Fluorescent light rained down, illuminating a figure bound to a chair in the center of the room.

"Oh, dear God," Rachel cried, and hurried inside.

When the phone rang Roger and Michael both jumped to answer it, bumping into each other in the process.

"Go ahead," Roger nodded. "It's your phone."

"Damn right," Michael muttered, picking up the receiver. "Hello?" he said cautiously.

"Mr. Gabriel," a man's voice asked, and Michael sighed. This wasn't the voice he had come to hate over the past few weeks.

"Yes, who's this?"

"It's George. From the security team at Miss Taylor's house."

Michael tensed. "Is something wrong?" Until now he'd only received nightly reports from the surveillance team.

"I don't know, sir. A woman came to the house and talked to Miss Taylor's friend. Then they drove off together. I figured maybe the friend was leaving, except she didn't take her bags. A little while later Miss Taylor came out and tore off in her car. Might be nothing, but I thought you might want to know about this, given the situation and all."

"What did this woman look like?"

"Tall, light hair, late thirties. One of the reporters hanging around out front heard her give the name Dorothy Myers."

Michael couldn't breathe. "Dorothy?" he asked, certain he hadn't heard correctly.

"That's right. Is there a problem?"

"Stay there. I'll be right over."

Michael slammed down the phone and ran from the room. He stopped in the living room to tuck the .38 into the waistband of his jeans, then he headed for the back door. He was outside before Roger caught up with him, grabbing his arm and spinning him around.

"Where's the fire, Mike?"

"Rachel's friend took off with a woman whose name is Dorothy Myers. And Rachel was right behind them." Michael let out an exasperated sigh at the blank look on Roger's face. "Remember the letters—the weird fan letters no one could trace?"

"Aw, hell," Roger groaned, then sprinted ahead of Michael toward the car. Michael had barely shut the door before Roger started down the driveway.

Roger opened the front gate by remote and drove through the throng of reporters on the other side. Michael watched as they all scrambled for their cars like ants whose hill had just been destroyed.

"I knew those letters were trouble the minute you showed them to me," Roger muttered.

"That's why I showed them to you," Michael said wryly. "Go to Rachel's."

"I thought she left."

"She did. But since I don't know where she went, maybe we can find something at her house that will give us a clue. Otherwise we can question the reporters on her lawn."

Roger nodded. "Better call the cops. I don't like the smell of this."

Michael didn't either. He was already dialing the car phone. "I need to speak with Detective

Hamilton." He listened, then shouted, "This *is* an emergency. I don't care where he is; just find him and send him to Rachel Taylor's."

"He's unavailable, I take it," Roger said.

"Out on another emergency. They'll send someone over, though."

Roger slammed on the brakes in front of Rachel's house. The front-porch light was on, casting a yellow glow around the yard. The place looked deserted.

"Weird," Michael muttered as he got out of the car.

"I suppose the reporters followed her just like they followed us when we left." Roger turned and looked back in the direction they'd come.

Not a headlight on the street. No one was following them. He glanced back at Michael and shrugged.

"They must have gotten a hotter tip," Michael said, and walked toward Rachel's front door. He stopped on the porch and turned. His gaze swept the empty yard. "Where's the guard?"

Roger bent down and picked up a buzzing cellular phone from the ground. "I have a feeling we'll find him in the desert somewhere if we look hard enough."

"No time now. Let the police handle that," Michael said as he tried the front doorknob. It twisted easily in his hand and he frowned. Before he could enter, Roger shoved him aside and went in first. Michael flinched, fearing he might hear the sharp report of a gun, but quiet reigned. He stepped inside behind Roger and knew immediately that the house was empty, though all the lights blazed a welcome. A quick search proved his instinct correct but revealed no clues to Rachel's whereabouts.

"Now what?" Michael asked.

As if in answer, the phone rang.

Michael jumped toward it, barking a terse greeting into the receiver.

"You're quick. But not quick enough for me. Too bad no one was there to greet you." The high-pitched laughter Michael had come to hate so well filled the electric silence. "Sorry I had to knock your hired gun on the head, but he was in my way. I'll be waiting for you at the studio. In your favorite place. The time has come, Michael."

Michael didn't even try to reason with the caller. He knew now whoever stalked him was beyond reason. Many pieces of the puzzle were falling into place. All except the most important. Who was Dorothy Myers, and why was she doing this?

"Let's go," he said to Roger.

"Where?"

"The studio."

"You told the cops to meet us here."

"So call them back. I'm not waiting," Michael said tersely and left.

Minutes later they were back on the road,

this time with Michael behind the wheel. The tension within him had built to a painful pitch. He had to get to Rachel. Because of him she was in danger. He had misread the situation, and now she could suffer for his stupidity. He should never have let her out of his sight. What had he been thinking to trust the word of a lunatic?

The Lincoln skidded into the parking lot of Danfield Studios, narrowly missing a television truck parked near the rear. Blue-white lights blazed, illuminating the building like a baseball stadium during a night game.

Michael stopped the car, staring in amazement at the lot, which was filled to overflowing with people and vehicles. Reporters, photographers, television cameramen and announcers all vied with the police for a choice spot.

"What the hell?" Roger asked.

"Exactly," Michael said, his gaze locked on the power of the press in live action before him. "It *is* hell."

Michael couldn't move. There were hundreds of people milling around outside the studio. Had Rachel been hurt? That would explain why the police and the media had already arrived. Whatever the cause, he had to find Rachel. And that meant exposing his face to hundreds of people, most of them sporting cameras of some shape or size. He might have been on the front page of a national tabloid, but he still flinched at the thought of being stared at after so many years of solitude. Taking a deep breath, Michael opened the door and stepped from the cool confines of the car.

The whirring whine of motor-driven cameras filled the heavy air, but Michael ignored the sounds. Reporters shouted questions, but he walked past them all with his head held high. Roger pushed a path through the crowd with the combined use of his burly arms and ferocious glares. In minutes they reached the police line. Detective Hamilton waited to usher them past the barricades and away from the throng.

"What's going on here, Detective?" Michael demanded. "Shouldn't this area be secured? How did the press hear about this?"

Detective Hamilton grimaced. "The woman inside—she calls herself Dorothy Myers—called us and the press. We all arrived at the same time, and I'd rather deal with the hostage situation than waste time clearing the press out of here. They'll just take pictures with their telephoto lenses no matter how far back I push them."

Michael had to force his next words past the lump in his throat. "Hostage situation?"

Hamilton nodded. "This Dorothy's got a gun on Rachel Taylor and her friend. The woman's pretty worked up. We've been talking to her on the phone, and she insists she'll deal with no one but you. I'd like to see what you can accomplish before I send in the crisis reaction team."

"I'll do what I can, Detective," Michael said.

Hamilton motioned to one of his officers, who brought him a phone. He dialed, then handed the receiver to Michael.

"Michael?"

The voice was unfamiliar, and Michael frowned. This wasn't the voice that had haunted his waking and sleeping hours for several weeks. But there *was* something familiar about it.

"Yes," he answered. "What do you want?"

"Come inside," she whispered. "Alone."

"I don't know if they'll let me."

"Is everyone here?" She sounded pleased. "Things are working out just as planned."

"Is Rachel all right? What about her friend?"

"They're fine. For now. But you'd better come in here like I asked or they won't be for long."

Dorothy hung up, and Michael turned to the detective. "She wants me to come in. Alone."

"I can't allow that, Gabriel."

"What do you plan to do?"

"It's out of my hands. I'll have to call crisis reaction now."

"Detective, the voice I just heard was different."

"What do you mean, different?"

"Different from the one that's called me before."

The detective shrugged. "I'm sure she tried

to disguise her voice before. Now she has no reason to."

"Maybe," Michael said. But he didn't think so.

The detective turned away and began issuing orders. Michael watched helplessly for several moments until a stray thought pricked at the back of his mind.

Danfield Studios was a self-contained studio. There were many buildings, some housing the recording studios, others the artists' offices, all connected by underground tunnels. If he entered through another building, he could go through the tunnels and reach Rachel before the detective's crisis team arrived. Michael knew with the gut-wrenching instinct of one in love that Rachel's life hung by too thin a thread to be left to chance.

Michael tapped Roger on the shoulder. While everyone's attention was focused on the unfolding tableau, they slipped away and went underground.

Michael ran through the darkened tunnel, the damp, cool air brushing his face like icy fingers. The dim light from the walls shifted and twisted, creating the illusion of candles in a night wind. He had the distinct impression that the walls were moving inward, inch by creeping inch, and he breathed a sigh of relief when they reached the end of the tunnel. Michael paused and checked his gun, making sure it was fully loaded. He tucked the weapon into the small of his back, yanking his shirt from the waistband to cover the gun's placement.

He nodded to Roger, and they climbed the stairs to the door. Michael reached out and turned the doorknob. It clicked but didn't move.

Michael slammed his fist against the locked door—once, twice, three times. The sound echoed into the tunnel and back.

The door didn't budge.

"Beth," Rachel cried as she ran to her friend's side.

When there was no response Rachel took Beth by the shoulders and shook her. She was rewarded with a mumble but nothing more.

"Hold on; I'll get you loose." Rachel struggled with the rope holding her friend to the chair. "Who did this, Beth? Why?" she mumbled as she loosened the knots. "We've got to get out of here before they come back."

Finally she had her friend free, but Beth remained unconscious. Looking into her face, Rachel noticed a bruise darkening her friend's cheek. Further investigation revealed a lump on Beth's temple.

Rachel ran to the phone and picked it up. She had dialed three numbers before she realized the line was dead. Her fear increased. Crossing the room, she attempted to lift her friend. They were going to get out of here somehow.

Behind her, the doorknob clicked. The door swung slowly open. Rachel caught her breath.

A woman entered. A woman with a gun. She smiled at Rachel as though they were having afternoon tea and shut the door, locking it with a sharp click.

Rachel watched the woman warily, trying to remember whether she had seen her somewhere before. Tall and raw-boned, perhaps in her late thirties, she wore a stylish pantsuit with flat, serviceable shoes. Her nondescript dishwater blond hair was pulled back into a severe ponytail. If she had seen the woman before, Rachel couldn't remember where or when.

"Hello," the woman said, glancing at Beth on the floor. Her face twisted with dislike, and Rachel took a protective step toward her friend. The woman looked up at her and chuckled. "Don't worry. I won't do anything more to her."

"Who are you?"

"Dorothy Myers."

"Do I know you?"

"No. But before this night's through you will. You're in for some surprises, Rachel." She laughed, as though she had told a great joke before crossing the room. Rachel flinched back from the woman as she passed. "I can't wait to see your face when he comes through the door."

"Who?"

"Ah, ah, ah. I'm not allowed to tell. The three of us will just wait here until he comes."

"Are you talking about Michael? You're the one who's been calling him," Rachel said. "Why?"

Dorothy took a chair facing the door, keeping the cocked gun pointed at Rachel all the while. She waited so long to answer, Rachel thought the woman had lapsed into silence for good.

"There's a lot you don't know. Like I said, you'll just have to wait. All you need to know is that I did what I did because I love him."

Beth groaned and shifted. Rachel went down on her knees next to her friend. "Beth? Wake up, honey. It's Rachel."

"Leave her."

Dorothy's voice was venomous, and Rachel looked up at her with a frown. *What did the woman have against Beth?*

"No one loves him like I do. No one ever has, and no one ever will. Do you understand?"

Rachel nodded. She didn't understand, but she wasn't going to tell Dorothy that with the woman pointing a loaded gun in her face. She glanced down at Beth. Her friend was still unconscious.

"How did you get her to come here?" Rachel asked with a nod in Beth's direction.

"Easy. I told her I was a friend of yours and we were going to play a little game on you."

"The notes."

"Yeah. She wrote them out, we put them where they needed to go, and then just waited for you to show up. By the time you got here I think she figured out I wasn't your friend."

Rachel stifled the urge to fly at Dorothy and scratch her eyes out. How could the woman talk about what she'd done to Beth as if they'd merely been playing bridge.

"Rachel?" Beth whispered.

"Yes. I'm here." Rachel leaned closer to Beth. "Can you open your eyes?"

"No. Head hurts." Beth moved her head weakly, then groaned. "Where are we?"

"At the studio. Don't worry. I'll take care of you."

Dorothy snorted. "Not if I have anything to say about it."

"What do you have against Beth? I'm the one who's been with Michael. She has nothing to do with this."

"Oh, but she does. More than you know. What happened between you and Michael is between you and . . . and him."

Rachel stifled an angry retort. Instead she took a deep breath and tried to speak in a reasonable voice. "Beth needs a doctor. Let me at least get someone in here to take her out. I'll stay with you."

"No! You're both to stay here. I have my orders."

"Orders? From who?"

"You'll see." Dorothy got up and moved to

the door. "I'll just check and find out what's holding up the show." She slipped from the room and locked the door behind her.

Beth moaned and grabbed at Rachel's hand. Rachel's attention immediately went to her friend.

"You never knew him like I did," Beth said, her voice barely above a whisper. "You only saw him the way he wanted you to see him."

"Beth, don't try to talk. Just rest. We can talk later."

"No. You have to hear this. I never said anything because I loved him too much. I always thought it was something I did wrong that set him off. Something I wasn't giving him to make him happy."

"We don't need to talk about Bobby now." Rachel smoothed Beth's hair away from her brow.

"What's happening right here, right now, is all about Bobby. You just don't see it yet. There was something inside him, Rachel. Something dark and twisted. He never let you see him that way because he needed your adulation. That's why he wanted to be an actor. He craved the attention."

"Don't we all?"

"He craved it to a point beyond reason. When he didn't get his way he got violent. Crazy sometimes."

Rachel went very still. "What are you saying, Beth?"

"I just want you to know, in case anything happens to me." Beth's eyelids fluttered, but she lost the battle to open her eyes. Instead she squeezed Rachel's hand weakly. "You deserve a chance at happiness. I think you can have it with Michael. Believe what he tells you about Bobby."

"That Bobby tried to kill him? Over a part?"

"Believe it, Rachel. Bobby was capable of anything when he thought his career was being threatened."

"How do you know this?"

Beth was silent for a moment, as though gathering the strength to go on. "Once I thought I was pregnant." She stopped and drew in a shaky breath. Rachel hovered closer, fear clutching her as she watched her friend's too pale face. "I tried to get him to marry me. He went into a rage. Told me he'd kill me before he let me ruin his career. I didn't believe him." She sighed, a long, slow moan. "Until he broke my arm."

"Beth! No!"

"That's not important now. What's important is that you realize what he was really like. You've got to let him go. We both do. The only way he can keep hurting us is if we let him."

Rachel remained silent, remembering the brother she had adored. The things Beth was saying about him concerned a side of her brother she had never seen. But what purpose would Beth have for lying now?

"Rachel?" Beth said, her voice fading.

"I'm right here." She squeezed her friend's fingers firmly. "Thanks for telling me about Bobby. We can talk about it when we get out of here. We've got a bigger problem on our hands right now than my brother."

Beth didn't answer, and Rachel leaned closer. Her friend had slipped once more into unconsciousness. Panic gripped Rachel, and she jumped up. She ran to the door and began to pound on it, screaming for help.

Seconds later the lock clicked, and as the door swung open, Rachel backed away. The figure filling the doorway wasn't that of Dorothy Myers. Instead, silhouetted in the lights from the hall was the figure of a man.

Rachel tilted her head, squinting against the encroaching darkness. So familiar. He almost looked like . . .

The man stepped into the room, and the overhead lights revealed his face. Rachel gasped and reached out for support. The man's face swayed before her eyes, and then the entire world went black.

Chapter Thirteen

"Out of my way, Mike." Roger shoved him aside and squatted in front of the door. He grunted, then rose to pull something from his pocket.

"What are you doing?"

"Picking the lock."

Michael's shoulders slumped. Why hadn't he thought of that? He was so focused on getting to Rachel, he couldn't think of anything else.

Roger swore.

"What's wrong?"

"Light's bad and the lock's old. But I'll get it. Most of the time locks have to be picked in the dark anyway. It'll just take me a little longer than usual."

Michael leaned against the wall, striving for patience. He didn't know what awaited him inside the studio. Rachel could be hurt or dead. Had he made the correct decision, coming in here? He was no hero, just a man trying to save the woman he loved. If only he knew who he was fighting against and why.

"There," Roger said, and the door swung open.

Michael surged forward, but Roger's heavy arm prevented him from entering the studio. "Move it, Rog. I'm in no mood."

"At least let me check it out before you charge in like the cavalry. This isn't a movie, Mike. If you get shot here, you won't get up after the director yells 'cut.' "

"Let's just get on with it." Michael shoved at Roger's arm.

The bodyguard proceeded into the studio, with Michael right behind. The place looked the same as it had every other night they had come there: silent, dark, peaceful. But this time Michael knew something evil lurked inside. All he had to do was find it.

"I want to check Rachel's practice room," he said to Roger.

His friend nodded and turned down the next corridor. The two men stopped in front of the door. Michael listened but didn't hear anything.

He shrugged and reached for the doorknob.

"No," Roger hissed.

Even as the word left his mouth the door opened, and they both froze. Then Michael recognized the woman in the doorway and relaxed.

"Susan? What are you doing here?"

His agent's partner ignored his question. Instead she motioned for them to enter the room. "Come in, Michael."

"We can't. We're looking for someone."

Susan withdrew her hand from behind her back. Michael's eyes widened at the sight of the gun.

"Get in here. Both of you," she ordered.

The two men walked past her and into the room. Roger immediately went down on his knees next to the unconscious woman.

"Beth?" Michael asked.

"Uh huh." Roger ran his hands over her head and pulled her eyelids up to look into her eyes. "Maybe a concussion." He bent to pick her up. "I'll take her outside."

"You'll stay right here," Susan said.

"She needs help," Michael said. "Let Roger take her outside. I'll stay here."

"Yes, you will." Susan stood with her back against the closed door, gun pointed at Michael. "For a few minutes anyway. Then you're going to go on a little treasure hunt."

"Susan, why are you here? Are you the one who's been calling me?"

"No. But you'll soon find out who has. You'll soon find out a lot of things."

"Do you know Dorothy Myers?"

Susan laughed. "You might say that. She's

me. Or I'm her. Whatever you prefer."

Michael frowned. "I don't understand. Why would you send me fan letters?"

"Because he asked me to. He wanted to keep you away from *her*. Miss Songbird, he calls her. He figured that eventually you'd suspect Rachel of the calls, and you did. Too bad even that couldn't keep the two of you apart. He's very angry that you touched her."

"Who's he?"

"You'll find out."

"Where's Rachel?"

"With him. They had a lot to talk about. When they're caught up—then it's your turn."

Michael found it hard to believe that this woman, someone he had known for years, was behind all of his problems. Who could the mysterious "he" be? His agent, Bill? Obviously someone with money, brains and knowledge about both Michael and Rachel's pasts.

"Susan, I trusted you," Michael said, putting all the reproach her could muster into his voice. He took a tentative step toward her. "You were my friend when I needed one very badly. I've always appreciated that."

For a moment Susan hesitated, and the gun dropped an inch. Michael saw Roger tense from the corner of his eye. So did Susan. The gun came up as she frowned.

"Don't try it. I'm pretty good with a gun. And I'd like nothing better than to shoot you and maybe hit the cutie pie behind you while

I'm at it. He wouldn't be happy but . . ." She shrugged. " . . . accidents happen."

Beep, beep, beep.

Susan raised the hand that didn't hold a gun and glanced at her watch. "Time to get on with the fun," she announced, shutting off the alarm. "You," she pointed at Roger with the gun. "Take her out to the cops. You," she pointed at Michael. "Come with me."

"No," Roger said, straightening to his full seven foot height.

"You don't scare me. A bullet will kill you just as dead as anyone. Care to try it out?" She pointed the gun at Roger's chest.

"Go," Michael said. "I'll be fine."

"I won't leave you with her. She's nuts."

"Hey, watch your mouth," Susan snapped.

"Beth needs help. If Susan will let you take her out, you've got to do it." Michael turned to his friend and looked into Roger's eyes. "This has got to end. Rachel's in trouble. She needs me."

Roger stared into Michael's eyes for several seconds, then dropped his gaze. "All right. You're the boss."

Michael let out a sigh of relief. As Roger walked by with Beth in his arms, the bodyguard whispered a message for Michael's ears alone: "And I do know the way back in."

Rachel was adrift in a great black ocean. The water was cold, thick, impossible to swim through. She floundered. She thrashed. She screamed for help.

"Relax," said a voice. "I'm here. I love you. I'll take care of you."

"Michael," she whispered, and reached out for his hand.

"No." The voice was angry, though Rachel couldn't fathom why. "Forget him. He's dead to you. Or he will be soon."

She went under again. Cold, thick, deep water. Over her head. She was frightened. Alone. Confused.

"Who's there?" she cried.

"Open your eyes, Rachel. Open your eyes and see."

She knew that voice from somewhere in the depths of her past. Energy surged into her tired limbs, and she shot upward, breaking the surface of the ocean. She took deep cleansing breaths, and the surface of consciousness nudged into her mind.

Rachel opened her eyes. A face hovered above her. At first too blurry to comprehend and then . . .

"Bobby," she gasped, and sat up.

The earth moved again, and she put her hand to her head, trying to keep it from falling off her shoulders.

Dear God, I'm dreaming.

She rubbed her eyes and tried again. The face was still the same. Her dead brother kneeled next to the couch where she lay in what looked to be Harry's office.

"Hi," he said, and smiled with all the innocence of their youth.

"I'm dead," she said in wonder. "How did that happen?"

"No, you're not."

"If I'm not dead, then why are you here?"

"Because I'm alive."

"No, that's impossible. I went to your funeral." She nodded and was pleased to find her head was now firmly attached to her shoulders. "You're very definitely dead."

"Damn it, Rachel." Bobby stood and walked a few steps away from her.

Rachel frowned. Bobby limped. He had never limped when he was alive.

"See?" she said, pointing at his leg. Bobby turned around. "You never limped."

"I do now. Broke the damn leg. At the time I didn't have the funds to get it set right." At Rachel's continued look of suspicion he let out an exasperated sigh. "I fell off a cliff. Remember?"

She remembered—all too well. Slowly she sat up, leaned forward, and reached out a hand to touch his pants. Real denim. She went a step further and touched his leg. Real flesh.

Her eyes filled with tears. She got to her feet and threw herself into Bobby's arms.

"You're real," she whispered.

"Told you so."

"This is impossible." She pulled back, but only far enough to see his face. Now that she had her brother in her arms, she was loathe to let him go. He looked much older than the last time she'd seen him—his face creased where it had once been smooth. His white-blond hair hung past his collar and showed a streak of silver at the temples. But what struck her most about Bobby was his eyes. She had always known danger was on the way when her brother's eyes darkened to navy blue. Right now they were near black, and something lurked in their depths that she had never seen before.

She reached up and touched his cheek. "Where have you been?" she asked. "What happened?"

"Whoa, little sister. We don't have much time before we'll have company. I'll just fill you in on a few of the details." He disengaged himself from her hold. "Sit." He nodded at the couch she had just vacated.

"This had better be good, big brother." Rachel sat while Bobby continued to stand in front of her.

"It is," Bobby began, then fixed her with a glare. "What the hell have you been playing at with Michael Gabriel?"

"I . . . ah . . ." Rachel stopped. She didn't know herself. What could she tell Bobby?

"Yeah, I figured that. He always had a way with women."

"I don't want to talk about Michael right

now. I want to know what *you've* been playing at. Mother and Father nearly died when they thought they'd lost you. You'd better have a good explanation, Robert Matthew Taylor."

"Don't start. I'm sorry for everything you had to go through. Do you think I'd have hurt you if I didn't have to?"

Rachel swallowed the angry words perched on the tip of her tongue. "I suppose not. But I don't understand where you've been all this time. What happened?"

"It was Gabriel." Bobby looked away, staring into the distance, as if he saw something Rachel did not. "He stole everything from me I ever wanted. If I wanted a girl, she wanted him. If I had a friend, they became his friend, too, as soon as they met him. Any part I mentioned, he got there first. I had no choice but to get rid of him. Then everything went wrong. But I wasn't going to let him win."

"You tried to kill him."

"He told you that." Bobby turned back to her, and a sudden chill came over Rachel at the hate in her brother's eyes. "You believed him?"

"I don't know what to believe," she said in the soothing tone she'd always used with Bobby in their youth. "Why don't you tell me?"

He nodded. "You always loved me, Rachel. That means everything to me. I would never have hurt you. I only said I would to keep you away from him. He takes everything from me that matters."

So Bobby, not Dorothy, had been behind the phone calls and the threats. That explained how the person in her home had known her nickname and the game she and Beth played as children.

"What happened at the Canyon?" Rachel asked. "Tell me the way you remember it."

"We fell over and hit the ledge below." He flinched, as though living again the agony of the impact. "I went over the edge, but I caught Gabriel's leg. He started to slide over. Then I think he grabbed something, and we stopped falling."

So far, the tale was the same as Michael had told her that day at the Canyon. Except her brother had conveniently left out *why* he and Michael had gone over the edge in the first place, an omission on which she planned to question him once he finished the story.

"He started to pull his leg back, and I started to lose my grip. I screamed for him to stop, but he kept pulling." Bobby looked into her eyes. "He wanted me to fall."

"No," Rachel gasped. "He would never do that."

Bobby took a step toward her, raising his hand as if to strike, and Rachel cringed back in her chair. "What do you know about it?" he shouted. "Were you there? Or did you just hear his side and believe it over the word of your own flesh and blood?" Bobby made a disgusted sound and lowered his hand before turning away.

Rachel didn't answer him. This man frightened her with the wildness in his eyes. She was unsure of what to say to him, or if he even wanted her to answer his questions. She had thought to tell him Michael's side of the story, try to make him see reason. But so far any mention of Michael only made Bobby furious. After the way he'd been acting she had no desire to anger her brother any further.

"He pulled his leg away and I started to lose my grip," Bobby repeated, slowly and clearly, as though he wanted to make sure she understood and believed. "I looked down and saw another ledge a few feet below. So I let go and landed on it. Then I screamed to make Gabriel think I'd fallen."

"Why on earth would you do that?"

Bobby turned back toward her and shrugged. "To scare him. I don't know. I just did it. Turned out to be a good thing because when he passed out he thought I was dead."

"We all did. How did you get off that ledge, Bobby?"

Her brother opened his mouth to answer, but just then a short tap sounded on the door, and then the knob began to turn. Bobby smiled and picked something up from the table behind him. Rachel's eyes widened as she saw the gun in his hand.

"What are you doing?" she demanded.

"Time to end this once and for all. I've wanted to kill Gabriel for years, and now I'll finally get my chance."

Rachel glanced at the door, which had begun to open.

"Michael," she screamed. "Run. He's going to kill you."

Bobby backhanded her across the mouth. Her head snapped back, and Rachel learned what it meant to see stars. Then the door crashed open.

Bobby whirled toward the sound. Rachel tensed in preparation for the sharp report of the gun. Nothing happened.

The doorway remained empty.

Michael froze when Rachel shouted her warning. The door swung open, but he hung back, out of sight. Then he heard the unmistakable sound of flesh striking flesh. Susan shoved him from behind with the butt of the gun, catching him off guard. He fell through the open door and landed on his knees. A gun was cocked right next to his ear. He slowly raised his head.

Robert Matthews began to laugh. "Hello, Gabriel. Bet you never thought to see me again." He put his foot on Michael's shoulder and shoved. Michael reeled backward, landing on his rear with a thud. "Get up. Join my sister where I can see you both." Robert glanced at Rachel. "Touching scene, Sis. Did you think

I'd leave anything to chance this time around? Gabriel's not getting away. At least not alive."

Michael got to his feet and took a seat next to Rachel. His mind was still reeling at the sight of Rob—alive. He looked at Rachel, frowning at the red mark that marred her cheek. She saw his anger and shook her head slightly.

Robert turned to Susan. "Thanks. Wait outside until we're done. Make sure I'm not interrupted."

Susan looked at Robert adoringly and nodded before leaving the room.

"Who the hell is Susan?" Rachel demanded. "I thought her name was Dorothy."

"She's my agent's partner," Michael said. "Apparently your brother has been using her to help him all these years. And poor Susan loves him enough to do anything. I have a feeling she's been embezzling from her company to finance this fiasco."

"Once you have money, there are a hundred ways to make more. All illegally, of course," Rob said.

Michael ignored him and continued. "Susan even wrote some fan letters to me, using the name Dorothy so I'd think you were after me."

"Had you going there for a while, didn't I?" Rob snickered. "Too bad you couldn't keep your hands off my sister, even when you thought she was out to kill you."

"Leave Rachel out of this, Rob. It's between you and me. Let her go."

"Not yet. She needs to know what kind of man you are. We were just discussing that memorable camping trip the two of us took. Ring a bell?"

"Yes. I'd like to know why you let everyone believe you were dead, and how you did it."

"I'm pretty proud of the scheme." Robert smiled. "Especially since I had to concoct it off the cuff. Lucky for me a climber came by and heard me calling."

"Someone else was there?" Michael sat up with interest. "Why didn't the police ever talk to him?"

"Because he ended up at the bottom of the Canyon, chewed up and dragged around by God knows what animals. Worked out well for my plans, not so good for him. Too bad really, since I appreciated his helping me out."

"Let me get this straight," Michael said. "A climber came by, helped you out, and then you threw him off the cliff?"

"Bingo. No moss growin' on your brain, Gabriel."

"Why didn't you kill me then?" Michael asked.

"Good question. I could have had the climber pull me up to your ledge, then dump you off. But I suspected that might upset him a bit and send him for the police. So I told him I thought your back or neck was broken, and we'd better get an emergency team in before we moved you. Then, when I got to the top . . ."

Rob made a diving motion with his hand. "Off he went."

"I—I—c—can't believe this," Rachel stammered, leaning forward and clutching her stomach. "You're admitting to coldblooded murder."

Michael heard the near hysteria in her voice and reached over to take her hand.

"Don't touch her," Robert said. The softness of his voice did nothing to disguise the barely suppressed violence in his tone. "Just keep your filthy hands off my sister, Gabriel."

Michael gritted his teeth and tightened his hold on Rachel. He was getting sick of taking orders from this nut case. Robert's face darkened in anger at Michael's refusal to obey, and his hand shook as he raised the gun.

"No!" Rachel yanked her hand away from Michael. "It's all right. I'm fine. See?" She held up both her hands for Rob's inspection. "Go on with what you were saying."

Robert continued to stare at Michael for another moment. Finally he relaxed and glanced at Rachel. "I had to kill the guy. He'd seen me alive. I'd realized by then what a great opportunity I had. Although I'd planned to kill Gabriel that day, I figured I could finish him off another time, if he lived. Then I could have the added fun of tormenting him a bit. Just as he tormented me."

"I never tormented you, Rob."

"Really? You helped me with my career,

pretended to be my friend, but every time I turned around you took something away from me. And just when I thought things were going my way you destroyed everything I'd dreamed of."

"I didn't mean to hurt you. I was young and selfish and stupid. We both were."

"No. I was never stupid. Not then and not now. And I won't let someone live who betrayed me the way you did. Shit, even Camilla preferred you, though God knows why." He laughed. "But I had the last laugh in the end. Once you weren't so pretty, she ran straight to me."

"Camilla knew you were alive?" Michael couldn't belive she'd spoken to him as she had over the phone and never given a hint that Rob was behind everything. If he ever got out of this mess, his first stop was going to be Melody Lanes so he could wring Camilla's neck.

"Sure. I needed help to stay in hiding this long. Susan and Camilla were more than happy to accommodate me."

"Who's Camilla?" Rachel asked.

"Never mind." Robert and Michael spoke together, neither of them looking at her. They just kept staring at each other like two wary dogs with a steak between them.

"The place is crawling with cops. How do you propose to get away with this?" Michael asked.

"I've had years to plan. Do you think I haven't thought of everything? I'll take care of you and get away too."

"Why did you bring everyone here, Rob? It would have been easier to just kill me in the dark somewhere."

"Easier, but not half as fun. I know how much you hate the press. I wanted them here to photograph your dead body."

Rachel let out a small sob, and Michael glanced over at her. Her face had turned pale, making the darkening bruise on her cheek all the more visible, even in the dim light. Michael's anger flared anew. He had to get her out of here, and then he would deal with Rob.

"What about Rachel?" he asked.

"What about her? She's my sister." Rob smacked his chest with his free hand. "*My* sister. I don't think you understand what that means, Gabriel. You may have slept with her, but blood is thicker than sex. In the end, she goes with me."

"We'll see about that, won't we, Rob?"

"Yeah, I guess we will."

"Stop it," Rachel cried. She stood up and placed herself between them. "Stop talking about me as if I weren't here. I'll go where I want, when I want, with whomever I want. And there won't be any more talk about killing. Do you hear me, Bobby? You've had your revenge. You've tormented Michael enough and now you're done. We'll see if we can talk our way out of this mess with the police. Then we can go home, and you can explain to Mother and Father. I only hope the sight of you doesn't give them both fatal heart attacks."

"I don't think you understand yet, Sis. I mean to kill him. It's all that's kept me going for the past three years. If you don't want to watch, I suggest you go outside with Susan."

Rachel looked back and forth between the two men, her eyes reflecting her panic. She knew Rob was serious; she just didn't want to admit it.

"Go, Rachel," Michael said.

"Are you crazy? I'm not leaving you. No way."

Robert moved quickly and grabbed her by the upper arm, yanking her toward him. She let out a startled cry, and Michael tensed. Rob looked at him and smiled. "Go ahead, Gabriel. Protect her. I'll shoot you before you get two feet."

Michael didn't move. He wasn't worried about Rob killing him; he just didn't want the bastard to do it in front of Rachel.

Rob saw his capitulation and turned his attention back to his sister. Unfortunately, he kept a tight hold on his gun and a sporadic gaze on Michael. "I told you to get out." He shoved Rachel toward the door. "Now get."

Rachel dug in her heels and hung back. "What's the matter with you? Aren't you even concerned about Beth? Do you know what your little love slave did to her?" Rachel yanked her arm from her brother's grasp. "She's got a concussion at the least. She's been beaten up pretty good. Was that part of your precious plan, Bobby?"

Robert stared at her coldly. "I don't care about her. I haven't for a long time. I told Susan to bring her here so you would come. I knew Gabriel would follow. She was a means to this end. That's all."

Rachel stared at him with wide eyes. "Beth was right: I don't know you. When did you turn into such a sadistic bastard?"

Robert's eyes narrowed, and he took a step toward Rachel.

"Don't," Michael said. "Don't touch her again, Rob."

"Or what? I'm the one holding all the cards." He looked down at the gun in his hand. "Or all the guns, in this case. I'll do whatever the hell I want with her."

Michael stood. Rob swung up the gun until it was pointed at Michael's head.

"Sit down, Gabriel."

"No."

"Michael, do what he says," Rachel pleaded. "Don't antagonize him."

"What's the point? He's going to kill me anyway. But I'm not going to let him hurt you again."

"Oh, you're so noble, Gabriel. So noble you make me want to puke. But then, you always were. Helping the poor, stupid kid from Kansas. Just enough so he actually had hope. Then taking it away. You must have laughed yourself sick every night." Robert jerked his head toward the door. "Get out, Rachel. Now. Unless you want to see him die."

"Bobby, please." Rachel's voice broke. "Please. Let him go."

"You've got to be kidding. I've waited three years for this. I've lived it, dreamed it, planned it until I couldn't think of anything else. There's nothing you can say or do that will change my mind."

Rachel bit her lip, obviously trying to think of a way to make her brother listen to her. "Remember when we were kids?" she asked, her desperation coming through in her voice. "We had that tree house, and we used to go up there and do plays?"

"Yeah?" Rob frowned in confusion at her change of subject. "So?"

"We had so much fun. We both wanted the same thing. No one else understood us, but we understood each other. We were best friends. We made it through those days together."

Robert nodded. "Yeah. You were a cute little thing. Always following me and begging to play the leading lady."

"I wanted to be just like you. I loved you. I still do." She moved closer and touched his shoulder. Rob looked down into her face and smiled. "Let him go, Bobby. Please."

For a moment Michael thought Rob was going to give in. The gun wavered, and Michael tensed, prepared to spring forward and take the weapon away if he got the chance.

"Please don't hurt him," Rachel whispered. "I love him."

Robert's head snapped up. His eyes met Michael's, and hate burned in their depths.

"You'll learn to live without him, Sis. Where we're going there'll be plenty of guys to take his place. All rich and tanned, with villas like you wouldn't believe. You'll love it." Robert grabbed her by the arm and dragged her toward the door. Rachel struggled, but Rob kept the gun steady on Michael as he dealt with his sister. He kicked the door. "Susan, open up and get her out of here."

Immediately, the door flew open and Susan appeared. She pointed her gun at Rachel. "Don't give me any trouble," Susan said. "Your brother may not want to shoot you, but I will. I'll do whatever it takes to protect him and get us out of here safe."

"Take her to the roof and wait for the helicopter. I'll be there in five minutes."

Susan nodded and jammed the barrel of her gun into Rachel's side. The door closed behind the two women, and Michael turned back to Robert.

In Rob's eyes, murder shone.

Chapter Fourteen

Rachel flinched away from the hard metal pressing into her ribs. She was terrified that at any moment she would hear the report of a gun from inside the room. The entire situation had taken on a surrealistic air. How could her brother still be alive? And how could he have turned into such a monster? Rachel kept expecting to wake up at home, and that all this was a very vivid dream. But the jab of the gun into her flesh was real.

She had to figure a way out of this.

"Move. We're going upstairs," Susan said, punctuating her words with another vicious jab to the ribs.

"Ouch. Watch it with that thing, would you?" Rachel moved a few steps forward.

"Just do what I say. This whole thing makes me nervous."

"I don't understand how you can stand by and let him murder Michael. Michael thought you were his friend."

"That's what he was supposed to think." Susan's voice reflected no remorse at her duplicity. Rachel gritted her teeth. She wanted to berate Susan for her blind devotion to Bobby, but the words would fall on deaf ears. Rachel had to find another way to get away from her jailer.

"The police aren't going to let this go. They'll hunt you down. And kidnapping is a federal offense."

"Shut up. Where we're going no one will find us. No one will care who we've killed or why. Drug runners aren't particular."

"Sounds like a nice place."

"Anyplace is fine with me as long as I'm there with Robert. I don't know why we have to bring you along, but I'm willing to adjust."

"Where are we going?"

"None of your damned business."

Susan shoved Rachel harder this time, and Rachel stumbled forward into the wall. She allowed herself to slide to the floor, pretending she was hurt. Susan came up behind her to yank her to her feet, and Rachel drove her elbow upward into the woman's face. The crunch of Susan's nose as it broke was a gratifying sound. Even more gratifying was the clatter of the gun when it hit the floor.

Rachel reached for the weapon, but she had underestimated Susan. Even with blood gushing from her nose the woman could still function. She kicked the gun away and grabbed Rachel around the neck with the crook of her arm. Susan tightened her hold, inch by inch, driving the breath from Rachel's lungs. Black spots did the cha-cha with white spots before Rachel's eyes.

She thought she saw a shadowy movement to her left, but she couldn't be sure with the entire world swaying. Then she was free. She fell to her knees, gasping for air. When Rachel regained awareness the gun lay on the floor only a few feet ahead of her, its barrel glinting silver in the glow from an overhead security light. She dove for the weapon, expecting at any second to have Susan slam into her from behind.

Rachel's fingers grasped the gun without mishap. She rolled onto her back and pointed the gun where Susan should have been.

But it wasn't Susan behind her anymore. Susan lay on the floor at the feet of . . .

"Roger," Rachel croaked, her throat swollen and aching.

"Where's Mike?"

"Inside." She nodded at the door. Roger immediately turned and started toward it. "Be careful. My brother—" She began to cough.

"Your brother?" Roger glanced over his shoulder.

Rachel nodded.

"The dead one?"

"Yes," she gasped. "Not dead—anymore."

"Shit." Roger held out his hand for the gun. "Better give me that thing."

Rachel handed him the weapon. "Don't hurt him."

"I'll do whatever I have to, babe."

Rachel closed her eyes and uttered a quick prayer that no one would be killed. Then, without warning, everything began to happen at once.

Susan sat up and grabbed Roger's leg. The big man, off balance as he turned to go after Michael, fell heavily on top of the woman. The two grappled for the gun.

Bobby's voice rose from behind the studio door. "Say good-bye, Gabriel."

Rachel jumped to her feet and leapt over the two struggling people on the floor, bursting into the room.

"No, Bobby," she screamed. "Stop!"

Bobby turned toward her. His face twisted in anger. Then he focused on something behind her. "Get down, Rachel," he shouted, and aimed the gun directly at her chest.

Rachel froze. Roger must be behind her. She couldn't dive for the floor and allow him to be shot. Bobby wouldn't shoot her. He couldn't.

Instead of getting down, she clenched her fists and stood her ground.

Her brother's eyes narrowed, and his finger tightened on the trigger. "I warned you, Sis."

The deafening report of a gun made her jump. Her heart raced painfully.

Funny. It doesn't hurt, she thought, and looked down.

No blood marred her shirt.

She glanced up just in time to see her brother fall to the floor, his face reflecting the shock flowing through Rachel at that moment. She looked behind her. Roger stood in the doorway as she'd expected, but his hands were empty. He shrugged and nodded at Michael.

Rachel turned back. Michael stood in the same place. His arm still outstretched, his fingers clutching a gun. He stared fixedly at Bobby, on the floor in front of him.

She ran forward and fell to her knees next to her brother. A patch of red spread across his white cotton T-shirt. She could tell by the gray tinge to his skin that Bobby's life would be measured in minutes from that point on. His eyelids fluttered, then opened.

"Sis."

His voice was weak, and Rachel leaned forward to better hear him. Out of the corner of her eye she saw Michael make an involuntary move toward her, as though to keep her from getting too close. She shook her head sharply and waved him back.

"I'm here," she told her brother.

"Can't see you too good. Hold my hand."

Rachel groped for his hand. Ice-cold fingers clasped hers, which were suddenly fiery hot.

"There," she said. "Can you feel that?"

"Yeah. Thanks. Guess this is it. I figured I'd die young. Just never thought it'd be this way."

"Don't talk. We'll get you to a hospital. You'll be fine."

"No hospital. Even if they managed to work a miracle, I'll only end up in prison. Rather be dead than go there."

"Oh, Bobby." Rachel started to cry. "What happened to you? You were never like this—so full of hate."

"I was. You just didn't—" He coughed, and blood welled on his lower lip.

Rachel smoothed it away with her finger, then brushed his damp hair back from his forehead. "Hush," she whispered.

Bobby let out a short laugh, which turned into a watery cough. When he had regained his voice he said, "I never deserved a sister as loving as you. You're loyal to the end. Even though I would have killed your lover boy without a second thought. God, Rachel, you've got to wise up."

Rachel was squeezing his hand so hard, she never knew when Bobby's fingers went slack. Rachel sat upright when she realized that the sound of her brother struggling to breathe no longer filled the room. She wiped at her tears with the back of her free hand. Bobby's eyes fluttered closed, and he whispered one final word.

"Sorry."

Rachel stared at his still face. Hot tears ran down her cheeks and dripped off the tip of her nose. They fell on Bobby's chest, but he was past caring now.

She couldn't believe she had found her brother only to lose him again, this time right in her arms. It was impossible to assimilate all the things she had learned about Bobby in the past few hours. The gamut of emotions she had experienced—from joy to fear to anger and shock—had left Rachel numb. She stared at her brother's face, but her mind was a blank.

"Rachel?"

Someone called to her. She didn't want to talk. Not to anyone. She wanted to stay in the quiet place with Bobby.

"Babe." *Click, click.* "Snap out of it."

Rachel frowned. Something wasn't right. Michael should be with her, but it wasn't Michael's voice she heard.

Rachel looked up. Roger loomed over her. He snapped his fingers in front of her face, and she blinked, then slapped his hand away. He smiled at her irritation and straightened. Behind Roger stood Detective Hamilton and several other officers. One held Susan by the arm as she struggled to get free. When had everyone come into the room? Where was . . .

"Michael?" she asked.

"He needed to be alone," Roger said. He held out his hand to her, this time palm up, offering assistance. "Come on. Let your brother go. There's nothing more you can do."

"No." She gathered Bobby to her and held on tightly. "I just want to hold him awhile longer."

"We've got some questions to ask, Miss Taylor." Detective Hamilton stepped forward.

Roger swung around, and the detective took a quick step back. "Lay off, man. Can't you see she's not ready for that yet? I'll take care of her. Why don't you go back outside until she can let him go."

The detective frowned and opened his mouth to argue. Then Hamilton glanced uneasily at Roger's face. Whatever he saw there made him shrug and turn away. He waved at the officer who was restraining Susan. "Let's get this woman downtown. You can send them in for Taylor later."

The door closed behind the police, leaving Roger and Rachel alone.

"I know how you feel," Roger began.

"Do you?" Rachel snapped. She didn't know why she was striking out at Roger, who was only trying to help, but she couldn't seem to stop herself. "Have you ever had anyone you love die in your arms?"

"Actually, yes."

Rachel looked up at Roger in surprise. He

was gazing into space, obviously remembering the occasion.

"I'm sorry. I didn't know." Rachel felt like an idiot.

"No. No one does. Not even Mike. It's not something you want to remember or talk about. But you get past it. You never forget. You just learn to go on."

"I hope so. I thought I was beginning to get over his death, and then he turned up alive. And so different from what I remembered."

Roger nodded. "No one knows what goes on in another's heart and mind and soul. You might think you do, but you don't."

Roger's understanding touched her where the hard knot of numbness dwelled in her chest. The urge to strike out melted away. With its loss, the pain trickled in. She laid her brother gently on the floor and rubbed her tired eyes with her fingers.

"I'm so angry," she said, surprised at such an emotion given the situation. "Why is that? Bobby's dead, and I just want to break something into tiny pieces."

"It'll pass. I put my hand through a door." Roger flexed his fingers, as if remembering the pain. "Broke it good."

"Did you feel better?"

"A little."

"Maybe I'll try it."

"It's not something I'd recommend. Besides, I'd have to stop you. Mike would have my head if I let you get hurt. Even if you were stupid enough to hurt yourself."

"You love him, don't you?"

Instead of answering, Roger asked a question of his own. "Don't you?"

"Of course. But I don't know if he'll believe me. I don't know if we can get past all this." She looked down at Bobby once again and traced his brow gently with her fingertip. "Michael saved my life."

"He did. But he's having a hard time with what he had to do. He's thought for years he killed Rob. Now he's really done it. Mike needs you now, babe. More than him." Roger nodded at her brother. "Say your good-byes. Then I'll take you where you can do some good."

Rachel nodded. Leaning over, she kissed her brother one last time. "I love you, too, Robert Matthew Taylor. I'll miss you forever." She stood and followed Roger from the room without looking back.

Michael sat on the floor in a soundproof studio. He hadn't bothered to turn on the lights. The pressing blackness suited his mood.

He closed his eyes and leaned back against the wall. The sound of the gun going off filled his head. He experienced again the jerk of the weapon in his hand, saw the splotch of red spread on Rob's shirt, witnessed the shock in Rachel's brother's eyes.

This time he really had done it—killed her

brother right in front of her. Michael knew he'd had no choice. Rob would have killed him, though he hadn't been prepared to kill the man to prevent that. But when the gun had turned toward Rachel the fear flooding him had dictated his actions. No matter what, he wouldn't allow Rachel to be hurt.

He had begun to hope that he and Rachel could get past the ghost of her brother hovering between them. But that was before Rob had reappeared and Michael had killed him—this time for good. He doubted if she could ever forgive or forget this night's work.

Watching Rachel hold Rob in her arms with that dazed look of shock on her face had been too much for him. He'd left her with Roger and sought the darkness that had soothed him in the past. He wouldn't force Rachel to look her brother's murderer in the face ever again. It was the least he could do for her.

Now that the movie was done, he would go back to the life he'd lived before—existing in the shadows, working in the dark, living on the outskirts of life. Rachel could get on with her career and forget she'd ever known Michael Gabriel.

But he would never forget her. For the rest of his life he would remember the touch of her lips on his scarred cheek, the smell of her hair as it brushed across his chest, the sound of her voice as she called out his name in the midst of her ecstasy. At least he would have those memories to keep him somewhat sane during the darkest nights.

The door to the studio opened, but Michael's eyes remained closed. After a second's hesitation someone stepped inside and shut the door.

Footsteps approached and stopped directly in front of him.

"Is she gone?" Michael asked.

Silence met his question.

"Dammit, Roger," Michael exploded. "Answer me. Is she gone? Can we get out of here now?"

"No," Rachel answered. "*She's* not gone. *She's* not going anywhere without you."

Michael's eyes flew open, but he could see nothing in the complete darkness. "Rachel?"

He heard her move, and her next words drifted to him on the same level as his face. She must have sat down on the floor beside him. "Of course it's Rachel. Did you think I'd face that mess outside alone?"

Michael reached a tentative hand forward and touched her face. She leaned her cheek into his palm, then turned and kissed his fingers.

"I thought you'd leave. That you'd never want to see me again after what I did."

"You think I'd treat you like that after you saved my life?"

"I killed your brother."

"That wasn't my brother."

"What?" Michael's mind grasped for her meaning.

"My brother was happy and fun. A wonderful man to look up to. Maybe the person I believed him to be was a lie, but I believed it just the same. The man who just died wasn't the man I adored through childhood. Sure, that might have been the body of Bobby, but the soul I once loved was gone. I prefer to remember him the way he was in Kansas."

"You don't hate me?"

"No. My heart is too filled with love for you to fit in anything else."

Michael remained silent. He couldn't believe what he had just heard. He was afraid to believe it. If what she said was true, every dream he'd conjured up since the first moment he'd set eyes on her would have a chance of coming true.

"Michael?"

Rachel's voice shook, as though she was on the verge of tears.

"What's wrong?"

"That depends on you."

"Me?"

"If you love me, too, then the future looks pretty good about now. If not, well . . ." She gave a wobbly laugh. "If not, I feel like the world's biggest fool."

"No, you're not a fool. Never that. Come here."

Suddenly she was in his arms, and Michael kissed her with all the love he had never expressed. He could hardly believe what he was hearing. She didn't blame him. Could he, perhaps, stop blaming himself?

Rachel settled herself more securely upon his lap and snuggled against him. "Michael, Bobby was like a rabid dog in there. I could see it in his eyes: the pain, the hate, the madness. Rabid dogs have to be shot before they spread their poison to others. He'd already ruined Susan. He had to be stopped."

"I only wish I wasn't the one who had to do it."

"I know." She rubbed her cheek against his chest and tightened her hold on him. "But it's done. I'll spend the rest of my life, if I have to, telling you that you did what you had to do. We've got to go on, Michael. If we don't, then Bobby's won. You'll be alive, but he'll still have taken your life. You can't let him get away with that."

Michael nodded slowly, still unable to let go completely of the guilt he'd carried for so long. "I don't understand why he hated me so much. I never realized . . ."

"No one did. That's the tragedy. My brother needed help, and no one saw it. If anyone should feel guilty here, it's me. I never saw beyond what I wanted to see in him."

The door opened again, threading light across them. Then Roger's immense form interrupted it.

"Looks like everything's all right in here," he

observed. "Sorry to break this up, but we have to go to the hospital."

Rachel stiffened in Michael's arms. "Beth," she whispered.

"She's fine," Roger assured her. "Just dizzy. The doc wants to keep her overnight. The hospital needs to have insurance info and stuff like that, so I said I'd bring you over."

"We'll go together," Michael said. They both got to their feet.

"Hamilton is pretty hot to talk to you too. I told him he could meet us at the hospital."

"Thanks, Roger," Rachel said.

"They found some kind of diary on your brother. Seems he wrote down everything he's been up to for the past three years. It's as good as a confession and solves a lot of the mysteries. Should have seen the detective; he was nearly dancing with joy when he got a look at it."

"We'll be right out," Michael said pointedly.

Roger nodded. "Sorry, Rachel. I know you're upset. I shouldn't be so . . ." He shrugged.

"I'm all right. I'm glad Bobby wrote it all down. Maybe I can understand better why he did what he did once I read it."

Roger left, shutting the door behind him and throwing the room into total blackness once more.

"We really should get to the hospital," Rachel said.

"In a minute." Michael took her into his arms. "I want to kiss you one last time in the dark.

From this moment on no more shadows—around us or between us."

"No more shadows," Rachel murmured, as though the idea were new and intriguing. "Sounds too good to be true."

She was probably right, but Michael had hope. There would be no more guilt, no more nightmares. Perhaps Rachel's parents could finally heal, once they learned the truth of that terrible day three years in the past.

"Does this mean you're ready to come back into the light with me?" Rachel's voice cut into his thoughts. "You've been gone a long time."

In response Michael kissed her the way he had the very first time they'd touched in the darkness. Then he took her hand, and together they left the soundproof studio.

Roger fell in behind them and the three of them walked to the entrance of Danfield Studios. Michael looked down at Rachel and smiled. Then he shoved open the door and drew her with him outside.

The merciless Arizona sun flooded over them as Michael raised their joined hands in a sign of victory. Cameras whirred and the crowd cheered, placing Rachel and Michael in the eye of the storm.

Epilogue

"Ladies and gentlemen, I'm coming to you live from the premiere of Danfield Studio's latest film. But will the film live up to its press? We'll soon know for sure. I'm certain all of you have followed the papers and read of the scandalous events surrounding the making of this movie. Not to mention the real-life love affair between the two stars. And here they are now."

The white stretch limousine slid to a stop at the curb in front of the theater. Roger left the driver's seat, imposing in a black leather suit, long hair pulled sharply away from his face with a leather thong. The passenger door opened and Beth stepped out, the rows of white fringe on her ankle-length dress swinging with her movements. She smiled at Roger and stepped back from the car, ignoring the questions shouted to her from the crowd.

Roger returned her smile, then swept a dark, probing gaze over the throng. They gave an uneasy murmur and fell back as he made his way around the car and opened the rear door.

A ruby-red high heel, followed by a long, slim leg, shot from the opening. Then Rachel Taylor appeared, wearing a white dress, fitted and awash with sequins. When she walked, the thigh-high slits on either side shimmered open and closed around her legs.

She smiled at the crowd and waved her satin-gloved hand in response to their cheers. Then she turned and held out the same hand to the final occupant of the limousine.

Resplendent in black, Michael Gabriel emerged to stand tall and proud next to her. Long ebony hair brushed past his shoulders, but his arresting face was visible for all to see. A few in the crowd whispered at the sight of his horribly scarred cheek, but he seemed not to hear the stirring within the audience.

Flanked by their friends, Rachel and Michael approached a podium in front of the theater. Their producer, Harold P. Stanhope, their director, and the other actors responsible for the voices in the movie awaited them. Michael stepped up to the microphone, and the crowd fell silent.

"Thank you all for coming. I can't tell you what an experience making this movie has been for me. I nearly lost my life." He glanced at Rachel and she returned his smile. "Then I found it." The crowd cheered. "I'm sure everyone will enjoy this latest creation from Danfield. As for my next project, I've just signed to direct an action-adventure film with Rachel as the star. We'll begin shooting next month when we return from our honeymoon."

Crossing the short distance to Rachel, Michael looked deeply into her eyes, then kissed her as the crowd cheered on and on.

THE
OUTBACK
SAGA
AARON FLETCHER

Futuristic Romance

Love in another time, another place.

LADY ROGUE

New York Times Bestselling Author Phoebe Conn writing as Cinnamon Burke!

Smooth as silk, delicate as porcelain, Ivory Diamond is every inch a lady. She is also a ruthless player in her father's pirate empire. Equally comfortable behind an easel creating artistic masterpieces or behind a celestial cannon enforcing her father's edicts, Ivory has but one weakness: She wants a man to love.

Sent to the pirate stronghold to infiltrate Spider Diamond's operation, Drew Jordan finds himself in an impossible situation. Handpicked by Spider as a suitable "pet" for his daughter, Drew has to win her love or lose his life. But once he's initiated Ivory into the delights of lovemaking, he knows he can never turn her over to the authorities. For he has found a vulnerable woman's heart within the formidable lady rogue.

__3558-8 $5.99 US/$6.99 CAN

LEISURE BOOKS
ATTN: Order Department
276 5th Avenue, New York, NY 10001

Please add $1.50 for shipping and handling for the first book and $.35 for each book thereafter. PA., N.Y.S. and N.Y.C. residents, please add appropriate sales tax. No cash, stamps, or C.O.D.s. All orders shipped within 6 weeks via postal service book rate. Canadian orders require $2.00 extra postage and must be paid in U.S. dollars through a U.S. banking facility.

Name ____

Address ______________________________________

City ______________________ State ______ Zip ______

I have enclosed $______ in payment for the checked book(s).

Payment must accompany all orders. ☐ Please send a free catalog.

LOVE SPELL